BECOMING
EMILY NOVAK

ISBN: 979-8-9854265-4-0

author.audreybethstein.com

For Mom
For Zack
For Amber

BECOMING EMILY NOVAK

a novel

AUDREY BETH STEIN

Prologue: A Photograph

The four Novaks are busy making a dreidel. All are in the basement together—two parents, daughter Emily already in kindergarten, son Zack in preschool. Emily had brought home the instructions in a packet from Hebrew school, *Chanukah Activities for the Whole Family*. Yesterday Emily and Zack picked out the paint colors together, silvery and golden. Mom selected the wood with as much care as she tucks them in each night. Dad shaped the dreidel as all of them watched, cutting and sanding the point until it would spin. Because of Zack's peanut allergy they are making wooden peanuts too, small pieces of pine which Dad cut out and Mom sanded last night after bedtime. Dad arranges the tripod and sets the self-timer for his camera, the very same Pentax camera that he will give to Emily many years later when she signs up for her first photography class. He tells them all to ignore the camera. Emily and Zack instead look up and make funny faces, but almost immediately return to dreidel-making.

Dad is carving the letters, *Shin*, put one in, *Gimel*, take all. Emily is ready with a waving paintbrush and the silver paint. Zack and Mom, surrounded by crayons, are coloring wooden peanuts blue and green. All are engrossed, all are happy, all are content.

The shutter clicks.

Emily could hear the phone conversation from the dining room where she sat with her mother and her father's parents, eating breakfast. She could hear that something was wrong. "What is it?" Emily's mother asked, eyes red, crumpled tissue in hand. "Elliot, what's going on?"

Emily's father shushed her. "I'm trying to find out," he said from the kitchen. "I can't hear when you're talking to me." He said it more nicely than usual because Mom's father had just died, but Emily could still tell he was annoyed about being interrupted.

Grandma and Grandpa Novak had stopped eating and were looking in the direction of their son's voice. Emily's brother Zack, who was only eleven, was outside in the backyard picking raspberries. Emily eyed the cream cheese, out of reach. She could wait. She took a bite of dry bagel and hoped Zack would leave her some raspberries.

"Uy," Dad said, when he got off the phone. "The funeral home told me that the service is tomorrow at ten, which is not what your brother-in-law said, but they wouldn't tell me the cemetery."

"What do you mean, they wouldn't tell you the cemetery?"

"Apparently your sister told them not to tell anyone."

"Uy vey," said Grandma Novak.

"I knew I was right not to trust her," said Mom. "Now you see why I asked you to call the funeral parlor to double-check?"

"Did you tell them Daisy is Irv's daughter?" asked Grandpa Novak.

3

"I told them," said Dad.

"Uy," said Grandpa.

Mom wasn't saying anything. Wasn't looking at anyone. Wasn't crying. Her small frame, usually restless with energy, sat stiff in the wooden chair. "It's the same plot as my mother," she finally said. "Elliot, if you go upstairs, it's written on my little brown calendar in the front zippered pocket of my purse."

"How do you know they won't bury him in a different plot?" Dad asked. "If they're acting this idiotic."

"I'll get your purse, Mom," Emily said, and then jumped up and headed up the stairs before anyone could stop her. She opened the zippered compartment and found the green spearmint Tic-Tacs her mother always carried, and a lipstick and the round marbled-blue mirror Emily had liked to play with when she was younger, and then the calendar.

She heard the door slam as she came downstairs. "Where's Dad going?" she asked.

"To find the rabbi," said Mom. "Thank you for getting my calendar."

They were staying with Grandma and Grandpa Novak in Queens, Emily sleeping in the tiny bedroom which had once been her father's. They had driven down the previous night from Oaktown, CT, where they lived, first to the hospital on Long Island to say what turned out to be goodbye to a semi-conscious Grandpa Irv, then backtracking the half hour to Queens to sleep. Emily had stayed under the covers that morning after her father told her the news, thinking about Grandpa Irv, until Grandma Novak called up to say that breakfast was ready. Under the covers, Emily had cried a little bit. When the tears stopped it seemed too soon—she had cried more than that when her gerbil died—so Emily had tried to remember things. She remembered the poem Grandpa Irv had written her when she was born, the one she had memorized in sixth grade. That memory triggered a few more tears. Then she had remembered the big purple ring he always wore, and the scratchiness of his face when he leaned down for a kiss, but no more tears would come.

When she'd come downstairs for breakfast, Emily had given her mother a hug and been surprised at how tightly her mother had hugged back, how long she'd held on. She could tell by their eyes that her mother had been crying and her father and Zack had not. She had watched Mom cling to Zack too, long and tight, Zack letting her for once smooth down his hair, while he eyed the kitchen. The smell of frying onions permeated the air.

They had all eaten breakfast with Grandma and Grandpa Novak, bagels and lox and scrambled eggs with onions and fake bacon bits, except for Mom who sat with a glass of orange juice but no food. "I can't keep it down," she had said, when Grandma Novak tried to get her to eat. But Mom never ate much breakfast anyway so that wasn't new. Her father had eaten quickly like he always did, and then before Emily had even put cream cheese on the second half of her bagel, he was on the phone in the kitchen, calling to find out when the funeral was.

Mom wasn't touching the calendar, which lay on the table next to her empty orange juice glass, so Grandma Novak reached for it and began flipping through. "Oh, my glasses are upstairs," Grandma Novak said, squinting. She handed the calendar to Grandpa Novak and started clearing dishes. "Emily," she said, "please bring in the orange juice and the butter, then take a bowl and go out and help your brother get some raspberries for lunch."

"There might be some tomatoes too," Grandpa Novak said, as Emily watched Grandma Novak close the cream cheese container and take it into the kitchen. "You remember how to tell if a tomato is ripe?"

Emily remembered. She nodded, and pantomimed gently, *gently*, tugging on a palm-sized red tomato.

"Okay then."

Outside, Zack had already polished off the ripe raspberries from the large bush—more into his mouth than into the bowl Grandma Novak had given him, from the looks of it—so Emily started in on one of the two smaller bushes. There didn't appear to be many raspberries on that bush either. "Thanks a lot, Zack," Emily said, sticking her tongue out at her brother. She picked the last three raspberries from her bush and then popped them in her mouth.

"What's that for?" said Zack, automatically sticking his tongue out in return. "Mom told me to eat more fruits and vegetables."

Zack must have finished the third raspberry bush, Emily decided, because he had stepped away from it and was now standing over the spot where Grandpa Novak usually dug up the horseradish for Passover. "Why don't you eat horseradish then?" she shot back, a little delayed.

"Horseradish counts as a vegetable?" Zack asked.

"Last time I checked," said Emily, who had never checked but didn't want to admit she wasn't sure.

"Dare you to eat a hunk as big as my thumb." Zack was digging in the dirt.

"No," Emily said. "Besides, you're gonna get in trouble."

Zack ignored her, digging away. Emily watched him get a shovel then come back and hack at the ground.

"Aren't you sad about Grandpa Irv?" Emily asked.

Zack kept hacking. "I don't know," he finally said.

Emily stared. How could you not *know?* But he had only been two when Grandpa Irv had gotten sick.

"Do you think he'll have an open casket?" Zack asked, not looking up. "Like Gram?"

Emily had forgotten about the open casket. Her mother had covered Emily's eyes so she wouldn't have to look, but Zack had been the one to discover it, entering the funeral home room first and asking, "How come Gram looks waxy?"

"I don't know if he will," Emily answered. "Jews aren't supposed to have open caskets. I'm not sure why Gram had one."

"Maybe Aunt Ninian just wanted to see Gram again," Zack said. He was quiet for a second. "Gram was her mother."

"Are *you* going to look this time?" Emily asked. "If it's open again?"

"Yes," Zack said.

"You had nightmares last time," Emily reminded him.

"Well what if I don't look and then wish I had?" Zack answered. "I can't just dig him up again."

"That's gross, Zack."

"Duh. Are you going to look?"

"No."

"I bet I'm the only one who looks," Zack said. He had hacked away a piece of the horseradish and brought it under the hose at the side of the house to rinse off. "Dare you," he said again, holding the rinsed-off-but-still-dirty hunk of horseradish towards Emily.

"You need to cut off the outside part," Emily said, shaking her head vehemently.

"You want to go back in there for a knife?" Zack popped the whole hunk of horseradish in his mouth, chewed, grimaced, and swallowed.

Eventually Dad came home with a confirmation of the time and cemetery plot and a promise from the rabbi to contact them directly if there were any last-minute changes. Later that night, Aunt Ninian called. Mom refused to take the phone, so Dad spoke. He pulled the long phone cord from the kitchen through to the living room where they were all spread out, and tried—wordlessly— a couple of times during the conversation to get Mom to pick up the other extension and talk to her sister, but Emily could see from her mother's raised eyebrows and the way her jaw-bone pulled back that she wasn't budging. Emily didn't blame her mother. Aunt Ninian hadn't even told them Grandpa Irv was in the hospital—Mom had found *that* out from the nursing home.

Emily was confused by her aunt's behavior, which had started right before Gram died. *My ex-aunt,* Emily had started calling Aunt Ninian in her head. She listened to Dad's phone conversation, trying to guess what was being said on the other end. Zack was on the floor with a puzzle, absorbed and oblivious, but Emily could tell her mother and grandparents were listening as well.

"She told me the correct information," Dad said to Mom when he got off the phone. "She apologized."

"The rabbi probably told her you stopped by," said Mom.

"Daisy, people do strange things when they're upset."

"You're defending her? After all this you're defending her?"

"I'm not defending her. I just think it helps to have family when bad things happen. We all know she's crazy. Holding a grudge hurts you more than it hurts her."

"She's the one who started it. Screaming at me over our mother's deathbed, for god sake. I have family. Right here," she looked at the five of them, "I have family. I don't need her kind of family."

The funeral home was large, and impersonal, and smelled like stale carpet and aftershave. Somber men pointed out the washrooms and directed them towards the gathering room for their deceased. A placard next to the open door read *Funeral of Irving Horn*. Dad led them into the room, where they stood, speaking in hushed voices, and waiting. There were people all around them, almost none of whom Emily recognized. She didn't see a casket. While Emily was trying to discreetly adjust her bra, which didn't have much to hold it in place, Aunt Ninian approached them. Aunt Ninian wore an ill-fitting black suit jacket over a sequined dress more appropriate for a cocktail party, and her shaggy haircut made her look like an unwashed horse. "Let's be together as sisters today," she said to Mom. "Let bygones be bygones. We shouldn't be fighting on such an occasion."

Mom was gracious, and polite, and Emily knew she was holding her tongue. "How are you all holding up?" she asked. "How are the girls?" The girls were Emily's two cousins, whom she hadn't seen since Gram's funeral. They were sitting on the other side of the room on a broad dark couch, surrounded by people, and Emily didn't know if she wanted them to come over or not. Emily held her father's hand. His other arm was around Mom. That left Mom's other hand for Zack, but it was clenched.

Emily looked around. Zack was in between Grandma and Grandpa Novak, Grandpa's hand on Zack's shoulder. Good. He was okay there. That was good because Emily didn't want to let go of her father's hand. She was thirteen and by Jewish law already an adult, but as long as Zack was okay she could be whatever age she wanted. Emily was being five inside, so she could hold her father's hand and not have to use words besides "I love you" to make her mother feel better. "I'm sorry" was what you were usually supposed to say, but that was too hard, and Emily didn't know if "I'm sorry" still applied when it was your own grandfather.

Aunt Ninian introduced them all to a few people nearby, who said their condolences, and as the rabbi came to usher them all into the room for the service, Aunt Ninian leaned in towards each of the Novaks in turn. Emily received the wet peck on her left cheek, but didn't reciprocate. As Aunt Ninian leaned in towards Zack, Emily tried discreetly to wipe it off with her sleeve.

"The bitch," Mom whispered to Dad once Aunt Ninian was out of earshot. "You know she just wanted me to be the one to make a scene, so she would look good in front of all her friends. She certainly wouldn't have come up to me if no one was watching."

After the cemetery it was the four of them, Mom and Dad and Emily and Zack, at the Burger King drive-thru. The sign by the drive-thru window advertised watches for one ninety-nine with the purchase of a Whopper. "Can I have a watch?" Emily asked, more to hear her parents' voices than anything else. Mom and Dad never got those sort of things for her and Zack. *We're not wasting our money on cheap junk*, they would always say.

There was a choice of colors and Dad got her blue, her favorite. A red one for Zack. Emily sensed that if she had asked for a ten-speed bicycle he would have bought that too. Her mother was in the passenger seat and Emily watched her, waiting for her to object, but Mom just looked at Dad as if she didn't care, just as long as he drove her out of all this.

Only a few short months ago, Emily had four living grandparents, and on Mother's Day she had seen them all. That Mother's Day morning began with Emily burning French toast and Zack spilling orange juice. Later that day, Mom would tell both sets of grandparents how her kids had made her breakfast in bed, not mentioning either the spill or the burn.

After breakfast, they climbed into the Valiant, Emily and Zack fighting over who got to pick the radio station until Dad shut it off and started singing. There was traffic on the way to New York, then a line at the diner that Grandma Novak had chosen for lunch. Glare from the sun once they finally sat down caused Dad to squint strangely and Mom to laugh at the faces he was making. Dad's sister showed up alone, leaving her husband Max and sons to clean up the incredible mess that one of them—none would fess up—had caused by accidentally clogging the toilet and letting it overflow.

"I came downstairs," Aunt Sarah told them, "and my husband and eldest son were just standing there, watching the water spread through the living room."

"What a Mother's Day gift," said Grandpa Novak, as the waitress arrived at their table.

Aunt Sarah laughed. "I never liked that carpet much anyway." After the waitress had taken their orders, Aunt Sarah said, "I suppose I could get mad, but it's not going to change them. So I just shut off the toilet and left them the fun part."

Emily was puzzled by something. "*You* got the water to stop? You didn't have to call a plumber?"

"Sure," said Aunt Sarah. "Your grandma showed me how when I was little."

Zack perked up. "*Grandma* fixes toilets?"

"You never knew that your grandma worked as a plumber to put me through optometry school?" said Grandpa Novak. "Not an easy job for a woman back then."

Grandma Novak nodded, a bit proud. "But it sure paid better than secretarial work."

Once the food arrived, Emily and Zack fought over the plastic stirrers and the colored-tinseled toothpicks, then practiced sword-fighting until Dad frowned at them. Grandpa Novak told his favorite joke again. Grandma Novak whispered to the waitress who brought Emily and Zack each an extra orange juice with *two* stirrers. Mom ordered her all-time favorite New York dessert, a slice of cheesecake with strawberries on top, and pronounced it the best slice she had eaten since nineteen seventy-seven. Dad and Grandpa Novak both reached for the check simultaneously, Dad's hand faster, then Grandpa Novak snuck off and exchanged credit cards—Dad would never succeed in paying when Grandpa Novak was around.

As they were leaving, Aunt Sarah winked at Emily and told her, "There's usually a knob on one of the pipes in back—if the water in the bowl is getting high, turn it to the right and it should stop the flow. *Then* plunge."

At a stop sign on the way from one set of grandparents to the other, as Emily and Zack were playing the plane game, Emily felt the car go *thunk*. "Time out," said Zack, as Mom whipped her head around to the back seat and Emily spied a plane that now wouldn't count.

"Are you two okay?" Mom asked.

Emily nodded, still watching the plane. "What was that?"

"I'm fine," said Zack.

"Are *you* okay?" Dad asked Mom, looking at her and rolling down the window. "We're all fine," he called out to the driver of the other car, who was walking towards them. Dad got out of the car and Emily watched as the two of them talked, then walked around both vehicles, then shook hands and returned to their respective cars. Mom copied down the other license plate as it drove away, in case they turned out to need it later, which they wouldn't. Just a minor fender bender, no one hurt, nothing broken, but the yellow Valiant would have a blue stripe on it for the rest of its life.

"Game on," said Zack. "I see a plane." He pointed, and Emily wondered if it could be the one she'd spied five minutes earlier.

The score was tied 3-3 when they arrived, with Emily still scanning the sky for planes as Gram and Aunt Ninian came out to the car to meet them, but Emily promptly forgot about winning the plane game when her cousins appeared. Gram nodded at Dad, gave Mom a stiff barely-touching hug, and pointed Emily to her left cheek while Aunt Ninian plastered Zack with a very wet specimen of what she called a smooch. "I got a new Cabbage Patch," announced the older cousin, who had recently turned eight. "He has glasses and can hold a crayon."

"Did you bring Pooh?" asked the little one, the six-year-old, as one of Aunt Ninian's smooches landed on Emily's cheek.

"Yep," said Emily, hugging her cousin and then lifting her upside-down so her hair dangled in the grass. "Put me down, put me down," said the six-year-old, tugging on Emily's shoelace as the eight-year-old stuck a painted-toenail foot in front of her face.

"Go say hello to Grandpa Irv," Mom instructed Emily, "and then you can all go play in the backyard."

Grandpa Irv was snoring on the brown recliner when Emily went inside, her eyes slowly adjusting to the absence of sunlight, and at first she didn't even see her uncle, just the television channels mysteriously flipping themselves. "Pop," he said. "Your other grandkids are here."

Grandpa Irv stirred.

"He's not doing so hot today," Emily's uncle told her. "But go give him a kiss, he always likes to see you. Maybe he'll be more awake later."

Emily did as she was told, leaning in nervously, then gave her uncle the hug he was expecting and ran back outside where her cousins were waiting. For the next couple of hours the three of them played on the backyard swing set and with their dolls—this was one place Emily wasn't made fun of for still playing with dolls, although she overheard Mom and Gram discussing it when she ran back inside for the six-year-old's frog. Zack joined them on the swing set for a short while, showing off his skill on the monkey bars, then disappeared inside.

Eventually they got hungry and the eight-year-old remembered that there were popsicles in the freezer, so they headed towards the kitchen. "A-ha," said Dad, grabbing the little one as they passed, "is this my youngest niece, who forgot to give her Uncle Elliot a hug when he arrived?" He tossed her up in the air, caught her in a hug, and began tickling her as she laughed and laughed.

"Me next," said the eight-year-old, already licking her popsicle.

"You're eating," Dad said. "I'll wait until you're done eating. But *Emily* here," he said, putting down the six-year-old and reaching wiggling fingers towards Emily as she squeezed her arms against her body, "Emily is about to get caught by the tickle monster."

Dad's fingers worked their way into Emily's underarms while she twisted and turned, trying to get away. There was a chair blocking her on one side and the kitchen counter on the other. "Stop it," she said. "Dad, stop it." But he wasn't listening so she pulled her hands into fists and wrenched her left arm sideways into Dad's stomach, then her right fist into his upper arm.

"Ouch," Dad said, grabbing Emily's wrists. "Emily, don't do that."

"Don't tickle me then," Emily said, yanking her arms but unable to escape Dad's grip. "Let go."

Dad held the grip. "You're a kid, it's my job to tickle you." He let go. Emily's hands were still balled into fists.

"Tickle your nieces. They want to be tickled."

"I'm done with my popsicle, Uncle Elliot," said the eight-year-old.

Dad was still facing Emily, his fingers wiggling again. Emily looked at Mom for help. Mom frowned at Dad, and then both the eight-year-old and the six-year-old were jumping on Dad, one per leg, and Dad shifted his attention, one tickle-monster hand for each of them.

"Elliot," Mom said when Dad finally looked up again, "Emily *is* getting a little too old for that, don't you think?"

"Never," said Dad, tossing the eight-year-old up in the air. "Hey, wasn't there an exhibit of your father's you wanted to see today, Daisy?"

The six females squeezed into the Valiant to visit the exhibit— a dozen of Grandpa Irv's poems interspersed with other people's needlepoint and watercolors and clay menorahs in a hallway of the temple where the cousins went to Hebrew school. Zack stayed behind to play on the cousins' new computer, Dad stayed to watch Zack, and the uncle stayed to watch Grandpa Irv, who lay all afternoon in the recliner and didn't much respond to anything.

The six-year-old raced down the shiny halls, taking off her shoes and sliding in stocking feet. The eight-year-old tried to turn a cartwheel. Gram watched, talking to Mom and Aunt Ninian about Grandpa Irv's pill regimen, insisting that no she didn't need a vacation, didn't want a part-time nurse to come in to help, what would Irv think if a stranger was taking care of him. Emily demonstrated her own cartwheel, listening to Mom and Aunt Ninian disagree with Gram and each other about what would be best. Aunt Ninian kept interrupting Mom, Mom glaring at her and repeating, *let me finish.* The eight-year-old peeked into a locked classroom door, pointing out her desk and chair to Emily. The six-year-old slid back up the hallway, tugging on Emily's hand, then pulled her towards the first-grade door. Emily's rubber soles stuck to the floor.

Emily skipped back to Mom to ask if she could take her own shoes off. Mom was talking, trying to convince Gram to visit the doctor, Aunt Ninian nodding now and Gram shaking her head. *Don't you start with me too, Ninian,* Gram was saying.

Emily stood next to Mom, shifting her weight from one foot to the other, waiting for a break in the conversation. Mom still talking, her hands now gently moving in Emily's hair, absentmindedly French-braiding. Emily could feel Mom's fingers untangling the knots, separating and twisting segments of hair into strands, lightly tugging up and back, weaving over and under. The gentle touch of love on Emily's scalp.

The last day of shiva for Grandpa Irv, after the sun went down, Emily helped her mother uncover the mirrors and bring the extra chairs back down to the basement while Dad took Zack shopping for soccer cleats. The next morning, Mom would return to work and Emily expected that everything would return to normal, except that Mom would continue to stand and say *kaddish* in synagogue for another eleven months. Emily wrestled the last chair into place and bounded up the two flights of stairs. Mom stood in her bedroom, staring into the newly-uncovered mirror over the dresser. "I've aged," she said.

"No you haven't," Emily said, but then she looked and it was true, her mother *did* look older than she had a week ago. It wasn't just the lack of makeup which Mom always wore.

"See," said Mom, reading Emily's face next to her in the mirror. "You see it too." She sighed and turned, so Emily could only see her back in the mirror as she changed into a nightgown and started to unmake the bed. It was barely seven-thirty.

"Are you going to sleep?" Emily asked, studying the zit that was emerging on her chin.

Mom shrugged, listless. She pulled herself into the bed, propped up by pillows.

Emily turned. "Will you quiz me in Latin? I have a test to make up."

Mom nodded. "Bring it here."

But Mom's concentration was elsewhere, or nowhere, and they

16

hadn't even made it through half a page of vocabulary words by the time Dad and Zack got home, Zack racing up the stairs.

"Mom, Mom, check out my new cleats!" They were in his hands, the box and shoe-paper having lightly thumped to the ground in the hall behind him. He traced the side-stitching, "It's a Z for Zack, well it's backwards on the other one but still, and it *glows*—"

"Do they fit?" Mom asked, looking from the sneaker to Zack and then to Dad, who stood near the doorway, eyeing the nightgown.

"—so I can play soccer in the dark—"

"You're not playing soccer in the dark, Zack," said Dad.

"Do they fit?" Mom asked again.

Dad shrugged. "He says so."

"You didn't check the toe?"

"Daisy, there was a salesperson helping us, they're fine, if you want to check them yourself and go back with him tomorrow, feel free."

"—and they have glow-in-the-dark laces you can buy but Dad says I have to use my allowance so can we go back next Sunday, Mom?"

"We'll see," said Dad. "Now don't you have homework left?"

"Just social studies and science," said Zack. "Emily, like my cleats?"

Emily looked up from *amo, amare, amavi*, antsy. "Sure. Mom?"

"Mom," Zack said, "Can you quiz me in social studies?"

"Can Dad do it this time, Zack?" Mom said, as Emily reached towards her with the Latin book again.

Dad caught Emily's eye and shook his head, gesturing towards the door.

"Mom's quizzing me," Emily protested.

"No fair," said Zack.

"Five more minutes," Dad told Emily, leading Zack out of the room. "Then give her some peace and quiet. Daisy, I'll bring you a cup of tea in a bit, unless you'd rather some ice cream."

"Thanks, but don't bother," Mom said, closing her eyes to indicate she'd rather go to sleep.

Dad allowed Emily and Zack to stay up an extra half hour that night. He tucked them in, as he had all week, and when Emily had a sudden urge to be read a bedtime story, which hadn't happened in years, Dad didn't say she was too old. Instead, he picked up the heaviest book within reach, which turned out to be Emily's Earth Science textbook, and read a paragraph. Then Dad laughed, kissed Emily's forehead, and settled in to read her the first chapter of *Tuck Everlasting*, seeming rather happy to have been asked.

Emily didn't shout *hello* like she usually did, because neither of her parents were supposed to be home and Zack had gotten off the school bus with a friend at another stop. It was a Thursday afternoon in the fall, a few weeks before the seventh and eighth grade Sadie Hawkins dance. Emily had it all figured out. She would call because it seemed easier by phone than at school, and of course Spencer would say yes because it wasn't nice not to. Then he would reciprocate by asking her to the movies. She would respond in kind, and before you knew it they would be going out.

She dropped her book bag in the hall and sat down at the kitchen table with Triscuits and cheddar cheese and the phone book, thumbing through to find the "T"s. Although technically Emily had had two boyfriends already, she didn't want to count the second one—which had lasted for twelve days of the sixth grade—because he was the class geek, and she couldn't count the first one anymore because she had only been in elementary school. She wanted a *real* boyfriend, someone who would hold her hand at school on the way to gym, and take her to the movies and kiss her goodnight on Saturday nights.

Spencer was cute, and almost popular. They were part of the same eighth-grade crowd, Spencer and one or two other boys and lots of girls, not quite cool, kind of in the middle. Emily didn't care about coolness as long as she wasn't considered too uncool to slow dance with. Although no boy had actually asked Emily to dance yet, Emily didn't like standing by the side watching, so she would ask boys to dance and sometimes they said yes. She had never asked Spencer because he was always dancing with someone already, and in any case she had only started liking him a month ago, after the last school dance.

Now Emily found the number, and she dialed. There were lots of nines and it was a rotary phone, so it took a while. He answered on the third ring. She knew it was him but she had expected his mother to answer, so she still asked, "Is Spencer there?"

"This is Spencer. Who's this?"

"It's Emily."

"Oh, *Emily*. How *are* you?" He was using the tone of voice that she liked, the one that made you feel important when it was directed at you. Made you want that attention on you all the time. Made you not know what to say next.

"I'm good, um, did you get the Geography homework assignment?"

"*Emily*, did you *forget* to write down the homework? Oh. My. God. *What* is Mr. Randall going to think?"

Emily felt herself blushing. Years later, she would learn the term *flaming queen* and understand that it had been tailor-made for Spencer, but now she just knew how his fleeting attentions made her feel. Flustered, she said, "I didn't exactly *forget*. I just missed a couple of page numbers. Do you have it?"

"Yeah, hold on."

She could hear him rustling around, the familiar click of his three-ring-binder opening, then he was back.

"Pages two-eighty-seven through three-ten," he said. "And exercises one through ten on page three-thirty-four."

Emily of course had written down the assignment already in class, so she was surprised when he mentioned the exercises.

"Exercises? I thought we just had to read."

"See what *happens* when you don't pay attention in class? I bet you didn't hear him mention the *test* on Monday either."

"There's a test? On what? How can we have a test? We just had one."

Spencer started laughing.

"Did you know," he asked, "that gullible's not in the dictionary?"

Oh.

Emily wasn't sure what to say next.

"Are you still there?" Spencer asked.

"Yeah."

"Well, I should probably—"

"Um, Spencer," Emily interrupted him. "Would you go to the Sadie Hawkins dance with me?"

She was so relieved to have finally said it that she hardly noticed that he hadn't said anything.

"Uhhh, when is it?"

Emily was flustered again. It was the only thing anyone had been talking about all week—how could he not know when it was? "Um, the week um, let me check my calendar, hang on." She walked over to the fridge with the phone and counted out three weeks. "The twenty-second. Friday."

"I think um I think I'm doing something with my dad that night."

That wasn't what she expected him to say. Emily didn't understand how doing something with his dad could take precedence over a school dance, but she knew the rules about spending time with parents were different if they were divorced. "Oh, well let me know if you can go."

"Okay, sure."

"Are you watching *Wonder Years* tonight?"

"Probably. Um, Emily, I have to go do my Geography homework now."

"Right."

"Bye."

"Um, are the exercises really part of our homework?"

But he had already hung up.

It was then Emily noticed her mother's car in the driveway. Sitting there with no one inside like it had been there the whole time. Emily listened, but couldn't hear anything, which was good because it meant, hopefully, that her mother hadn't heard her conversation.

She went upstairs, shouting *hello* now, heading towards to her parents' bedroom as usual, then stopping short because she could hear her mother crying again. *Dad please come home,* Emily whispered to herself.

Alone with Not-Mom was the hardest because *nothing* that Emily did worked, nothing seemed right. If she'd try to hug or comfort her mother. If she tried to pretend nothing was wrong, or ask her mother for something, or didn't ask. If she tried to vacuum—that time her mother snapped at her that she had a migraine—or make dinner—that time her mother said she was already defrosting something, then left Dad to finish while she stayed upstairs. Nothing helped, whether Emily needed Mom or tried to *be* a mom. Nothing.

This time, Emily crept past her mother's open door into her own bedroom and picked up Whitney, cuddling her close to her chest. "It's okay, Whitney," she told the doll, "it's gonna be okay," not knowing what the doll was upset about but knowing she needed comfort. She held Whitney out in front of her after a while so they could look at each other. Whitney tried to smile, and Emily smiled back, as best she could. Whitney's braids were coming out, so Emily fixed them, tightening the white bow on the left one, remaking the orange yarn braid on the right. With Emily's hands under her arms, Whitney made a somersault to thank her, then whispered in Emily's ear. It was true—Emily *could* play Oregon Trail on the computer now without Zack interrupting, and Dad wasn't there to tell her to do her homework. She gave Whitney another kiss and stretched her out on the bed next to Pooh, gave Pooh a kiss and a hug, then crept past her mother's room, closing *that* door quietly so her mother wouldn't be disturbed by computer noise, and went into the den.

Half an hour later Emily was absorbed in the game when she heard an "Emily" that made her jump.

"You scared me," Not-Mom said, standing in the doorway. "I didn't know you were home."

Emily felt her heart pounding quickly still, hoping it would slow. There was a blizzard on the trail. One of the horses had tripped and injured itself—she was bargaining for another horse with the food she'd need for the next leg of the journey.

"When did you get home?" her mother asked.

One of the people in Emily's wagon was bound to die before they reached Oregon.

Emily shrugged.

"Don't scare me like that."

Scare *you?* Emily wanted to say—but she held her tongue and returned to her game, scared somehow to say anything and wishing she had brought Whitney with her into the den. Wishing for someone to ask kind and gentle questions about the upcoming dance, explaining how to make sure a boy said *yes* like he was supposed to, even if it was Emily asking.

Dad prepared dinner that night, Emily and Zack helping. No one said much. Zack set out three place settings. When they heard the footsteps on the stairs, Emily and Zack looked at each other, and Zack scrambled to add a fourth place setting. Emily could see the hope in Zack's face that she felt inside. Was Mom actually joining them for dinner? She looked at Dad. His face was expressionless. Emily followed Dad's eyes to Not-Mom in the doorway. She wanted her mother back.

Emily's mother had been Not-Mom every night that week. She didn't even know that on Monday Zack had gotten caught listening to *Guns-n-Roses* on his walkman at Hebrew school. The principal had sent a note home, and Emily was worried because Zack hadn't gotten punished. Dad had signed the note and said *we'll discuss it when your mother gets home from work,* but Not-Mom had shown up, gone straight into her room yet again and shut the door and stayed there. Dad had brought her dinner on a tray. How much time did she need to mourn? Emily's friend Adena's grandpa had died a month after Emily's, and Adena's mom wasn't crying, she was redecorating the kitchen and teaching them how to make hummus.

"Can you pass the bread?" Emily asked for the second time. It was sitting in front of her mother, who was absently chewing and staring into space. Her father reached over and passed it to Emily. Her mother didn't even blink.

Emily needed to do *something.* "Did you tell Mom about the note?" Emily asked Zack. She knew she shouldn't bring it up, but he was supposed to get in trouble eventually.

Zack glared at her.

Emily couldn't tell if her father was consciously ignoring this or just absorbed in cutting his meat. Her mother was still staring into space.

"Mom, Zack keeps listening to his walkman in Hebrew school."

Mom blinked, jolted, like she had just remembered she was a parent. She glanced at Dad, and Emily recognized the damn-him-he's-not-getting-involved look cross her mother's face. "Zack?" Mom asked. "Is this true?"

"We're studying the same things we studied last year," Zack said. "It's boring. So I listen to the tape the cantor made of my *haftarah* so I can practice. I still got the second-highest grade in my class on the test last week." Now he gave Emily a look, the one he usually gave her for bragging about her good grades. Zack got good grades too, but not quite as high as Emily, and he didn't usually mention them unless asked.

"Zack," Mom said, "That's not very respectful of your teacher."

"I'm discreet," Zack said.

"It's not his haftarah he's listening to," Emily said, chewing.

"Zack," Dad said, in his disapproving tone. But that was all he said.

"Emily," Mom said, which meant *stay out of this.* For once, Emily was relieved to hear this tone of Mom's voice.

"I'll get the tape if you want to see it," Zack said, starting to get up from his seat.

"Zack, sit down," Mom said. He sat. "It's your education, not ours." Her expression said as much as her words.

Dad reached to pour himself more juice, which meant the discussion was over. No punishment. Emily took a moment to spit a half-chewed piece of meat into her napkin while no one was looking.

"Did Emily tell you she's using a computer dating service to find a date for the Sadie Hawkins dance?" Zack asked.

"I am not," Emily said, glaring at him, hoping he wouldn't find out about Spencer.

Zack grinned. "She got matched with Bert from *Sesame Street*."

That Saturday Mom woke up with a headache again, so Emily and Zack and Dad went alone to synagogue for Shabbat services. Dad frowned when Emily motioned that she was going to leave the sanctuary right after her friend Adena had slipped out, but he didn't stop her, so she and Adena spent most of the service hanging out in the lounge that was connected to the ladies bathroom until Adena's mom came in and told them to get back in time for *Aleinu.* Zack, Emily knew by the sounds coming through the door, had likewise slipped out of junior congregation and was playing catch in the hallway until the junior congregation leader dragged the truant kids back into the service. After services, Dad gave permission to invite Adena to come back to the Novaks' house, as long as they played outside or in the basement—so as not to disturb Mom—and Emily helped to carry in groceries when Dad got back from Shop-Rite.

Dad made the four of them grilled cheese sandwiches and brought Mom a toasted bagel, then left for the grocery store, opening the door for Zack's friend Keith, who lived in the neighborhood. Zack and Keith promptly headed to the basement, Zack leaving his crust-filled plate behind, and Emily cleared her place and Adena's then the two of them went out on the front porch.

"No peeking!" the boys shouted an hour later, when Emily and Adena tired of the porch swing and opened the basement door. Emily heard hammering, then something being pushed away.

"Zack, can Adena borrow your bike?"

"No."

"For ten bucks," Keith called back.

"It's not even yours, Keith."

"Fine," Keith said, appearing with Zack at the bottom of the stairs. "No, she can't borrow it. We might go riding later."

"Oh, well," Emily said loudly to Adena. "I guess we'll just go into the basement and make those jigsaw puzzles then."

"Wait," Zack called up. "If you bike to the store and get us some bubble gum, you can use it for an hour."

Emily looked at Adena, who shrugged. The store was their destination anyway. "Do you have money?" Emily called down.

"I'm letting you use the bike."

"One pack," Emily said. "And we each get a piece."

"Hubba Bubba," Zack said. "Not Bubblelicious." Keith said something to Zack they couldn't hear. "Grape Hubba Bubba," Zack clarified. "And you can *share* one piece—we need the other four for our experiment."

"What are they building down there?" Adena asked, once she and Emily were biking up the street.

"I have no idea," Emily said. "Something stupid, probably."

"Keith's kind of cute," said Adena.

"Adena, he's a *sixth* grader."

"So?"

This both exasperated and thrilled Emily about her friendship with Adena—unlike when she was with her classmates, Emily was definitely the mature one.

"Come on, let's see if the new *Sassy* magazine is out."

At that moment, Emily felt her tires slide out from underneath her. A passing car had sprayed gravel onto the sidewalk, and Emily had pedaled right into it. "Ow!" And then, "Owwww!" She was tangled up in the bike, scraped and bruised and when she got up she realized she had twisted her ankle. "I'm fine," she said, wincing as Adena rode back to see what had happened. "Let's go."

"Are you sure," Adena asked. "It looks like there's a piece of gravel stuck in your kneecap."

There was. Emily sat on the grass and examined it. It didn't hurt much, at least not compared to her ankle or scraped wrist, but when she pulled the rock out—it was about the size of her pinky nail, and sharp—her knee started bleeding and it wouldn't stop.

"We'd better go back," said Adena.

"We're not supposed to disturb Mom."

"We'd better go back."

Dad was pulling in the driveway when they made it back to the alley. "Good," he said to them. "Just in time to unload groceries."

"Elliot," Adena said. "Emily's bleeding."

At that Dad looked at Emily. The blood was dripping down her leg, soaking the top of her sock, so it looked worse than it was, and Emily did hurt quite a bit now that the shock was wearing off.

"Uy," Dad said. "Let's get you inside. Adena, can you please find Zack and ask him to help with the groceries?"

Dad got the gauze from the medicine cabinet and started wrapping Emily's knee while she sat on the back porch steps.

"You need to clean it out first," Emily said. He was rough with the cotton balls and awkward with the Bactine, accidentally squirting some on Emily's shorts. Not like Mom. And then he told Emily not to bike on it anymore that afternoon, even though it had stopped hurting.

"By the way," Dad said, as he wound an Ace bandage around Emily's ankle—which might or might not have been necessary—"You put pads on the shopping list, but not what kind, or how many, so I got a couple of college-ruled letter-sized pads with holes so you can fit them in a three-ring binder."

"I meant maxi pads," Emily said.

"You mean legal-sized?" Dad asked.

"No. *Maxi pads.* Sanitary napkins. For when you have your period." Emily whispered the last part, not sure if she should be embarrassed or not.

"Oh," Dad said. *He* was clearly embarrassed. "Well, put them on the shopping list again, maybe with a brand name this time."

"Dad, you need to go back."

"We can get it next shopping trip."

"Dad, I *need* them."

Keith had taken off on Zack's bike once it was clear that Dad wouldn't let Emily go biking again, but the boys had erected KEEP OUT signs on the basement door and there wasn't enough time left to make jigsaw puzzles anyway, since Adena was being picked up at three. So Emily and Adena wound up sitting on the swing again, which wasn't as much fun the second time around, but better than shoving food into the refrigerator. Emily wondered how long it would take before Mom noticed and rearranged the mess Zack and Dad were undoubtedly creating.

They heard Keith skid to a stop, then a short while later, Zack called out, "Catch," and Emily looked up to see a box of lemon-heads flying at her. She missed, but it landed in her lap.

"Thanks."

"Figured we borrowed from your secret stash of quarters, we should get you something."

"Zack!" But he and Keith were already thumping back down to the basement. Emily picked up the box—it was already half-empty—and dumped a few lemonheads into Adena's waiting hand. They sat and ate lemonheads until Adena's dad arrived to pick her up.

Her migraine had gotten better, but Mom skipped dinner again that night, and lunch the next day. She said no when Emily asked if they could bake cookies together and suggested Zack ask Dad to quiz him for his vocabulary test. She asked them not to disturb her until dinnertime so she could rest. Emily was mixing the batter for mint chocolate chip cookies on her own, Dad was out running errands, and Zack was upstairs, probably on the computer, when the phone rang. Emily let it ring three times, then when it seemed like no one else was going to answer, she picked up.

"Hello?" Zack said at the same time.

"Hello!" said Grandpa Novak. "Honey," he called, his mouth presumably away from the phone, "pick up!"

Grandma Novak picked up the extension and for the next ten minutes Grandma and Grandpa Novak learned about Zack's vocabulary test and Emily's bandaged kneecap and the spaceship that Zack and Keith were building in the basement.

"How are you planning to make it fly?" Grandpa asked.

"Firecrackers," Zack answered.

"Might want to run that by your Dad first," Grandpa suggested.

"Speaking of," Grandpa said, "are your parents there?"

"Which one?"

"Both of them. We want to wish them a happy anniversary."

Emily had forgotten. Usually there were presents in the morning—invariably, some kind of chocolate—and Emily and Zack home with a babysitter or, more recently, by themselves in the evening while their parents went somewhere to celebrate.

"Nineteen years," said Grandma Novak. "Well, tell them we called, and we'll try again after dinner."

"If we got Mom and Dad movie tickets," Zack said, entering the kitchen and swiping a fingerful of batter from the bowl, "would they go?"

Emily swatted Zack's hand away, too late. "If you eat it all there won't be any cookies." She went back to greasing a cookie sheet. "Maybe. How would we buy the tickets? We don't have a way to get to the theater."

"We could give them money and *tell* them what it's for."

Emily thought about that. "You don't have any money."

Zack pulled a small wad of singles from his pocket.

"Why'd you take my quarters then?"

Zack shrugged. Emily reached for the wad of cash, extracting a single grubby dollar which fluttered and landed in the batter before Zack could pull his hand away. Emily grabbed the dollar and wiped it on Zack's moving sleeve, then shoved it into her own pocket as he tucked away the rest of the bills. He wasn't trying to get it back. "You borrowed a dollar?"

"Fifty cents," Zack said. "But Keith might have taken a quarter or two while I wasn't looking."

"You let Keith into my bedroom?"

"So are we getting Mom and Dad movie tickets or not? Dad's gonna be home soon."

Emily thought about it. "Okay. You make the card. Wait here, and *don't* touch the batter." She ran upstairs and grabbed her cash box, along with the key from its secret hiding place, and came back down. She opened up the cash box and counted out four dollars.

"It's more than that," Zack said. "It's not a matinee, and they're adults."

Emily counted out the remainder, and Zack added his wad to the pile. She had a dollar left to her name, not counting the bat mitzvah and birthday gift money in her savings account that she wasn't supposed to touch. She would have to wait until next week's allowance to get *Sassy* magazine. "We can give them cookies to take instead of popcorn."

Zack dug around in the pantry to make a card, while Emily started spooning individual clumps of batter onto the cookie sheets. As Zack drew the card, both of them glancing periodically at the kitchen window for Dad's car and listening for Mom's footsteps, Emily wondered if Dad wanted to divorce Mom, if that was why there had been no chocolates. Adena's aunt and uncle were divorced. So were Spencer's parents. And Keith's mom had been married once before marrying Keith's dad. Emily was nervous.

Did Zack think about things like this? Was he still too young? He didn't seem to get upset like she was about Not-Mom.

"Why do you think Dad's still with Mom? All she does now is sit in bed and pretend to read the newspaper."

Zack was tracing over a "D" in thick black ink. "Where else would he go?"

Where else would he go? It was a good question, and Emily's mind was blank. She couldn't imagine him anywhere else. Maybe she was worried for no reason. But just to be sure, she rolled a big piece of dough between her fingers, then stretched it onto the cookie sheet. Then another, shaping it. When she was done, the first cookie sheet said "1" and the second said "9." If there was enough time before Mom and Dad reappeared, she would shape the remainder—sans the bit that Zack had just stolen from the bowl—into a heart. That evening, Emily imagined, Mom would see the cookie and kiss Dad and they would go off to the movies and when they came home that night, everything would be okay again.

Instead, that evening, when Not-Mom saw the dozen roses that Dad had placed in front of her seat at the dinner table, she looked embarrassed and said, "I'm sorry, Elliot. I completely forgot."

It was an awkward meal, ravioli and leftover salad and no sauce or dressing because they had run out and no one had put the ingredients on the shopping list. When all of them had finished, Zack leaving behind salad and Mom leaving behind almost everything, Zack kicked Emily under the table and she got up and fetched the cookies and Zack handed their parents the card.

Not-Mom smiled and ate a bite. Dad took a large bite. He would later polish off the rest. Not-Mom opened the card with the money inside and they read it together. Not-Mom whispered something to Dad. Dad said how much they appreciated the present and that they wanted Zack and Emily to enjoy the movie for them; he had already rented one to watch with Mom, a Woody Allen movie. Emily recognized it as the one that had come out right after Gram had died.

"But it's for you," Zack said.

"We'll enjoy it vicariously," Dad said, and as Dad then explained to Zack and Emily what *vicariously* meant, Emily felt herself deflate again inside. She noticed, too, that Zack's facial expression was inscrutable, and in the dark theater when his shoulders were shaking and she put her arm tight around him, he didn't stop her, and his tears kept coming through three previews and the opening credits.

When she would wonder, in the future, about her parents getting a divorce, she would remember the roses, and her father watching the end of the Woody Allen movie alone because Mom had fallen asleep, and she would come back to Zack's question, *where else would he go?* And when things got bad again as they got older, she would notice how Dad retreated into books, joined a bowling league, learned more Hebrew and started leading Thursday morning services at the synagogue—all ways to escape for a while without leaving home.

The winter after Grandpa's unveiling, they celebrated Zack's bar mitzvah, the sanctuary nearly full to capacity with friends and congregants and Dad's extended family. During the ceremony, Emily sat between Mom and Grandma Novak and mouthed the words of the *haftarah* blessings along with her brother. She clutched a yellow and a grape sourball in her hand, waiting to throw them in congratulations.

"It's almost time to duck," Emily reminded Grandma Novak in a whisper. "Not everyone has good aim."

Zack finished his *haftarah* and the whole congregation sang out, "A-men," as a cascade of sourballs arced from their hands towards the *bimah* where he stood. Some fell short, so Emily re-tossed a green one and another yellow, and popped an orange sourball into her mouth. Zack was grinning, waving at the new baby cousin, pantomiming throwing sourballs at the row of Hebrew school classmates. Dad was leading the congregation in singing *Siman Tov u Mazel Tov*, Grandma Novak was ducking and clapping and singing loudly, Grandpa Novak was standing up and tossing sourballs. Emily looked to her left and saw on Mom's face that she was happy and proud and tearing up, all at once.

For the most part, Mom had snapped out of being Not-Mom when it came time to plan the bar mitzvah. Selecting invitations, a caterer, the menu, clothing, flowers for the *bimah,* table decorations, and what felt to Emily like a million other details, with an overwhelming intensity that almost passed for enthusiasm. There were still episodes occasionally that would set Mom off, and Not-Mom would hover under the surface. Her words and actions would still be Mom, but the rest of the family could tell something was not quite right. It was like an actor playing Mom. Emily had learned to tread lightly, and to avoid discussing certain topics— like Mom's family, or Mom's entire childhood—to keep Not-Mom from breaking through that fragile surface.

When the singing ended, there was Zack's speech, and the Rabbi's speech, and the Mourner's Kaddish which Mom didn't have to stand up for anymore, and the rest of the service which felt short because of the distraction of the sourballs that had landed all around them, and then the service was over and they stood on the receiving line, greeting people.

Emily wore a new dress Mom had made her for the occasion. The two of them had found a fabric Emily loved, and a design which looked nice in the pattern book. Mom had whistled Chopin, working away at the sewing machine again, and Emily wished Zack could have a bar mitzvah every year, just for that. Zack and Dad wore new *kippot* Mom had made which matched their store-bought new suits and ties, and Mom wore a new dress suit with a stylish hat. Emily thought they all looked quite nice, except for her.

She couldn't quite put her finger on why. It wasn't Mom's sewing skills, which were impeccable. And the dress looked just fine on the hanger. It was something fundamental about girls dressing up. Pastels were too frilly and the slinky black dresses that the beautiful girls wore made Emily feel too exposed, but even when she tried a dress like this that her mom said was *very Emily,* it still didn't work. There were uncomfortable shoes and stockings, a handbag to keep track of, jewelry that had to work well with the necklines and collars. Not to mention nail polish to apply and the lipstick that Mom thought Emily should wear on special occasions. Emily envied her brother and father who could have two suits with big pockets and a pair of sturdy dress shoes and be done with it. Emily liked the uniformity. She liked the requirement of wearing *kippot,* a simple defined visible-from-afar way to declare your Judaism and your personality at the same time. Girls didn't have anything comparable. Boys had a strict basic dress code, and about the only thing you could do to mess up was show up in a bow tie.

"Mazel tov, mazel tov," the friends and relatives and congregants said as they passed, shaking Emily's hand or kissing her cheek or hugging her.

"Thank you," Emily said, over and over. "Shabbat shalom. Thanks for coming."

No one mentioned Mom's family but their absence was tangible, especially in the contrast with Dad's family that was so present. Cousin after cousin, and great aunts and great uncles and of course Grandma and Grandpa Novak and Dad's sister and her whole family.

Once they were all in the social hall, with musicians playing *hava nagilah* and Grandpa Novak leading everyone in a *hora,* Uncle Max and his sons lifted Zack up on a chair, dancing it above the crowd.

Mom's turn was next, and she gripped the sides of the chair as it tipped and one of the great uncles jumped in to help hold it steady. Then Dad, letting go just long enough to raise his arms up victoriously, laughing the whole time. Then all eyes were on Emily, and she wished she was behind her camera lens instead of being pulled into the center of the circle by Adena and being lifted up in the air on a shaky seat with people watching. And then all of them were on the ground again, and the *hora* kept going and going. Emily saw her mom tear up again once or twice. *I always do this at happy occasions,* Mom said, and Emily wondered whether she was crying because Gram and Grandpa Irv were dead, or because they wouldn't have appreciated this anyway, or because even if all Mom's relatives were at the bar mitzvah and happy and getting along, Dad's family was still bigger with more love to go around.

Back home after the official party, Emily took photograph after photograph. She photographed the new baby cousin and all the boy cousins and Zack and his friends and even a few of the great aunts and uncles, although she wasn't as interested in the pictures of adults. Without a camera, around lots of people, Emily felt stiff. She had taken a photo class at her new prep school and joined the yearbook staff, and everyone at school knew her as the freshman with the camera around her neck.

Zack's friends and the boy cousins around her age put up their middle fingers so she wouldn't take the pictures but she clicked away anyway. She missed her girl cousins. Dad's whole side of the family had boys. Usually Emily tried not to think about her mother's side of the family anymore, but she wished her cousins were there.

The last time Emily had seen her girl cousins was across her grandfather's grave, and the last time before that had been at her grandmother's funeral. *They're still your cousins,* her parents had said then to her and Zack. *This fight is between your mom and your aunt, it's not about you and your cousins. We want you to be able to still have a relationship with them.* But Emily had also heard them use the word *brainwashing, they're so young, eight and six, Ninian is brainwashing them.* The littler cousin, the six year old, had waved at Emily across the hole in the ground, so she had waved back, but then she had looked away and the rest of the funeral she had looked at the scuffing on her shoes and her father's, and the velcro on Zack's sneakers which was half undone, and the pointiness of her mother's scuffless high heels.

Do you miss them? Emily wanted now to ask her mom. But couldn't. Her mother was laughing, talking to friends in the dining room, so proud of Zack. Happy for once, glowing, happy like Emily hadn't seen her in so long. Emily knew she couldn't interrupt the joyous occasion with the question.

The summer in between the funerals, soon after her bat mitzvah which none of her mother's relatives had attended, the cousins had each sent her a letter. Emily's parents stood there as she read and Emily knew she was supposed to turn them over, let her parents read, so she did. She stood there and listened to her parent's voices and almost wished her cousins hadn't written at all as Mom's mood changed and she began ranting about Aunt Ninian yet again. *Ninian wrote this one I can recognize her handwriting,* Mom declared, and Dad debated back and forth with her, *your niece might have dictated the letter,* and Emily asked, *did Aunt Ninian write this one too?* and Mom said, *your cousin probably wrote that one,* and asked Dad, *should Emily write back what do you think?*

Emily wanted to write back to her cousins, *Pooh and Whitney miss playing with your Cabbage Patch Kids,* but Dad was agreeing with Mom, *I'm sure Ninian would read the letter first, no I don't think she would throw it away, we should probably see what Emily sends,* and then they told Emily, you can write back if you want, we'd like to look at the letter before you send it. And Emily was trapped. If she wrote to her cousins, she was betraying Mom. If she didn't, Mom would feel guilty about the severed relationship and cry again. But who was she writing to? The way her parents talked, the cousins she had played with were gone, had been or were going to be brainwashed and didn't exist like that anymore.

So Emily had written a letter, but it had felt like someone else was moving the pen, and she hadn't known what to say. She didn't remember anymore what she had written. She'd given the letter unsealed to Dad, who read it and showed it to Mom, and Emily didn't listen to their conversation that time. Then the letters were on the counter in the kitchen waiting to be mailed, and then they were gone so someone had mailed them, but there wasn't ever another letter back.

Do you miss Gram and Grandpa Irv? Emily wanted to ask her mother. *Do you hate them? Should I hate them?* These weren't questions she could ask either. She didn't miss them. She didn't hate her grandfather. He was gone and it was a little sad but not really. She was mostly just glad to not ever have to go to the nursing home anymore. Maybe she hated Gram though.

Gram had gotten breast cancer and not told anybody. She had let it grow for five years until it was black and the size of a baseball, keeping it hidden. Gram and Grandpa Irv had been living in Aunt Ninian's in-law apartment at the time, babysitting Emily's two favorite cousins every day and dependent on Aunt Ninian for anything that involved leaving the apartment. Gram had for years refused to let Aunt Ninian take her to the doctor for a checkup. And then Aunt Ninian had finally managed to get Gram to the doctor and saw the lump and called Mom to say Gram had late-stage cancer, one month to live if they were lucky.

Aunt Ninian had lashed out at Mom on the phone that night, angry when Mom said she couldn't make the three-hour drive to see Gram until the end of the weekend, and then lashed out again two days later in Gram's hospital room as Emily watched. The two sisters had stopped speaking to each other after the scene in the hospital, and Gram died the next week, and it had been messy and yucky ever since. Aunt Ninian's actions surrounding Grandpa Irv's death clarified for Emily that the ties were permanently severed now from both sides. They didn't even know where Aunt Ninian and her family were living now. And if Gram had just told someone about the lump like you were supposed to, Emily realized as she filled the camera frame with even more boys, Emily's girl cousins would be here right now, and maybe even Gram too.

The morning after Zack's bar mitzvah, Dad made them all French toast. As they ate, Emily made plans in her head to develop her four rolls of film on Monday during lunchtime and then make contact sheets as soon as class got out. She wondered how much it would cost to buy chemicals and make Dad's old darkroom usable again. She was about to ask when Dad spoke.

"So, Zack," Dad asked, "are you going to start coming to minyan with me on Thursday nights?"

Zack was in the middle of a gulp of orange juice, so he shook his head in response.

Dad had asked Emily the same question after her bat mitzvah. She'd actually gone once or twice, but she didn't like the Thursday night tunes very much, and then when she started high school, she didn't have the time.

"Zack," said Mom, "I think it would be nice if you went on occasion. It would show your commitment to Judaism."

"I'm through with synagogue," Zack announced.

"What?" said Dad.

"I'm through."

"Zack, your bar mitzvah is just the *beginning*," said Mom.

"Mom, I did all the learning to get to my bar mitzvah, just like you both wanted, and I didn't even complain about it like most of my friends did, and now I'm a man and I can make my own decisions. This is my decision." Zack went back to his French toast. "Anyway," he said with his mouth full, "I don't believe in God."

As Mom sighed and Dad for one brief second looked as though he was about to laugh, Emily realized she didn't know if she believed in God or not, or if her parents did. She could still remember the one time her parents had ever discussed God together.

She had been ten, Zack eight. Shabbat dinner, Zack holding the *kiddush* cup while their father read aloud the long English translation of the wine blessing. Zack couldn't sit through the whole blessing without fidgeting, and that particular Friday he was working the pedal on the sewing machine base that held up their kitchen table.

Mom had shaken her head at Zack and he had held his upper body still, eyes on Dad reading the passage about Creation. His feet were still moving, though, as Emily found out when she shifted her leg and felt the pedal come down on her left toe.

"Ouch."

"Sorry."

Dad had stopped reading. "Do it again, Zack, and you can forget playing Atari tonight." Zack took his feet off the pedal and listened to Dad repeat the passage from the beginning. It was at the part where "the heavens and the earth were finished, and all their host, and on the seventh day God rested" that Zack interrupted.

"What did God do on the eighth day?"

Mom and Dad ignored him. Dad kept reading. After they'd each tasted the *kiddush* wine and begun eating their salads, Zack had asked again. "They stop telling at seven. What did God do on the *eighth* day?"

Mom and Dad exchanged glances, each waiting for the other to speak. Dad led his fork between his salad and his mouth. The kitchen clock ticked loudly.

A flicker of something unrecognizable, fear perhaps, passed over Mom's face as her eyes traced Dad's moving Adam's apple. Zack's foot started working the pedal again, and Dad glanced up, mid-chew.

He swallowed. "God did the same things on the eighth day that he does every day." He spoke carefully, then he reached for the bread knife and began cutting himself another slice of *challah*.

"Does God have go to synagogue?" Zack wanted to know.

Emily took a bite of her own *challah* as Mom answered, "God is *always* in synagogue."

"He's everywhere," Emily said. "We talked about it in Hebrew School yesterday."

"That's right," Mom said, serving the brisket. "Did you start that unit on the Inquisition yet? At last night's Hebrew school board meeting we were told you would be studying the Inquisition."

They hadn't. "My great-grandmother's ancestors had to flee from Spain because of the Inquisition," said Dad. "It was a terrible thing."

"We're very fortunate," continued Mom, "to live in a country where we can practice Judaism openly." Mom and Dad were back in rhythm again, talking with Zack and Emily about religious freedom.

Upstairs that evening, Zack had set up Space Invaders on his Atari and showed Emily how to play. "As soon as I get old enough I'm not going to synagogue anymore," he said, blasting an alien.

"You have to," Emily told him.

"No I don't," he shot back. "If God is everywhere, I can pray to him while I play Atari."

Five years after that evening, here was her brother following through on his eight-year-old self's declaration. Zack didn't look argumentative, just determined.

"Zack," Mom said now, as Emily reached for another slice of French toast, "I'm not asking you to believe in God. I'm asking you to respect your tradition. Didn't all those years of Hebrew school mean anything to you?"

"Should we have sent you to Catholic Catechism instead?" Dad asked. Emily wasn't sure if he was making a joke, or just frustrated.

Mom and Dad tried to argue with Zack, then they tried to reason. Then they gave in. Emily knew they could have simply pulled rank, but they didn't. She liked that they didn't. And she respected Zack for rebelling—she herself felt compelled to follow her parents' rules and expectations. Later she overheard her parents talking with each other.

"Did we go wrong somewhere?" Mom asked. "I thought we'd taught him to care."

"Let him be," Dad responded. "He'll grow out of it. He'll be back in synagogue by the time he's a sophomore. Isn't that the age you started talking about religion with all your friends?"

"I hope you're right," Mom said.

Early in Zack's eighth-grade year, he suddenly became noticeably interested in girls. Before that, he would attend the seventh and eighth grade school dances—nearly everyone in the class did—but mostly stood on the side with friends, joking and eating and occasionally shooting rubber bands or daring each other to ask someone to slow-dance. Emily had also witnessed Zack at a few bar and bat mitzvahs, avoiding the dance floor except for the limbo and games of Coke and Pepsi. Come that fall, though, Zack had gotten strangely awkward whenever they saw Adena—who despite being nearly flat-chested and destined to stay that way, had developed an adolescently seductive way of carrying herself that Emily all at once hated and wondered at and envied. He had also started using deodorant without being told, and once when Emily and her brother were home alone she had caught him flipping through her yearbook with his hand down his shorts. The real turning point, though, came with the impending arrival of the first school dance of eighth grade, which would be a Sadie Hawkins dance.

Emily had recently begun a practice of not volunteering information—Mom would ask enough direct questions to find out almost everything anyway—but Zack hadn't quite mastered it. He told the family as they sat down to dinner, "Cindy Winthrop asked me to the Sadie Hawkins dance."

"Mazel Tov," said Dad. "Who's Cindy Winthrop?"

"That's wonderful," said Mom. "Do you know what you're wearing? Do you need a fifties outfit? Elliot, she's the daughter of Patty Winthrop who organizes the book sale every year."

Dad started to frown. "That doesn't sound like a—" Mom shot him a look. "It's not," she said.

"Trevor was supposed to find out for me at homeroom whether Deanna was gonna ask me," Zack continued. "But he was late today, and Cindy asked me on the way to gym, and so I said yes, and *then* Trevor told me in the locker room that Deanna *was* going to ask me."

"Well, next time there's a dance, you can ask Deanna," Mom informed Zack. "Under *no* circumstances do you tell *anyone*, 'I'd rather go with Deanna than Cindy.' You will hurt someone's feelings."

"You can dance with other girls too," said Dad. "Not just Cindy. Do the girls do the asking *at* the dance?"

Zack shrugged. "I don't know, I've never been to a Sadie Hawkins dance."

Emily noticed that none of them looked to her for an answer, either forgetting or simply not knowing in the first place that *she* had gone to a Sadie Hawkins dance.

After they had cleaned the dishes and gone upstairs, Emily caught a snippet of her parents' conversation. "Elliot, he's in eighth grade. We've talked about this. We're not in New York anymore, there aren't a million Jews in his class, he and Emily have known the kids in Hebrew school since kindergarten. If we want them to *have* a social life..."

"I'd still feel better if this Cindy was Jewish."

"Please don't bring it up to him. Believe me, your kids know how you feel, and Emily seems to have internalized it a little *too* much already."

"Good," Dad said.

"You know you don't really mean that. Elliot, most of us don't find the person we're going to marry on the first try. She needs to feel comfortable with the trying, or its only going to get harder when she's wanting to settle down."

Emily stopped listening at that point, because the phone was ringing. Clearly, she and Zack were not going to satisfy both parents.

The next day, word came back that someone named Matt had asked Deanna to the dance, ignoring the Sadie Hawkins rules, and that she had said yes, although Deanna had apparently told Trevor that she still liked Zack. Later that week, two girls who didn't know that Zack was going to the dance with Cindy asked him as well, the second one so nervous when Emily answered that she almost hung up before Zack got there to say, as Mom had coached him, "Thanks but I already have a date."

That weekend, the last weekend before the dance, Zack realized that if he was going with a date he would actually have to *dance.*

"You've been going to these things for a whole year and you've never actually danced?" said Mom.

"Just slow-danced," said Zack.

Mom gave him a strange look. "Elliot, were *your* school dances like this?"

Dad looked embarrassed. "I didn't go."

"Not 'til high school?" asked Emily.

Dad looked more embarrassed. "Not until college."

"Really?" said Mom. "I thought it was just dating that started late for you."

"When did Dad start dating?" Emily asked.

"College," Mom said. "When we met."

Zack was jumping around the den, in some vague attempt at dancing. Emily and Mom started laughing. Dad, Emily noticed, didn't. She went over and gave Dad a hug—for a split second, he seemed even younger than Zack.

"Let me show you," Mom said. She began to show him a few dance steps from the 1950s, saying, "It's Sadie Hawkins, I'm sure they'll have fifties music," but Emily and Zack both shook their heads.

"Top 40, Mom," Emily said.

"And some Zeppelin," Zack added.

Emily wasn't sure who Zeppelin was. "Stairway to Heaven?" Zack asked. Emily shook her head. He started singing it.

Now she remembered. It was the long song they played at the end of every eighth grade dance, the one that was endless except for the few times someone actually said yes to dance with her. She could still remember Winston's tall sweaty shoulder against the left side of her face, her hands around his waist, his on her mid-back.

Mom was demonstrating the bunny hop when Dad slinked away, and Emily was glad when Adena rang the bell.

Adena had her learner's permit, and she had driven over with her father, who would take over the wheel for an hour or so to run errands while Adena hung out, then pick her up so Adena could practice driving home. Adena watched the spectacle for a moment from the door of the den, waiting until Zack looked up and blushed before she followed Emily into her bedroom. Although Adena didn't have a boyfriend either, she'd come back from summer camp with stories of *two*, and a new talent for flirting. Today, later, when Zack passed by Emily's bedroom door, Adena called to him. "Zack my boy," she said, "you need a few lessons in *today's* dancing to round that out."

Zack came in, and Adena showed him some moves. He wasn't good—in fact, for Emily it was like watching a sitcom—but he was enthusiastic, and once he started, un-self-conscious, comfortable in his body. Emily envied him. She wanted to be up there practicing the electric slide—what Adena called "brushing up on the retro"—but just couldn't lift herself from where she perched on her bed. In her imagination, she was dancing just fine, but her body wouldn't follow. And anyway, now that she had babysitting most Saturday nights, she had an excuse not to go to dances—which weren't as big a deal in high school anyway.

When Adena's father sounded his horn, Adena gave Zack a kiss on the cheek, a move that made both Zack, receiving, and Emily, watching, turn red in the face. "Good luck, handsome," she said. "See you in Hebrew school, Emily."

"She's like that with everyone," Emily told Zack, once Adena had gone. He didn't seem to notice the tone behind Emily's words. "Don't get too hopeful."

Emily's jealousy—she didn't actually know what precisely she was jealous of—simmered until Dance Night, when Zack was rummaging through closets, making strange movements that only vaguely approximated dancing, and slicking back his hair like John Travolta in *Grease.* Mom hollered out, "Emily, you need to take pictures of this transformation for us."

Emily didn't want to take pictures. She didn't even want to be home, but her babysitting job didn't start for another hour.

"Don't you dare, Emily," Zack called out. "Mom, she takes pictures of me with my tongue sticking out and shows her friends."

"Maybe you shouldn't stick your tongue out," Mom suggested, while Emily said to him, meanly, "Don't worry, you look like an idiot. I'd break my camera."

Zack continued rummaging, hollering out, "Does anyone have a box I can roll up my sleeve like a pack of cigarettes?"

Emily had the perfect-sized box, but she kept her mouth shut, even when Mom emerged with a too-small jewelry box that only made Zack look stupid.

Zack again was oblivious to the meanness, which only made Emily feel worse. He seemed focused on how Mom's behavior was embarrassing him, particularly when Cindy showed up. Mom made Cindy's parents come in for cheese and crackers and she made Dad take pictures of the Sadie Hawkins couple with Emily's camera. Dad largely kept his mouth shut, appearing nearly as uncomfortable as Zack, until Cindy's father asked him something about politics, and then Dad began spewing, not willing to let a Republican have the last word, even if he was a guest of sorts. Out of earshot of their parents, before Mom finally let Zack and Cindy out the door, Zack said to Emily, "This is the last time I bring a date home." Emily would remember that statement when Zack started dating seriously in high school without their parents knowing, and again when Emily's first real relationship began.

After Zack and his date left, Emily was picked up for babysitting, which, except for the occasional movie with a classmate or sleepover with Adena, was her usual weekend night activity. Emily hadn't clicked into the school social scene, and actually preferred babysitting, particularly when she was able to get homework done after the kids went to bed. She was still doing extremely well in school, but it had gotten harder—it took a lot more work and time to *almost* keep up the kinds of grades she had been getting since the second week of kindergarten when she had suddenly picked up a book and started reading. That evening, the kids tired themselves out playing basketball in the yard and fell asleep early enough for Emily to finish all but her Latin homework.

At the end of the evening, Emily got a report from the kids' mother, who was a teacher at Zack's school and had been chaperoning that night. Emily learned that Zack had held his own, looking horrendous on the dance floor with his version of Adena's moves, but in a compelling way—people danced with him—the enthusiasm mattering more than the coordination. And for the one 50s song other than the twist, which everyone knew, Zack had been the only boy who had known what to do and had led his date in a respectable Lindy, which had brought him newfound attention from quite a few girls and thereby envied glares from a number of the boys. Emily pointedly didn't ask about slow-dancing, nor whether her brother had danced at all with Deanna, although the teacher did report that Matt and Deanna had snuck off during the 50s dance and were caught French-kissing behind the bleachers.

For the remainder of the year, Emily would continue getting updates from the teacher and learn that by April Zack had "gone out with" quite a few of the girls in his class, fitting into the maxim that the average eighth grade relationship lasted about two weeks. The only one that got mentioned at home was Noa, which overlapped a dance and therefore meant that whichever parent would be driving Zack to the dance would have to stop on the way to pick her up. Emily wasn't sure if Zack had planned most of his relationships and breakups to avoid the dances; she did notice, however, that when Zack mentioned Noa, Dad perked up and said, "Jewish?" And when Zack said that she was half-Jewish, on her mother's side, Dad sighed and said, "Well, at least it's the side that counts."

When Emily got home the night of the Sadie Hawkins dance, her little brother was listening to KC101, the door closed all but a crack, and she peeked in to watch him. Wild, awkward, weird, dancing. She knocked and opened the door. He was still dancing.

"They liked it, Emily. I look horrible when I dance. But they *liked* it. Isn't that strange?"

She flopped down on his bed. He flopped down next to her. "I thought maybe I'd gotten better," he said, gesturing towards the mirror. He shook his head furiously. "Nope. They *liked* it."

Zack had shot up about six inches over the summer, so he was now as tall as Emily and his voice had deepened just enough to disorient Emily whenever he spoke. He had acquired a certain cockiness that hadn't disappeared as Emily expected when he and his friends began to attend different high schools. Zack was only a freshman, and already he fit in better than Emily at school. It seemed effortless for him—anywhere he went, all his peers seemed to gravitate towards him. He was rarely home anymore. On this particular fall Sunday, he had gone hiking for the day with his friend Oliver, or at least that's what he had told Mom and Dad—Emily suspected he was with the junior he was rumored to be dating. Mom had gone food shopping, so just Emily and Dad were home.

They were in the basement, where Dad had set up a darkroom before Emily and Zack were born. More recently, he had replaced the decades-old chemicals so that Emily could use the darkroom for her own photography. Emily was printing pictures from Grandma and Grandpa Novak's forty-fifth anniversary party, and Dad was moving the images from the fixer to the wash and squeegeeing the finished prints. He had already printed a reproduction of his parents' wedding photo, and together he and Emily would make an album.

"Did Grandma and Grandpa know Gram and Grandpa Irv?" Emily asked, focusing an image of Grandma and Grandpa Novak dancing.

"Yes," answered Dad. "Don't you remember, they all used to come to your birthday parties?"

"Oh," Emily said, feeling stupid for not remembering that. "Were they *friends*?" she asked.

Dad hesitated. "No, not really. I don't think they *disliked* each other. They just didn't have very much in common." He used tongs to move another print to the running wash in the sink. "I remember them driving up here together a few times."

Emily considered that, sliding a sheet of paper under the easel and exposing it. "They came to Grandpa Irv's funeral."

"Yes."

"Do you think they know where Ninian went?"

"Doubtful," Dad said. "We know your aunt was planning—"

"My *ex*-aunt," Emily interrupted.

"Your *ex*-aunt," Dad continued, "was planning to move to Arizona somewhere. She told that to Gram's best friend at Grandpa Irv's funeral, and Helen told Mommy."

"Do I know Helen?" Emily asked. She hadn't realized Gram had *had* a best friend.

"You met her once or twice," Dad said. "She died a year or two ago. Anyway, we don't know if they wound up in Arizona or not, or even if they did, if they'd still be there. They could still be living in their old house for all we know."

Emily doubted that, because she had checked the telephone book at Grandma and Grandpa Novak's house once, and Ninian's husband's name wasn't listed anymore. She studied the image of Grandma and Grandpa Novak as it slowly appeared in the developer, glowing yellow and black under the safelight. You could tell how much they enjoyed life. Emily was glad to have half their genes.

"Do you want to look for your cousins?" Dad asked. "We could try writing them again."

"No," Emily said. "I was just curious."

The prints needed more time to dry before going in the album, so after having dinner with her parents, Emily decided to take a bath. She picked up the book she had started reading that morning, put a *Simon and Garfunkel* tape in her boom box, and carried them both towards the bathroom.

Her father called out to her from the den. "Emily, what are you doing with that radio?"

"Don't worry, Dad," she called back, knowing what he was concerned about. "I plug it in on the other side of the bathroom. It's nowhere near the tub."

"No," he said. He got up from the desk where he had been grading exams. "You could electrocute yourself." He walked towards Emily, hands outstretched. "Let me have that."

Emily held the boom box tighter. "I'm not going to touch it when I'm wet. I'm not even going to be near it. It's perfectly safe."

"It is *not* perfectly safe," he said. His voice was rising.

"It's fine, Dad. I've done it plenty of times." Was this really the first time he had noticed? "Nothing's—"

He cut her off. "It's *dangerous,* Emily. I don't know why you would even *think* about doing something so incredibly *stupid.*"

Emily stepped backward into the bathroom, realizing that Dad had gotten into his unreasonable mode again. Her father was mellower than anyone else Emily knew, except when he went into unreasonable mode. You couldn't predict when it would happen, and once it did, he wouldn't budge.

"What about if I used batteries?" Emily asked. "You can't get electrocuted on batteries."

"If you have batteries, you can listen to it," Dad said. "But not otherwise."

"Fine," Emily said, setting the boom box on the scale in the bathroom. Dad stood in the doorway, watching until she detached the plug and carried it into her room. When she got back to the bathroom, she pressed *play* but nothing happened. "The batteries are dead," she announced. "Dad, can you get me new batteries?"

"You're not helpless, Emily." When Dad said this in a light-hearted tone, he would sometimes do what she asked anyway, but Emily could tell from the fury in his voice that this was not one of those times. She thumped downstairs, shuddering at the creaks even though she was far too old to really believe there were monsters, and opened the refrigerator where they kept fresh batteries. She needed six C batteries. There were only two.

She stomped back upstairs. "We need more C batteries." Her father was back in the den with a stack of exams and didn't look up. Emily made sure he wasn't watching, then went into her room and fetched the plug and returned to the bathroom, where she closed the door and plugged in the boom box. She took off her shirt and pants and bra and started filling the tub. She pressed play and then sat down on the toilet, underpants around her feet.

She heard Dad's footsteps, but he couldn't come into the bathroom once the door was closed.

"Emily, is that thing on batteries?"

"Yes."

"Emily." His voice was right outside the door.

She ignored him.

His footsteps got softer and she knew he was heading towards her bedroom, and then they got louder again. "Don't lie to me. Hand me your radio or I'm coming in and taking it."

"I'm on the toilet," Emily said.

The door opened. Dad barely glanced at Emily, apparently not even registering her nakedness as he stormed in and unplugged the boom box and took it away, leaving the door open behind him.

In shock, for a moment Emily couldn't even move or speak. Dad had actually *opened* the bathroom door while Emily was on the toilet. Dad had come *into* the bathroom while Emily was sitting there naked. Dad had *left* the door open. Emily was now exposed on the toilet, with the open door out of reach.

"Close the door," she shouted. "Close the damn door at least."

"Don't use that kind of language," Dad said, turning around and abruptly turning back. He had clearly just recognized his faux pas, because he continued on to the den and shut *that* door. Emily got up and walked with the underwear around her feet to shut the bathroom door, slamming it feebly because she didn't have good leverage.

She peed and flushed and washed her hands and then settled into the tub with her book, turning the water off. Soon there was a knock at the door. "What."

"It's me, Emily," her mother said. "Can I come in and wash my face?"

Emily sighed, slid open the tub door enough to put the book down, open face on the second page of chapter three, closed the door and said, "Fine, come in."

She reached for the washcloth and held it out through a crack so her mother wouldn't have to open and reach in.

"Thanks."

Emily didn't say anything.

"Are you having a nice bath?"

"It would be better with music. *Why* does he have to get like that?"

"He's right that you shouldn't be plugging in your radio near water."

"It *wasn't*, Mom. I'm not going to get electrocuted. It was on the whole other side of the bathroom, on the scale."

Emily squeezed the Suave into her hand and worked it into her hair. Her hair was getting longer and she wondered if the extra maintenance and shampoo was worth the supposed benefits that came with long hair, the automatic perception of attractiveness.

"You know how he gets. You're not going to reason with him on this one, Emily. Just put batteries on the shopping list and be subtle about it next time, don't go trying to pick a fight."

Emily dunked her head underwater, rinsing off the shampoo.

Mom put toothpaste on her brush and then asked before putting the brush in her mouth, "Did you finish your homework for tomorrow?"

"Almost," Emily said. "All I have left is Calculus, and I can do that in study hall."

Mom finished brushing her upper teeth, then spit. "Are you sure that's enough time?"

"Yeah. I'm too tired to focus anymore tonight anyway."

"So you're not looking at your college material either?"

"Not tonight," Emily said, "*Top Gun* is on TV. What time is it?"

"Almost nine," Mom said, spitting for the last time then rinsing her toothbrush. She picked up the washcloth. "May I put my washcloth back?"

"Sure," said Emily, dunking under water a little more.

When Mom shut the door, Emily applied conditioner to her hair, rinsed it off, ran a washcloth over her body, then let out the stopper with her toes. She dried off, threw on pajamas, and headed into the empty den and turned on the television.

Dad shouted up from the bottom of the stairs. "Emily, do you want ice cream?"

She debated not answering. "Yeah. Two scoops of mint chip. Please."

He came up with three bowls.

Emily examined her bowl. Two Dad-sized scoops, which meant barely as much as she or Zack would put in one scoop. If Dad weren't being such a jerk, she might go down at the commercial for more, but she didn't want to set him off again.

"How was your bath?" Dad asked.

He was clearly pretending nothing had happened. Typical. Emily wasn't quite ready to let it go, but was glad he seemed to be out of unreasonable mode for the moment. "Fine," she said. "Ssh, the movie's starting."

The next morning, as Zack groggily wolfed down breakfast half-dressed and Emily remembered she didn't have study hall on Mondays, Mom announced a family pumpkin-picking trip for the following Saturday afternoon.

"I can't go," Emily said. "That's Adena's birthday, remember? We're going roller-skating, and then she's having a pizza-and-movie night."

"Roller-skating?" said Zack. "That's lame. I can't go either, Mom. I promised Oliver I'd help him test out his new canoe."

"Did we give you permission to go canoeing?" asked Dad.

"Since when do I need permission to go canoeing?" asked Zack. "It's a weekend. Oh, and I need a ride."

"We'll drop you off on the way back from pumpkin-picking," said Dad. 'We should be back by about four—that'll give you a whole half-hour to test the canoe before it starts getting dark."

Zack rolled his eyes. "Oliver invited me for eleven. Mom, can I go?"

Dad turned to Emily. "I don't remember you asking permission to go roller-skating either."

"I asked Mom last week and she said it was fine,"

Mom looked at Dad. "I guess this is life with two teenagers." She looked back at Zack and Emily. "Zack, you may go canoeing, but next time, please *ask* before making promises to your friends. And *I* will try to remember that my children have lives of their own before assuming that they might want to spend a pleasant fall afternoon with their parents. Elliot, would *you* like to pick out a pumpkin with me next weekend?"

A few weeks later, as the Sunday night movie was ending, the doorbell rang. Mom was already asleep, the bedroom door closed so she wouldn't hear the television. Zack was at Oliver's house studying for a Chemistry test. Emily and Dad were in the den watching the movie, Emily ostensibly reading college brochures during the commercials. "I wonder who's ringing the bell so late at night," Dad said.

"Maybe Zack forgot his keys," Emily suggested, even though that had never happened before.

The bell rang again, a double-ring, and Emily realized that it was the front doorbell. Dad looked worried, and he hurried downstairs with a different thud rhythm than usual. Everyone who knew them used the back door. Dad's nervousness made Emily nervous, and because she didn't know what else to do, she fetched her camera and crept over to the top of the stairs.

There was a cop standing in the doorway. Zack stood next to him.

"—found them drinking in the woods behind the library," the cop was saying. "Your son identified this backpack as his. There was a bag of marijuana inside."

The cop was looking at Dad. Dad was looking at Zack. Zack's eyes were directed towards Dad's hands, which were clenched. Emily didn't know if any of them had noticed she was there. She looked through the lens, not clicking because she wanted to sit and listen and not disturb. Would a cop arrest her for taking pictures? It was her house. But he was outside, on the porch. No, he was in the entry. He'd stepped inside.

"We could press charges, you understand," the cop continued. "Possession of marijuana is considered a misdemeanor. Fortunately for your son, his friend confessed to placing it in the backpack. The sergeant decided to let Zack off with a warning." He looked at Zack. "That won't happen next time, son, so don't let there be a next time."

"There won't," Dad said firmly. It was the first thing Emily had heard him say. Her father's voice registered first concern, then disbelief, as he continued speaking, but maintained its usual volume, just soft-spoken enough to keep Emily from making out the words.

Dad took the official warning notice the cop handed to him, and then shook his hand. Once the door was closed and locked, Dad's tone changed to fury. "What is *wrong* with you, Zack?" He spoke loud enough that Emily doubted either of them heard the camera click. They seemed oblivious to her presence. Emily listened, eyed the one big footprint on the burgundy carpet, a cop footprint. Her mother would be mad that he hadn't wiped his feet, *what kind of behavior is that for a law enforcement officer?* There was a Dustbuster in the pantry, maybe Emily could vacuum up the footprint before Mom woke up. "Are you out of your *mind?*" Dad was yelling now. "Zack Novak. *Look at me* when I'm talking to you." Click. Neither of them looked up, and Emily crept back up the final two stairs and into her bedroom. She closed the door and opened her book, one ear listening for the footsteps which would mean her dad and brother were coming upstairs.

Eventually Emily got drawn into her book. She didn't look up until her bladder decided it couldn't wait anymore, and on the way to the bathroom she noticed that the den door was closed, as was Zack's, and it was quiet. Light wasn't seeping into the hall from under the door of her parents' bedroom like it was for the other two rooms, so Emily concluded that Mom had slept through everything. After using the bathroom, Emily knocked on Zack's door.

"It's me," she said.

"It's open," said Zack.

Emily opened the door. Zack was lying on face up on his bed, hands behind his head.

"Are you in deep trouble?" Emily asked.

"No shit." Zack sighed. "He's waiting until tomorrow morning to get into it. When Mom wakes up."

"What happened?"

"Where's Dad?" Zack asked.

"In the den."

"Close the door."

Emily did. She sat down on Zack's bean bag chair. "Were you smoking pot?"

"Tonight," Zack said, "I was just meeting this guy to drop off a bootleg of a show. Me and Charlie stopped by on the way back from Oliver's house." He grimaced. "Just in time for the raid."

Charlie was known as the freshman class stoner. Oliver was another classmate. They had a study group together for Chemistry, or at least Zack had told their parents it was a study group. Now Emily wasn't so sure. And Zack had said *tonight* like on other nights he *did* go there to smoke pot.

"What was the bootleg?" Emily asked. She was trying to act cool, act like it was no big deal, but inside she was thinking, *my brother drinks, my brother smokes pot, my brother's messing his life up.*

"I don't see what the big deal is," Zack said to their parents the next night. "I simply stopped by for a few minutes to see my friends on my way back home, and unfortunately my timing coincided with that of the police."

Later incidents would have worse consequences, but in a way the cop's arrival at the front door would overshadow any others, because that was when the family lost their blinders. The four of them sat at the dinner table, food eaten but not yet put away. The conversation had been delayed so that Mom and Dad could have time earlier that afternoon to confer.

"Zack," Mom said, "the issue here is that you lied to us." There were two folded pieces of paper next to Mom's place setting, and Emily wondered what they were for. "You told us that you were studying with your friend Oliver—"

"I *did* study—"

"and instead you were in the woods behind the library, in the dark, with a bunch of people who were drinking and using drugs."

"I—"

"I don't even want to *think* about what could have happened back there."

Mom was quiet for a few long seconds, presumably letting the impact of her statement sink in. Emily sat uncomfortably. She didn't have a speaking role in this family meeting, but her presence was expected nonetheless.

"Your father and I have discussed it," Mom continued, "and we've decided to ground you for the next month. Hopefully by then you'll have found some more appropriate friends."

"We've also decided," Dad said, "that after the grounding is up, your new curfew on school nights will be ten-thirty."

Zack started to protest, and Mom cut him off. "If your study group needs to meet later than that, they can come *here*."

Emily looked at Zack. He had a look in his face that reminded Emily of her father in unreasonable mode. He wasn't trying to defend himself anymore. He wasn't arguing against the severity of the punishment. If her parents had hoped this would open the communication lines, they were far more out of touch with their son than they realized.

"Now," said Dad, "about what *was* happening last night—"

"Wait," Mom said. "Zack, do you understand everything we just said?"

"Yes," said Zack, his tone flat. "Grounding for a month, then ten-thirty curfew forever."

"At least for the remainder of the school year," Dad said. "Then we'll discuss it. Now would you like to tell us what actually happened last night?"

"Not particularly," Zack said.

"Were you drinking?" Mom asked.

"No."

"And why should we believe you?" asked Dad.

"You can believe what you want to believe," said Zack. "Would you like to interrogate Charlie and Oliver to see if their stories corroborate with mine?"

"You're taking this a little too far, Zack," Mom said.

"Me?" said Zack.

"The point is," Mom said, "we're worried about you. We don't want you hanging out with people who do these kinds of things. Who might pressure you into joining them. We don't want you lying to us. We want you to feel comfortable coming to us if you find yourself in a tough situation."

Now Zack rolled his eyes in Emily's direction, and she nodded back, imperceptibly enough so that her parents wouldn't notice. *Comfortable* was not exactly the message they were sending. Although Emily was thankful they were paying attention and cracking down.

"This applies to both of you," Mom said, turning to Emily for the first time. She pushed the sheets of paper towards Emily and Zack, one for each of them. "These came in the mail a few weeks ago as part of a Mothers Against Drunk Driving solicitation, and this afternoon your father and I decided it might be a good idea."

Emily skimmed the document in front of her. *Safe Driving Contract*, it was titled, *between Emily Novak (Teen) and Daisy and Elliot Novak (Parent(s)/Guardian(s))*. It promised a no-questions-asked ride home from Parent(s)/Guardian(s) at any time in exchange for Teen's agreement not to drive after drinking or accept a ride from anyone who had been drinking. Emily's parents—in her mother's handwriting—had added the phrase "or using drugs" in the relevant places on the document.

"This does not mean we're giving you permission to drink," Dad said. "It's illegal until you're twenty-one, for good reason. But sometimes things happen, and above all, we want you both to be *safe*."

"Do you have a pen?" Zack asked. Emily felt for the one in her pocket and reached out to put it in Zack's outstretched hand, but her father intercepted.

"*Read*, Zack," he said, "before you sign. This is not a game." He let go and Zack took the pen, tapping it on the table as he read. Finally they each signed—Mom and Dad and Emily on one contract, Mom and Dad and Zack on the other—and Emily was glad to see her parents' and Zack's signatures, though she didn't quite believe the part about no-questions-asked.

Their parents' trust in Zack had crumpled like a wad of aluminum foil after the cop incident. *They act like I'm going to become a heroin addict from having a beer once in a while,* Emily heard Zack tell one of his friends over the phone. She didn't know what Mom and Dad could do differently, but their actions were definitely pushing him away, and he seemed to be shutting out Emily as well. Emily escaped whenever she could to the darkroom, either at home or at school, hoping to avoid the interrogations and screaming matches that had become the most frequent form of communication between her parents and her brother.

It was from the rumor mill at school, not from Zack, that Emily learned that her brother and the junior had broken up and that Zack was now dating a girl named Kathryn. So when Emily first encountered Zack and his new girlfriend together in early January, she wasn't sure what the protocol was, particularly since Zack just seemed to assume she already knew. Emily had just left the office of her Physics teacher, where she'd been meeting about a failed pop quiz. She'd been warning her parents that the class was too hard, that she wanted to drop out of honors, that she couldn't be good at *every* subject, but her grades didn't reflect the difficulty. Now one finally had—she had *proof*—and suddenly she didn't want to tell them. It was the first academic anything she had failed, ever. It would be dropped—the teacher dropped the lowest quiz grade—but still. She didn't want to fail. She just wanted *room* to fail, for her *work* to be acknowledged and for the pressure and unfair expectations to go away. And now Emily was already ten minutes late for her next class, and she decided then and there to follow up her first "F" with her first cut class. And that's when she ran into Zack and Kathryn in Main Hall, pasting up the new Honor Roll.

Emily said hello and paused to look at the names.

"You're there," Kathryn said, pointing halfway down the junior column. She was perched on a stepstool pasting up the sophomores as Zack called out names and handed her letters.

"Did you make it?" Emily asked.

"Me? No." Kathryn laughed. "The only list I make is work crew. They tell me I'm in the running for most demerits ever by a freshman. Your brother, on the other hand, has the distinct honor of making *both* lists."

This was news to Emily.

"What can I say?" Zack shrugged, waving to a couple of friends down the hall. "I'm multi-talented."

"Yeah?" said Kathryn, flirtatiously. "So why I am doing all the work here? Hand me another letter."

Zack slid a letter into Kathryn's back pocket.

"Zack!" Kathryn climbed down from the stepstool. "You can do the rest." She turned to Emily. "Did Zack tell you he scored *Phish* tickets for next weekend?"

"Shh," said Zack. "She'll tell my parents."

"Fish tickets?" asked Emily, confused.

"No she won't," Kathryn said to Zack, then mouthed the words *road trip* to Emily as one of the deans passed by.

"Can I get a ride home with you?" Zack asked Emily. "I thought I had to stay late but practice is cancelled because of the weather."

"Sure," said Emily, as Zack's friends approached. "If you're ready *at* three. I'm not waiting."

"You sound like Mom," Zack said. "Three-fifteen. Don't leave without me."

At three-twenty, Zack showed up at the car, holding hands with Kathryn. For a moment Emily thought Kathryn was going to get in the car too, but instead Kathryn pushed Zack up against the passenger side for a lengthy public display of affection—something that was definitely against school rules—before scampering off with a wave. Zack was flushed when he climbed into the seat.

"Kathryn's just gonna get you in more trouble," Emily told Zack as they drove off.

"Jesus, Emily," said Zack. "Lighten up."

Mom was hanging laundry while Emily photographed her. It was September, Emily's senior year of high school. "Tell me about ballet," Emily asked.

"You've heard this before, Emily."

"Tell me again."

So Mom did, how she had been given her first ballet lessons as a birthday present when she turned six, and learned to dance so well that she was accepted into the High School of Performing Arts, and then been diagnosed with scoliosis and had to quit.

"Couldn't you have kept dancing anyway?" Emily asked. "Did it *hurt* your back?"

"No, it didn't," Mom said, "but I knew the scoliosis would get worse. I wouldn't have been able to be professional."

"Do you ever think about dancing again now?"

"Emily, do you know how long it's been?"

"Just for fun though."

"No."

Click. After the photo was developed, Emily would stare at the expression she had captured, trying to wrap her head around its intensity. Her mother had been fifteen, and yet the bitterness was as raw as if it had happened yesterday.

"Why are you so curious about ballet all of a sudden?" Mom asked.

"Just thinking about what I want to do with my life."

"Which is?"

"I'm just thinking about it."

Emily took another couple of shots of her mother, her mother's hands pinning the clothespins, extra pins between her lips so she wouldn't have to reach down after each one. She wandered off, taking a close-up on the lilies of the valley and then focusing on a squirrel, but deciding the background was too busy for it to be a good shot. She came back and perched on the porch railing near her mother, handing her items from the laundry basket. "I want to major in photography, I think."

Her mother stopped pinning the clothes and looked at her. "You want to make a *career* out of being a photographer?"

"I don't know. Maybe. I just want to study it more. Get better at it."

"Emily, if you want to be a photographer, you need to go to a trade school, not a liberal arts school. Which is fine, if you want to pay for it. Your dad and I have been saving all these years so you can get a liberal arts education. We're paying for you to learn to *think*, not to take pictures."

"I thought you liked my photography."

"We *do*, Emily. I love your photos, you know that. Why do you think I have them displayed all over the house, and point them out whenever we have company? But you don't need to major in photography to keep taking pictures. It's a waste of money. You have savings. If you want to major in photography, you can use your savings."

Emily brought it up with her father the next week, when her mother wasn't around. "Your mother mentioned that to me," he said. "I agree with her—if you want to study photography, you can go to a trade school with your own money. But I think it's important that you get a well-rounded education. I think you're too intelligent to *just* do photography, and I think you would get bored, and you wouldn't be challenged by your classmates, and I think if you attend a liberal arts school which offers a few photo classes and has a darkroom you can use, you'll be happier."

She wanted to do photography, but not enough. She didn't want to graduate with a photo degree and not have anything for afterwards. She didn't want to photograph bar mitzvahs or weddings or well-groomed toddlers in Sears. She didn't want to work for a newspaper. She just wanted to take pictures and have someone discover them and be able to photograph whatever she wanted. And she *did* want the other stuff too, the liberal arts thinking skills that her parents were so adamant about. So she wrote her essays for the schools the college counselor had picked out, Harvard and Penn and Yale and four others, and a few months later Emily called home right after class and Mom said there was an envelope from Harvard.

Emily had a meeting at school in another two hours. She drove home anyway. The envelope was sitting at her place at the table, and as Emily put the key in the door, she could see it through the window. She could see that it was large, and thick. Thick meant *yes*.

She turned the key slowly. Now that she knew she'd been accepted, she could pay attention to the other fact. The thing she'd first said to herself when she was eleven years old, when she switched from public school to private school and her parents warned her there would be other smart kids around, and that she wasn't necessarily going to be at the top of her class anymore, and she might even have to work a little. *I want to apply to Harvard because I want to know if I'll get in, but I don't want to go there.*

No one turns down Harvard, people invariably said whenever she had talked about this plan. *If you get in, you'll go.* But the truth was she really did like Penn better. She liked the people she'd met, the lack of pretension, the fact that the students seemed focused on things they really cared about rather than on being the best and staying the best and rubbing it in.

"Hello," Emily hollered. She dropped her bookbag on the floor, picked up the envelope and felt its weight, set it down again, then opened the fridge and took out a grapefruit from the collection

Grandma and Grandpa Novak had sent them from Florida. She got out two bowls and a grapefruit peeler, sat down at the table, and began peeling. The envelope sat next to her, unopened. She wanted to savor this.

Her parents were downstairs by the time she'd peeled off two pieces of rind. "Well?" Mom asked.

"Well, what?"

"What did Harvard say?" asked Mom.

It was Mom's tone of voice that made Emily realize she wanted to do this alone. "I don't know yet. I haven't opened the envelope."

"Are you going to?" Dad asked.

"After I eat my grapefruit," Emily said. "Don't worry, I'll let you know." She said this looking at Mom, who had started to sit down but stopped, visibly hurt.

"I think Emily wants us to go upstairs," Mom said, bitterly.

Dad shrugged. Emily felt bad, but this was *her* moment. She continued peeling her grapefruit, slowly, as Mom and Dad went upstairs. She peeled off the yellow rind first, then the white pith, putting it all into the first bowl. Then she started peeling apart the individual sections, so that the membrane came apart from the individual pieces of pulp. Those pieces only she put in the second bowl, and when she had enough, she let herself taste a few bites. She peeled the whole grapefruit this way, and when the second bowl was filled with chunks of membrane-less grapefruit, she dumped out the first bowl and washed her hands and opened up the envelope, tearing along the glued flap. *Congratulations*, the letter began.

Emily read the letter and set it carefully back inside the envelope—she might frame it one day—and then read the rest of the acceptance material as she ate the rest of the grapefruit. She was calm. Very calm. It was the calm of accomplishment, of doing something that wasn't entirely surprising but was momentous nonetheless. It was the calm of being able to put it in perspective, of not being so blown away by the mere act of accomplishment that she let it define what came next. It tasted like well-peeled grapefruit. After she had savored the calm long enough, she approached the stairs.

Her parents were up in the hall to meet her almost before she called out to them. "I got in," she said.

Mom squealed, grabbing Emily and hugging her and jumping up and down. "Emily! I'm so proud of you." Emily hugged back, but when she let her arms relax, hug time over, Mom was still clinging and jumping. Emily had never seen her this excited, and it frightened her. It was as if *Mom* was the one who had gotten into college.

"Congratulations, kiddo," said Dad, tousling her hair because Mom had taken a temporary monopoly on the hugging. "I expected nothing less from my best daughter."

"Thanks," Emily said.

"Aren't you excited?" Mom asked. "Emily, you just got into *Harvard*."

"I know," said Emily, wishing she was allowed to name her own feelings. "I guess I am. I mean, it's not like I'm planning to *go* there."

"You *still* want to go to Penn?" Mom asked.

"Mmhm."

"I was guessing you might change your mind if you got into Harvard. I thought you might be trying to keep yourself from being disappointed."

"Nope," Emily said.

"Well, I'm glad," Dad said. "I liked Penn better."

"I do think Penn's a better fit for you," said Mom. "I just want to make sure you make a decision you're happy with."

"Remember," Emily said, "I still haven't gotten *into* Penn."

"You really think that will be a problem?" Mom said.

"*Emily*," Dad said, which meant the same thing.

"My baby got into *Harvard*," Mom said, jumping and squealing again. "I remember when you were two years old and I told Dad that you were smarter than everyone else in day care. He accused me of being partial."

"I didn't say you were *wrong*," Dad protested.

Emily's Penn acceptance came the following week, and her parents sent in the deposit check and Emily started thinking about the classes that she wanted to take in the fall, and how much cooler she would be at college, where *everyone* must have stuck out as "the smart one" in their old school in order to get into Penn in the first place. Now that she was leaving, she was starting to feel nostalgic, and appreciative, and spend more time with her school friends. Her required exercise that term was Ultimate Frisbee, and she discovered that she actually enjoyed it. Someone invested in a glow-in-the-dark Frisbee and the juniors and seniors celebrated the night after the first AP exam with tubs of ice cream and an impromptu nighttime Frisbee game that turned into a mud fight.

Each equally engrossed in their separate worlds, Emily and Zack barely spoke these days, just coexisted in the same house. Occasionally when Emily emerged from the school darkroom or a library study carrel for a dose of daylight, she saw Zack's profile on the soccer field, practicing with the other junior varsity players or helping to coach the town youth soccer team that used their school's facilities. Usually Zack could be found working one-on-one with someone, demonstrating how to do a particular move or giving a goalie practice shots.

One Saturday morning, Emily woke to the raised voices of her father and Zack.

"No you may *not* have a lift to a soccer game. You're supposed to be *grounded*, remember? Or did you forget that you were *caught* the last time you snuck out after curfew to see your girlfriend?"

"Dad, I'm the assistant coach. They're counting on me."

"They'll have to make do."

"Fine, I'll call Coach Nate and see if he can pick me up."

"You are not leaving this house."

"What? Dad—"

"Zack, there will be no more discussion. I'm already late. And don't ask your mother for a ride either. When she wakes up, you can use the phone in our bedroom to call your coach and tell him you won't be there. I'm taking the other phones with me."

Emily heard Dad thumping through the house, into and out of all the rooms that had phones. He skipped her bedroom, thankfully, and she wondered if Zack would knock after Dad left and ask to use her phone. Instead, almost as soon as she heard Dad's car drive off, Zack's thumping could be heard, then the faint sound of the basement door. Emily looked out the window to see Zack biking down the driveway. Was he biking all the way to school?

A few hours later, as Emily was searching the pantry for something to eat for lunch and Dad was wiping his feet on the back porch and turning his key in the lock, Zack stood in the kitchen in his soccer jacket and cleats talking excitedly to Mom. "—actually *scored*. His first time Mom. And he did it with the kick I'd been teaching him last week."

"That's great, Zack," Mom said, the voice of someone who didn't appreciate sports but was trying for her son's sake.

At that moment the back door opened. Dad took one look at Zack, and Unreasonable Mode came on full force. "I told you not to leave the house."

Mom looked at Zack. "You didn't tell me you disobeyed your father's instructions. I said you could go to the game today *if* your father agreed."

"Mom, you can't let Dad have the final say when he gets like this. You *knew* it was important for me to be there today."

"Zack, whether you think we're being fair or not, no means no. I will *not* have you disobeying us."

"Clearly grounding isn't enough," Dad said. "For starters, you're quitting this coaching job. Completely."

"You can go to hell, Dad."

Zack stomped towards the entryway.

"Zack." Mom left no doubt where her loyalty had been cast.

"You too, Mom. Standing by your husband as he punishes a bunch of innocent ten-year-olds." The door slammed behind Zack as he ran up the driveway. "You can hurt me all you want," he shouted, "but I'm going to coach those kids."

Emily stared through the screen at her brother's receding figure. She imagined him going and going, not stopping until he'd run himself into a whole new life, a different family. She swallowed, a lump in her throat.

"Maybe," Mom's voice was shaky. "Maybe we went too far this time."

No one answered. Emily turned to look at her father. He, too, was staring out the window, his face impenetrable. It would stay that way long into the night, even after Zack made his silent, sullen, way back home.

The second time Zack got arrested, Emily was the only one home. Their parents were in New York at a college reunion. Emily had been letting the answering machine screen calls all evening so she could study for her Advanced Placement European History exam, and she wasn't sure what made her pick up that particular phone call.

"Emily, I need your help." Emily was instantly worried—why would Zack be calling *her*? Why not Kathryn or Oliver?

"Where are you?"

"The police station. You know where it is—right across from the library. I need you to meet me down here. Please, Emily."

"What—I mean, are you okay?"

"I'm fine. Oliver and I got arrested. Will you come? And bring my wallet? It'll be in the left front pocket of the jeans hanging over my desk chair."

"Left front pocket. Desk chair." Emily repeated the words, her brain not yet comprehending.

"*Thank* you." said Zack. "And Emily? Whatever you do, just—if Mom and Dad call, don't tell them."

"I can't *lie*, Zack."

"Em, you're smart, you'll think of something. Please."

The next few hours were a blur. Emily didn't remember driving, but there she was at the police station, handing over her own license for inspection and signing an affidavit that her brother was in fact Zack Novak and that his birthday was January eighteenth, nineteen seventy-seven, and that their parents would return from out of town the next day. Since Emily was still a minor, she wasn't permitted to take Zack home as he had intended, yet Zack elected not to call their parents. Instead he gave Emily a note—the sergeant insisted on reading it first—which explained the situation, suggesting that Emily leave it on the kitchen table and then make herself scarce when Mom and Dad returned. The note began, *Dear Mom and Dad, I am sorry to have to tell you that I have been arrested for consuming alcohol and this time I am not innocent.*

Back home, there were two messages from Emily's parents on the answering machine. The second one instructed Emily and Zack to leave a message with the hotel front desk confirming that that were okay, since Mom and Dad would be going to sleep shortly. Emily called the hotel as requested. She then dialed her friend Adena and made plans to go to Adena's house to study the next morning. That taken care of, Emily tried, unsuccessfully, to fall asleep.

"Drinking is no big deal," Adena advised Emily the next morning. "It's not like your family has a history of alcoholism. *Most* teens will have a drink or two at a party. *I've* done it. Heck, I even tried mushrooms a couple of times last summer and nothing happened. Not that I recommend it—it tastes weird and some guys won't go out with girls who shroom. Plus if you do it too much it can zap your brain cells."

Adena too? Emily thought to herself, not sure whether to be worried further, or relieved, or maybe both.

When Emily returned from Adena's late that afternoon, Zack was at home, grounded again, and scheduled for a hearing the following day at the same time as Emily's exam. There was a tense dinner, no one speaking much, and then Dad left for a meeting and Mom disappeared into her bedroom, closing the door. Zack knocked on Emily's bedroom door that night as she was reviewing her list of dates one more time. *1492—Spanish Inquisition and Columbus discovers America.* "Come in." *1517—Martin Luther publishes 95 Theses.*

Zack took a few steps into the room, then stood awkwardly. "Thanks for helping me out yesterday."

Emily, cross-legged on her bed surrounded by books and notes, looked up and studied him for a moment. Overgrown bangs, cutoffs, fabric belt, Phish t-shirt, Tevas, zits. *What would a judge see?* "I don't see what good it did. You still had to spend the night at the police station. You're still going to be in big trouble in court tomorrow."

"It let Dad cool off," Zack said.

"I guess."

"It gave *me* a little time."

"For what?"

Zack looked like he was about to say something, then stopped. "Imagine if I'd called them in New York," he said instead.

Emily thought about that. She imagined her parents being paged in the middle of their reunion festivities. Mom panicking that one of them had died. Dad snapping into unreasonable mode. Yes, Zack had been smart not to call. Though their parents seemed no less *worried*, and judging by the bong she had found in Zack's room—which Emily recognized from Just Say No television commercials—they were right to worry.

"Good luck tomorrow," Emily said. "I mean—I don't think you should be doing what you were doing, and I think you *should* be punished, so that you stop, but—I don't want you to go to *jail*."

"It would be a juvenile detention center," Zack explained. "Not jail. But I'd still prefer to have community service and prep school on my brag sheet."

"Zack." Emily wasn't sure how to make the words come out right. "Will you *stop*? Please?"

"Em, it's only beer and pot. It's not like what you—ah, I don't know how to explain it to you. You'll try it sometime, you'll see."

"Not me," Emily said. "*I* don't need that stuff."

"It's not about *need*."

Mom picked Emily up from school the next afternoon, driving straight from the courthouse, and Emily was glad to have her mother's attention diverted from the AP exam, which Emily wasn't sure she had passed. She suspected she'd gotten a 3, and you needed a 4 to get credit at Penn. She was trying not to care so much about grades now that she'd gotten into college, but it hadn't worked yet.

"Your brother was sentenced to one hundred fifty hours of community service. Your father nearly got into an argument with the judge, trying to keep him from sending Zack to reform school." Mom talked so fast that Emily couldn't get a word in edgewise. "Thank God it worked—reform school would have made this whole horrible situation worse."

The traffic light in front of them was yellow, but her mother wasn't slowing down. "Mom," Emily said, pointing. "The light."

It turned red as they reached it, Mom driving too fast to stop.

"Sorry," Mom said, once they had passed the intersection.

"He'll be grounded through the summer," Mom continued, "but since we've already made the reservations for Washington D.C. in June, and since that was meant to be our last family vacation before you left for college, all four of us will still go. You shouldn't lose out on time with your whole family just because of your brother's mistake."

Emily watched the cars go by, not sure what she was supposed to say to this.

"Oh, I found you sheets," Mom said. "While we were in New York, from Macy's. The extra-long twin size you need for your dorm."

"What color?" Emily asked. A safe question.

"Navy. The dark navy that you like. They were on sale, so I took a chance." Mom had picked out the same color that Emily would have chosen. "We still need to find you a comforter, though, and towels, and a hamper, and you probably want a reading lamp to put by your bed—I think I saw one on sale this week at Bradlees."

"Mom, I'm not leaving for college for another four months."

"I know, but the last time I blinked, you were just starting high school. I don't want to miss anything."

"Mom?"

"What?"

"I'm scared something bad is going to happen to Zack."

They were stopped at another light, and Mom looked over at Emily. "We're all worried about him, Emily. But I think this incident is really going to turn him around. He's agreed to see a therapist and I think all that community service will do him good." Emily sensed the lack of conviction in her mother's voice. Her mother looked back at the road, just in time for the light to turn green. She pressed the gas. "Your brother is a good kid who got into a bad crowd. We need to be a bit more firm with him for a while, that's all. He'll be fine. Concentrate on passing your AP exams and enjoying your first year of college—don't spend your energy on your brother."

Summer came and went. The trip to Washington, D.C. was uneventful. Emily spent two weeks of July at an arts camp and the rest of the time working at the local amusement park with Adena. Zack, single again, split his time between community service and a job at McDonalds. In September Mom and Dad drove Emily down to Penn for orientation, Zack staying behind for pre-season soccer camp. The first few weeks of college were an exhilarating whirlwind, but before Emily knew it October had arrived and the newness of the school year had already worn off.

She was taking the train home from college for fall break, her first visit home. Her seatmate looked like one of the cocky popular guys who usually intimidated her, but when he said he'd been visiting colleges in D.C. and she realized he was younger than her, she relaxed a little, and he turned out to be nice. He had a sketchbook with him, and he showed her some of the drawings. Plants. A baseball bat. A shoe. Simple subjects, but he could bring them alive in pencil. He didn't want to study art though. He didn't know what he wanted to study in college. For some reason Emily decided not to mention that she did photography, even though she sensed he'd be interested. So they talked about colleges, and the fall weather, and sketching.

The words came easily and Emily wondered if they would swap addresses at the end of the ride and decided that she would rather he be just someone she met once on a train. She liked the way he looked—his jaw line, his solid hands, the vein running up his lightly-muscled arm—and she wondered, what was keeping them from making out, right here, right now? Not that Emily had done anything remotely like that—making out with a stranger on a train, making out with *anybody*, for that matter—but that only made the thoughts come stronger.

What if, Emily thought, what if they slipped into one of the toilet booths, and he had a condom in his back pocket, and they had sex? And then his stop would come and he would get off without Emily giving him her address or asking for his and that would be it, Emily not a virgin anymore, Emily with a train adventure. Emily and this boy who seemed to like her, or at least be interested in talking to her, but she was afraid to ask if he was even remotely thinking the way she was. He would probably be shocked but what if? She imagined that boys didn't say no to such a proposal, sex no strings. But how would she even ask? So she kept talking about college and co-ed dorms and the differ-ent meal plans and how important it was to be near a city even though you never left campus, and he had a nice face, soft and defined like Matthew Broderick in *Ferris Bueller's Day Off*, and then the train pulled into New York's Penn Station and he got his bags and shook her hand and said thanks for the conversation and then, "I'm Rob by the way." And they both laughed because it had been nearly two hours with no introductions, and then she said "I'm Emily," and then he was gone.

It was a Saturday, and when Emily arrived at home it was nearly dinnertime and the table was already set for four. Mom had prepared one of Emily's favorite meals, roast chicken with butternut squash soup, and during the meal fed her question after question. Did Emily like her classes, and what were the people on her hall like, and had she become friends with the nice girl in the next room, and did she still like her roommate, and so on and so forth, not leaving space for Dad or Zack to speak. Her father seemed content, as usual, to let her mother drive the conversation. Zack ate quickly and kept glancing at the clock in between bites.

Emily didn't usually mind answering questions, but her mother had a way of nailing her insecurities. Like how Emily's roommate and the next-room neighbors had somehow become best friends in the month and a half since orientation, and Emily hadn't figured out how it happened or how she'd been excluded. And how the people who came to the Hillel cared mostly about services and kashrut and observing Shabbat to the letter of the law, and the other Jews on campus didn't seem to care at all about Judaism, and Emily didn't know where to find all the people who were in between and confused and liked to talk about what it all meant.

Emily was particularly on edge because the previous weekend, when everyone else in the dorm was at one frat party after another, she had spent three straight hours using lynx, a computer program that let you explore this new thing called the internet, and although she'd told herself she *wasn't* searching for her cousins, she'd uncovered an outdated work address for Aunt Ninian. The cousins would be fourteen and twelve now. In another four years the older one might be at college, and then maybe Emily could find out a little more. She didn't exactly want to see them, but she did want to *know*. And she *didn't* want Mom to know she was looking.

Her mother's questions kept coming until everyone else was done eating and Emily's plate was still half-full and Dad noticed and said, "Daisy, let's give Emily a chance to eat." It was quiet while Emily chewed and swallowed, chewed and swallowed, and then Zack said to Emily, "I have a scrimmage on Monday, if you want to come take pictures." Did she? Emily's mouth was full. Before she could even ask what time it started, there was a honk.

Emily could see a car pulled up in the driveway, maybe three people inside, and Zack looking at their mother and then their father, and then Mom and Dad exchanged a look and a shrug, and Mom said, "Clear your place and put the empty juice container in the recycling on your way out, and you may go."

"Thanks, Mom," Zack said. "Have fun, Emily."

"When do you expect to be home?" Dad asked him.

"Eleven-thirty? Twelve-thirty? I don't know. Keith will drop me off."

"No later than that," said Dad. "Your mother and I don't want to be waiting up all night, we have things to do tomorrow. And call us when you're leaving. Do you know where you're going to be?"

"Out," said Zack. "I don't know. Driving around. Maybe we'll go to a movie. Maybe we'll go to North Carolina." He looked at Mom, who wasn't saying anything because she didn't need to, her face gave it all away. "You know you don't have to wait up. I'll be fine. Can I go now? They're waiting."

"Do you have the cell phone?" Dad asked. Zack rolled his eyes. Dad got up, shuffled through the pile of sunglasses by the door and pulled out a cell phone. He opened it to check the remaining battery power, then handed it to Zack. "Take the cell phone. Emily, your mom just got her own cell phone last week, so you can use hers if you go out later."

Zack looked at Dad, the question in his eyebrows. "You can go," Dad said. "Have fun. Tell Keith to drive safely."

And then Zack was out the door and they all watched out the kitchen window as he bounded up the hill and got into the back seat and the car drove off.

"I'm surprised you let him go," Emily said.

"We worry regardless," Mom said, sighing. "I'd rather know than have him sneak out."

"If only he'd give up this stupid notion of not going to college," Dad said. "Except for that, he's been doing a lot better."

"That, and the drugs," Mom said.

"Daisy, you don't know that he's smoking marijuana."

"I know," said Mom. "A mother knows."

Dad started clearing the table, silent as Mom filled in Emily on the community news she had missed by being away.

"I was thinking," Mom said. "Maybe Zack could visit you at school. Maybe you could talk some sense into him. Or maybe if he just sees what college is like."

Mom had made the suggestion in her practiced casual voice, which meant she had discussed it with Dad. Emily could tell from

Dad's body language that he didn't think it would work, don't blame him for the idea. She wished her mother wasn't trying to put Emily in the middle. Emily shrugged as noncommittally as she could.

"Here's an extra-special activity for you," Dad said, tossing Emily the sponge. "I bet you haven't wiped a kitchen table all *month*."

"Did you want to see any of your friends tonight?" Mom asked, when the table was cleared and wiped. "You could use my car." Emily hadn't made any plans. She'd been so busy at school she'd almost forgotten to even get a train ticket, and really, now that she thought about it, she was tired and liked the idea of staying in. They all went upstairs, where Emily flipped channels on the television for a little while and then took a bath—something which was now a luxury, living in a dorm—before going to bed.

The next morning Emily slept in, then took another long bath, then let Dad make her French toast. In the afternoon she visited with high school friends. She ate dinner with her parents. She watched videos that evening at another friend's house, and slept in again the following morning. There was a certain comfort to being home. Like the way the leaves around her made her feel settled. She hadn't realized until she saw the fall-colored tree-filled landscape how much she'd been missing it. And the sunset off the front porch. Having trees everywhere. The feeling of driving in a car. The niceness of being able to eat breakfast in pajamas, read the box of cereal, use a spoon that felt familiar and soothing in her mouth. And of course her bedroom, a whole room all to herself.

On Monday Emily browsed through her parents' bookshelf before heading to the high school for Zack's scrimmage, picking out a mystery to read on the train and discovering that Mom had bought—and marked up—a new book on parenting problem teens. She wondered if that was part of why her parents had been acting differently towards Zack.

Emily stopped in to say hi to a couple of teachers, then headed to the soccer field. She didn't know or like soccer well enough to know when to press the shutter and she didn't own a good enough lens, but she tried to take a few action shots anyway. She photographed leaves, bleachers, stray soccer balls. As Zack headed off the field at halftime, Emily was struck by the particular expression on his face. She spent the rest of the scrimmage attempting unsuccessfully to capture that expression.

She closed her eyes, trying to memorize it at least, save it. Zack, happy. No, it wasn't quite that. It was the tension gone. The tension of their parents' reactions, of preparing for them. Emily recognized it because this was tension she felt too. She felt it whenever she thought about doing something they wouldn't approve of. Usually it stopped Emily from acting. It didn't stop Zack, so he constantly carried that tension around in anticipation of their reaction. But here on the field, Emily could see its absence, and Zack looked, not happy exactly, but lighter somehow. Then, as the game ended and he headed over to her, she saw the tension begin to return.

"Please don't try to force Zack to visit me if he doesn't want to," Emily said to her mother as they drove back to the train station.

"Emily, I can't force your brother to do anything," Mom said. It wasn't true, though. Her persistence alone wore people down.

That spring Emily experienced her first kiss, with a frat guy from her dorm she then avoided for the rest of the year, and then during a game of Truth or Dare over the summer at Adena's birthday party, her second and third. Number two was with the hottest boy at the party, whose kiss was slobbery and made her gag. Number three was Zack's friend Keith, who was surprisingly good and Emily wished briefly that he didn't have a girlfriend. Yet at the end of each kiss, Emily was still Emily, no wiser and maybe a little more confused.

For sophomore year, Emily convinced her parents to pay the

extra for a single room, using the argument that it would help her concentrate on her studies, and in exchange she acquiesced to the inevitable visit from her brother. It was October. Zack stood in Emily's dorm room with his jacket on, his hands in his pockets. He had taken the train down to Philly, and after meeting him at 30th Street station and taking the subway back to campus, Emily didn't know what to do next. She had gotten Zack a ticket for the *a cappella* show she'd be photographing that evening, but there were still a couple of hours before dinner. There was awkward silence, then Zack pulled out a joint from his jacket pocket. "Mind if I smoke?"

Emily looked at the rolled paper in her brother's hand. It was the first joint she had ever actually seen, not counting movies and anti-drug posters. Would the smell go through the vent? How much trouble would she be in if Zack was caught? What about Mom and Dad? Zack's hand tightened, and Emily looked up and saw the same look of tension she'd recognized the previous year as he approached her on the soccer field. Somehow, she knew the most important thing in this moment was to erase that tension, whatever the cost. Emily shrugged slightly, and Zack pulled out a lighter.

She watched as he inhaled, exhaled, studied her photos on the wall. "Nice," he said, pointing to one of the musician shots. Emily picked up her camera from her desk, loaded film, focused on her brother and the intricacies of his breathing smoke. It was beautiful to watch. It held gentleness. It held mystery. It held boldness. Inside her head the voices were loud, jumbled, daring, reprimanding.

Halfway into the roll, Emily gestured to the marijuana and asked, "Can I try?"

Zack nodded. Emily took the joint from his outstretched hand with unsteady fingers, serious and respectful as he showed her how to breathe in and then exhale.

She coughed a couple of times after her first inhalation, and then said, "Wow."

"It can be rough on your throat," Zack acknowledged.

"No," she said. "Not that." She passed the joint back to Zack, then stared at her hand, moving it around so she could see it from all sides. "I just held a joint. I, Emily Novak, just smoked pot."

She didn't get high, but it didn't matter. She would feel the effects for years to come, the slow blurring of the impermeable line between *Emily Novak* and *other*. As she photographed the *a cappella* show that night, immersed in capturing the expression of other people's joy, she could feel herself already beginning to see the world a little differently.

It was April, and Emily had a lull in homework just in time for Passover. Academics had become easier again—choosing the courses she wanted made the more rigorous classes not seem like work much of the time, and by letting go of her attachment to grades, she found herself actually *learning* more and writing more interesting papers. Most interesting of all, this new approach *wasn't* producing lower grades. Had she stressed out in high school for nothing?, she wondered on occasion. Emily took the train to New York, then another train to Queens and Grandma and Grandpa Novak met her at the station.

This year, Emily had managed to come up a day early. She was glad for grandparent time. Helping Grandpa plant peas in peat pots, helping Grandma make the veggie chopped liver they would bring to the seder, going out for dinner at the Chinese restaurant for one last bit of *chametz* before the holiday started, driving—just the three of them—to Aunt Sarah's where the seder would be held, and in between relaxing and poking around and a couple of errands and noticing the spring arriving.

Zack's high school graduation was a month away, and he hadn't applied to any schools. Mom had announced that she would only attend his graduation if he had a college acceptance letter in hand, and—she had told Emily on the phone—she was maintaining a list on the fridge of schools which maintained rolling admissions. Dad, Emily was sure, had been rolling his eyes as she said this, but he was equally upset. *You'd better have an alternate plan,* Mom and Dad had told Zack, *because you aren't living here rent-free if you're not in school.*

Don't worry, Zack had told them, *I'm not planning to stay here.* But he wouldn't say where he was planning to stay, even after showing up one day with a used Plymouth he'd purchased.

Though none of them could know how long it would actually be before Zack made it home for Passover again, they sensed the possibility that this was the last one together for a while.

Aunt Sarah's house was filled with people who cared about each other but didn't see each other often, and it took some time for everyone to sit down and stop conversing so Grandma Novak's brother could lead them in the opening *kiddush.* During the seder Emily could feel something stirring inside her as forty-three relatives and relatives of relatives took turns telling the story of her ancestors' journey from slavery to freedom.

"In each generation...," Mom read aloud from the *Haggadah,* and Emily wondered, what was her mother's journey? The escape from living under Gram and Grandpa Irv's roof? The schism with Aunt Ninian? Or had that just created a new form of slavery? Mom had severed a connection and now there wasn't room for repair. She was stunted. And you could see it in the crafted persona Mom showed, even here. Pretend-Mom was on display, and Emily hated her.

So many of Emily's relatives gave her hugs with warmth, and although some also interrogated her, Emily wondered how much more comfortable she might feel talking with them if Mom wasn't always, intentionally it seemed, in eavesdropping distance. What would it be like to truly ask her first cousins, or Aunt Sarah, "Did *you* ever do something that was completely unlike who you were brought up to be? What happened afterward?"

There had been that time alone with Grandma and Grandpa Novak, of course, but Emily thought of that as restful time, not question time. It was where you filled up on hugs and love after a long semester. You didn't complicate those relationships, you soaked in them.

At the seder itself Zack kept a low profile, evading questions. "I'll be working on a heroin farm," he told someone who wouldn't stop pestering him. "I'm going to be a traveling bong salesman," he told someone else, loud enough for his eavesdropping parents to hear clearly. But on the ride back—Emily, Zack, and Grandma and Grandpa Novak in one car, Mom and Dad in another—Zack asked Grandpa Novak about the garden, and Emily listened, and it was a refreshing change. Then he asked Grandma Novak about her years working as a plumber. Emily had never heard any of the stories Grandma Novak then told and she wished she and Zack could travel around to the whole family and have Zack ask these questions and Emily photograph. She wished Zack could do this with Aunt Ninian, even—but that was the thing, Zack *wasn't* asking the prying questions. He was asking questions that made her family *want* to talk. How had he learned to do that, Emily wondered. She felt guilty about being glad that he was still much like Emily around the adults in the big gathering, awkward, not asking anything at all, young, the child on display—although even there Zack was bolder and better than her at deflecting the questions. Emily envied the skill but not the consequence—she had overheard relatives asking, *what happened to Zack?* Emily, instead, had over and over repeated answers of *I'm majoring in American Studies, I have a work-study job with a history professor, no I don't want to teach, yes Philadelphia is a wonderful place to go to school.*

What about your friends, Grandma had asked earlier, and Emily had told her about meeting her newest friend Sean in a History of Film class and how they had become friendly working together on a final video project. "Tell me more about that movie boy," Grandma said now.

"He's really good," Emily said. "But he's always worked with friends who just see film as a fun teenage hobby, and I think he appreciates that I take him seriously. Like I call him on it when he's taking shortcuts and it shows, or doesn't have his concepts worked out before he starts shooting."

"Do you want to date him?" Grandma Novak asked.

"No," Emily said. "He dates boys most of the time." An exaggeration, but truthful enough.

"That could make things difficult," Grandma Novak said.

"Who else do you hang out with?" Zack asked.

Emily thought about that. There wasn't one set group of people. There were film people through Sean, who she liked but didn't hang out with apart from him. There were people in her classes, study groups that would start and end near exam time, people she would hang out with in the dorm common room or knocking on their doors when it was dinnertime to eat dinner together. There was Adena and a couple of high school friends who she saw—less frequently now—when she came home to Connecticut. There were people in the darkroom, good and bad photographers she felt close to in the dark as they shared the images appearing in the developer, and barely recognized when the lights were on.

Emily shrugged. "People." Zack's new skill, apparently, wasn't developed enough to talk to his sister. If he'd asked about photography, the new liquid light technique her class was experimenting with, the magic of an image appearing, the comfort of a dark glowing room with your music playing, she could talk.

"Zack," Grandma Novak said suddenly. "Explain to me why that school hasn't expelled you."

"They want our money," Zack said.

"What money?" That was Grandpa Novak.

"All of ours. Big alumni donations to thank them for the success of my older sister, which of course we won't give if her younger brother doesn't also graduate."

"That's not true—" Emily said.

"Of course it is," said Zack.

"He's on probation," Emily explained to her grandparents. "There's a limit to what they can do when something happens off-campus."

"And your grades?" Grandpa Novak asked. Emily was curious too.

Zack shrugged. "B's mostly."

"Humph," Grandma said, sounding proud. "My troublemaking grandson is still getting B's."

"And why isn't he making both trouble and A's?" Grandpa asked. *So that's where Dad gets it from,* Emily thought to herself.

"Different priorities, Grandpa," Zack said, but Emily thought he looked a little less confident than he was letting on. "Even Emily couldn't manage both."

That night, after everyone was asleep, Emily found herself crying. She didn't know why. She was on the edge of something. That joint of Zack's had brought her into unfamiliar territory and Emily didn't want to go back but she didn't know how to navigate. She felt it pulling her away from family, sensed that she would soon be losing something Zack had already lost. She had an urge to take out her camera and photograph herself in the dark. But she had left it behind in Philadelphia—sensing that it was time she attended a family event *without* a camera.

She heard footsteps. Grandpa, going to the bathroom. A flush. Footsteps again, then a knock.

He came in and sat on the edge of her bed and patted her hair. "Nightmare?" he asked. She had had those sometimes when she was little, and when her parents weren't there he or Grandma would sit with her.

"Kind of," she said.

He sat there, patting her hair, until her crying stopped and she finally fell asleep.

That summer Emily was home for Zack's graduation, which Mom did actually skip. Zack drove off the following evening, and Emily watched Mom staring out the window, long after Zack had driven away. Her parents both tense, Dad first trying to make Mom feel better and then retreating. Bowling, synagogue, Emily watched him find distance over the summer as she sought her own in that house cramped with tension. She had thought it would get better once Zack had left, but instead Zack's presence inhabited every interaction.

His first phone call came after three weeks. He said he was in Idaho somewhere, he was pumping gas, a barter of sorts to pay for a repair on his broken-down car. It was a pay-phone call, short, leaving them all with even more questions. Mom and Dad began fighting afterwards, Emily hearing the question *should we go get him* coming from both of them but even on the third day of fighting it wasn't clear who wanted what.

Emily spent the first half of the summer working at the amusement park again—no Adena this time—and babysitting and reading and doing photography, experimenting with liquid light and infrared and Grandpa Novak's macro lens, and shooting a band that broke up before she could develop the film. Towards August she quit the amusement park in order to work the concession stand at a movie theater, which got her free movies and sick of popcorn and a crush on one of the other workers that went nowhere but was at least distraction from what was going on at home.

When her parents' friends asked about Zack, Emily could sense embarrassment from her parents, particularly as the summer neared its end and they still didn't know what town he was in, what state even, what he was doing, if he was really okay. They seemed conflicted, too, about what they should do. The calls came sporadically, infrequently, and as often as not Zack would reach the machine and leave a short message and their parents would begin fighting again and continue for the weeks until the next call.

She wondered what kind of adventures Zack was having, whether it was fun or scary, whether he was glad he'd run off or wished he hadn't. Somehow she never managed to be home for his sur-prise phone calls, so everything she knew came filtered from her parents. She could feel, more than she had before, her distance from them, a distance disguised by a façade of closeness. She cultivated the façade. She was hurt when Dad one day decided to drive down to New York to visit his parents and didn't want Emily to come along, but hid the hurt.

Right before she went back to school, Emily was actually home for a phone call from Zack. She answered the phone and was so surprised that she didn't say much besides *how are you* before Mom figured out who it was and took the phone from her. Rather than fight or go to another extension, Emily picked up the camera in front of her and focused it on her mother, whose back was turned. She almost clicked, but the image disappeared too quickly, and then Mom turned and saw the camera and motioned with her arms for Emily to put it away, angry.

Emily shot that.

Mom, still listening to Zack, grabbed the camera from Emily and opened up the back, exposing the film. She pulled it out from the middle and Emily watched, stunned, as the strip was exposed to the light and thrown to the floor. "Don't you photograph me like that," Mom mouthed to Emily, then sat the camera roughly on the table and turned away.

That night after dinner, after Mom reported that Zack yet again wouldn't tell his whereabouts, and Dad washed dishes without commenting, Mom said, "Elliot, maybe we should go to that counselor again."

"Why? It didn't help. *You* said it didn't help."

"We learned that one technique. It seemed to have a positive impact on Zack."

"Real positive," Dad said wryly.

"Elliot. That's not helping."

Dad stopped washing dishes and lifted his hands up in the air with a shrug. "If you want to go, go. I'll pass. If you actually learn something new, I'm sure you'll tell me."

"What was it like when *I* left for school," Emily asked Dad the next day, as they made pizza for lunch.

"It was wonderful," he said. "We could finally get in to take showers again."

"No, really," Emily said.

"Really. And no one minded when I put anchovy on pizza."

Emily stuck out her tongue.

"We missed you," Dad said, giving her a hug. "We're glad you've been home for the summer."

"Do you miss Zack?"

"Yes. Although I think it's better that we let him go right now than forced him to stay, I wish he'd decided to run away a little closer to home."

Emily wanted to trust her father's sincerity. She almost did. She was practically sure he was telling the truth. But she wouldn't ask the next question—whether *Mom* missed Zack, truly missed *her* when she was gone. She didn't want to hear the answer she was afraid of, and sensed she wouldn't quite believe the one her father would give.

Zack landed eventually on the west coast, although neither his parents nor Emily knew exactly how or when he'd gotten there, and Emily's somewhat tamer pursuits found her taking one photo class and then another at the Art Institute downtown, having figured out how to get Penn credits for doing so, and hanging out more with Sean and his film buddies.

Although it didn't quite feel like she belonged with Sean's crowd, it was comfortable, and she was sorry most of them would be graduating that year. It was nice to have a group sort of a friendship for once. She called home less that year, and discovered that *Dad* began calling more, Dad who previously would often stay quiet on the line while Mom and Emily did the talking. Sean himself had become an even better friend, and she sensed that he was turning to her for what he wasn't getting from the crowd or from the people he dated on and off.

The summer after junior year, Emily stayed in the dorm, away from the tension that had only increased with Zack's physical absence, and worked for the Residential Life office. In addition to staffing the desk and doing office work she was given a special assignment to shoot photos to hang in one of the newly-renovated dorms. When she wasn't working or in the darkroom, printing images that would later get rejected by contests and magazines, she hung out with the film crowd, which was slowly dissipating as the graduates slowly got jobs or gave up on getting jobs and moved to LA or New York or back home to places like Texas and Singapore.

Fall came and went, and then it was Emily's final semester at college. The major assignment for the *Topics In Photography* class—which Emily had chosen because of the professor's reputation for teaching technical skills—was a study of a person. Photograph the same person regularly over the course of two months.

Emily approached Sean first. "You'll be my subject, right?" Emily asked over their now-habitual Wednesday night Indian buffet.

"If you'll let me film you in exchange," Sean said. He had been playing around with a Super 8 camera all month, trying to get footage to use for a film school application.

"No," she said. "I'll help you write your essay, though."

"Nope," Sean said. "I want to film you." He pantomimed a camera following her shaking head. "Why not?"

Emily felt herself automatically cowering before the imaginary camera. It was a gut feeling, no logic. "I stay on one side of the camera."

"Oh, well," said Sean. "So much for grad school." He smiled when he said it, so Emily knew he was only kidding, but he still wouldn't agree to be her subject. Should she drop the class? Who could she photograph?

When Emily got home that night, in a moment of bravery, she called up Rachel, and Rachel said *sure, why not?*

Emily had only met Rachel that fall at a Halloween party where Sean had dragged Emily, but she'd known Rachel's name and seen her around for quite a while before that. Rachel was a known figure at Penn, a personality, quoted in the newspaper and probably widely lusted after: she was the Big Dyke On Campus. She'd seemed too cool to speak to Emily, but on line for the bathroom in someone's crowded apartment—Rachel dressed as a tampon, Emily as a court jester—they had talked for a good five or ten minutes about Barbara Kingsolver and about Serrano's *Piss Christ* exhibit, and afterwards Emily had come up with reasons to email

Rachel a couple of times. They'd also seen each other at a Penn Queer Association fund-raiser Rachel had organized—Emily wearing her *Straight but not Narrow* button and fidgeting with an imaginary Pentax since she hadn't brought the real one—and then they had had an actual phone conversation which had lasted a while.

By the time of this second phone call, Emily knew that Rachel had spent part of her childhood in France, that she had one brother and one sister and no appendix, and that she had switched majors three times but was minoring in Women's Studies. What Emily didn't know was why she felt a slight tickle inside, even after Rachel had said yes and chosen a day for the first shoot.

"Wear solid colors if you can," Emily said. "Patterns and writing tend to be distracting in photos."

"Are nudes part of it?" Rachel asked.

"Um," Emily said after a moment, surprised by the question. "They can be." Her teacher had shown slides the first day from a previous class, which had included some photos of a naked man. Emily was uncomfortable even looking from afar while other people were in the room. Since Emily had been planning to shoot Sean, she had simply erased the option of nudes from her mind. Would photographing another woman be easier?

"You can't ask me to do Playmate poses," Rachel said. "They're too unnatural. I have very photogenic breasts, at least I think they're photogenic whenever I look in the mirror. I've never actually photographed them because I don't want some dead-beat Kodak guy jerking off to my picture. Anyway you need to show them candid. Maybe even have me doing jumping jacks or something—"

"I'm all about candids," Emily said. Was Rachel *offering*, or just talking?

They were in Rachel's dorm, a four-person apartment on the nineteenth floor. One roommate was napping with her door shut, the other two were out, and Emily was examining Rachel's bedroom door and refrigerator. The door was covered with rainbow stickers and pink triangles and other gay pride paraphernalia. There was an Ani Difranco poster, a *Philadelphia Inquirer* clipping with the headline, "Penn senior's ingenuity raises over $4000 for campus Queer Association library and mentor program," and a poster for a NOW pro-choice rally. She would have to find an artful way to photograph the door. On the fridge were magnetic poetry words and a few snapshots, blurry and off-center. Nothing annoyed Emily more than blurred photos, but she studied them anyway.

"Is that your girlfriend?" Emily asked. It was a photo of Rachel and another girl with their arms around each other, like every high school yearbook picture Emily had taken before she got the zoom lens and learned to catch people unaware. The two girls both wore pro-choice t-shirts, and the Washington Monument was in the background.

"No, my best friend from high school," Rachel said from the other side of the room. "She's bi, and she's awesome, but, I don't know, it would be like dating my sister."

Emily's camera lay against her stomach, right below her belly button. She cupped the zoom in her palm, gently thumbing the focus back and forth, then lifted it up to double-check the ASA. She was using TMAX 400 film, which she'd loaded on the way over, and it was light enough to shoot indoors.

She'd hoped to take a dozen or so shots that afternoon, just to help Rachel get used to her with a camera. Used to Emily, period, since this was already the longest time they'd spent alone together. It made for more natural photos, Emily had found, when people could forget about the camera, and it was worth wasting part of a roll of film to get to that point.

Emily shot a few images as Rachel sat on the living room couch, talking about the rally. The line of the couch, the white of the wall, and the corner of poster in the upper right of the frame all distracted Emily. She could see that smile of Rachel's she liked and might have even captured it, but the background irked her.

"Want to try something else?" Emily asked. "Another location?"

Rachel shrugged. "You're the photographer." She led the way

into her bedroom, sat down on the edge of the desk with her feet on her desk chair—which left her half-made bed as the only other place to sit—and pulled off her t-shirt, then her bra.

Emily wished she had sat down before this. She felt the crease of her right sock, which had slipped down, underneath her heel. She shifted her weight to her left foot.

"What are you waiting for?" Rachel asked.

Emily was too nervous to do anything but put the camera in front of her face. Once she was looking through the lens, she could let herself see Rachel's breasts, the nipples larger and darker than her own. She shot, forgetting to check the light meter. Then adjusted and shot again, and then zoomed in. Zooming in she could capture Rachel's face, her utter comfort with her half-nude body, and not shoot the body itself. No one would be able to see Emily's emotions during this scene. More comfortable, she kept shooting, trying to capture the particular expressions that she thought of as the essence of Rachel.

"No fair," said Rachel after a few minutes. "Using the zoom lens. I feel like you're spying."

"I'm not," Emily said. Thinking, *I'm not, no I am, no I'm watching, I'm getting closer.*

But Rachel insisted she switch to the other lens, the fifty millimeter. The one that was closest to what she could see with her naked eye.

Emily was shooting scared then, unable to move close enough to frame the shots she wanted. She knew that they would be bad pictures. When the roll was finished, she said, "I think that's enough for today." She rewound the film and packed up the bag, not looking at Rachel who had put on her bra—a turquoise shiny thing—but wasn't making any move to put her shirt back on.

The next session took place outdoors, wandering around Rittenhouse Square. Emily had conveniently forgotten to bring contact sheets from the first shoot, even more nervous about showing the pictures than she'd been taking them.

"Were they good?" Rachel asked, walking towards the park fountain.

"Some," Emily said honestly, but vaguely. The best was the first breast shot, in which a wide sliver of Emily's own reflection showed in the mirror that Emily had accidentally captured in the right edge of the photo. No way was Emily showing that to anyone, especially Rachel, who had been looking away at the time. "After I develop today's batch, I'll pick three or four to print for our first critique."

Emily used her zoom to photograph Rachel feeding birds, and since Rachel didn't say anything about the lens, Emily continued shooting with it. They talked about music, and about Rachel's brother who had Down Syndrome. It started getting dark. Emily switched to the fifty millimeter because it didn't require as much light. She used the distance, playing with angles and backgrounds like a fashion shoot. Emily told Rachel about how Zack had taken off after high school graduation, buying a used Plymouth and driving west.

"I still remember how my mom stood there at the screen door," Emily said. "And how my parents jumped every time the phone rang."

"Did he finally call?" Rachel asked.

"Yeah, after a few weeks. He actually does keep in touch with them, but it's sporadic, and not nearly as often as my parents would like." Emily thought about the desperation in her mother's voice the times he had called that first summer, her mother afraid it would be the last time she ever spoke to him. "I figure if Zack wasn't planning to ever come home," Emily told Rachel, pointing out a particularly vivid area of sunset as she packed up her camera, "he wouldn't bother calling. I just don't know *when* he'll be back, or what might happen in the meantime."

"Where is he now?" Rachel asked, looking up at the sky. "Ooh, that's beautiful."

"Seattle," Emily said. "He gave my parents a number to use in case of emergency, but my mom's being stubborn."

"Do you have the number too?"

Emily patted her left pants pocket, where her wallet bulged, and nodded. "I just don't want to get in the middle of it. If I haven't heard from him by graduation, I'll call."

For the third shoot, it was cold, so they stayed inside. Emily used the fifty millimeter, perched on Rachel's desk chair, and Rachel kept her clothes on. Emily took picture after picture, and sometimes let the camera drop from her face, and it was starting to get comfortable. She had brought Rachel four prints and now Rachel was putting rings of scotch tape on the back of one. Rachel taped it to the door, then stood back so Emily could see. It was the one with breast, mirror carefully cropped out by Emily.

"I hope my roommate doesn't try to get me in trouble for this," said Rachel. She lowered her voice to a whisper. "She's a closet L-E-S-B-I-A-N." In a normal tone, Rachel continued, "I try to provoke her whenever I can, for her own good."

Emily waited for Rachel to say more, but Rachel was done with that subject. She was looking at Emily's camera. "How close can you get and still be in focus?" Rachel asked.

Emily started telling her about Grandpa Novak's macro lens which she had borrowed the previous summer, how you could use it for close-ups. She told Rachel about the crayon picture, and the photo of the leather knot on her shoe—putting her fingers like a frame up to the Eastlands she still wore—and Rachel listened and said she wanted to see those photos sometime, and Emily said, deep breath first, "How about tomorrow night?" Not believing she was actually saying it, Emily said, "Want to come over tomorrow night, you could see the photos and then maybe we can do dinner or something?"

And Rachel said *sure* and Emily wasn't sure if this was chemistry or just Rachel being nice, but she had asked and Rachel had said *sure* and it was the first time she had asked anything like this—with the tickle inside—since Spencer in eighth grade. That mattered. Even if Rachel only thought it was friends, that mattered. And then Rachel said, "But how close can you get with *that* lens?"

And there was nothing to do but move in close, as close as Emily could go and still be in focus, which she knew from blurry self-portraits was just a tad more than an arm's length, but somehow that distance seemed a lot closer now. "Stay like that," Rachel said. "Shoot me from there."

"Aren't I the photographer?" Emily asked. Excited and nervous and trembling inside. Rachel was so close, almost close enough to touch, and she was looking at her, and now Rachel didn't seem so cool and distant anymore, she seemed a little nervous too. When the camera clicked on the last frame, Emily let it drop. She tried to keep looking at Rachel, and she could feel something in the air between them—a charge, aliveness, alive *air*—and for a moment their eyes met. Emily thought maybe they were actually going to kiss but one or both of them looked away, Emily wasn't sure who, and she tried to will herself to look up again but she couldn't.

Then it was Friday evening and they were both sitting cross-legged on Emily's bed looking at photos. Rachel's knee was touching Emily's thigh, and their arms would occasionally brush. "Do you believe in God?" Emily asked.

"No," Rachel said. "I believe in something though. More of a spirit, although sometimes I call it a goddess because I like to think of a woman being in charge up there. When I'm hiking I feel it most. It's harder in the city."

Emily waited for Rachel to ask her the question back, but she didn't. The pile of mounted photos was getting smaller, and they flipped through more quietly, Emily only occasionally giving narration. "My dad had to hold the canoe steady so I could take this one," she said about the photo titled *New England Fall.* She didn't say anything about the crayon photo—a segment of colors poking out of the box, taken so close that you could see all the angles where the tips had been pressed to paper, the fading letters p-e-r on the periwinkle. Rachel took that one and grinned. "Nice," Rachel said, expanding the word to mean it was an understatement.

"Here's my first joint," Emily said, handing Rachel a picture of Zack, inhaling, surrounded by smoke. She'd already told Rachel the story behind it, and Rachel nodded almost reverently.

Emily handed Rachel the next photo. It was a silhouette of bird on rock, *Sunrise on Masada*. Instead of saying *ooh* or *wow* like Emily expected, Rachel said, "I think I'm falling for you." And Emily's breath caught and she was almost afraid to look and she didn't speak. When she turned her head Rachel was still looking at *Sunrise on Masada* but then Rachel looked up and Emily didn't know which of them moved first but then they were kissing. They were kissing.

After that Friday, Emily and Rachel were on the phone every night and spending almost every spare moment with each other, and a few weeks later, they decided to cut their hair together. Sean loaned his buzz cutter for the occasion. Emily set up her tripod in Rachel's bathtub, focusing on the space above and in front of the closed toilet seat where they took turns sitting and standing.

Scissors and Sean's buzz cutter and the feeling of closeness, physical closeness and its undercurrents, even when they weren't touching. Emily alternated the self-timer with an air cable release.

"What's that?" Rachel asked, when Emily first attached the air cable release to the camera.

"It's like a remote control on a string," Emily said, squeezing the black bulb and thereby capturing Rachel's amused expression.

"Can I try?"

Emily advanced the shutter and handed her the bulb.

"Sit down," Rachel directed.

Emily sat. Rachel approached her with the buzz cutter in one hand and air cable release in the other. "Not too short," Emily said, as Rachel knelt down, buzzing the back of Emily's head and then kissing her as she squeezed the release.

Shorter, kiss. Emily had cautiously checked a calendar before agreeing to this activity, calculated the shortest length which would be able to grow out again before she next saw her parents. Shorter, kiss, shorter, kiss. Long kiss. Buzz. Now reckless abandon took over. Emily was the one who discovered Rachel's roommate's hair dye, giving Rachel purple streaks and then selecting turquoise for her own. In the photographs, both colors would shine grey.

They had really only kissed. No one who saw them together would have guessed that though. They held hands whenever it seemed safe and some places where it probably wasn't. They cuddled and showed affection like they were only vaguely aware of others noticing. But public affection was easier than private. The moments in private when one might reach, or slip off a bra strap, Rachel also hesitated.

Emily was subconsciously grateful for the roommate interruptions, the homework, the conflicting morning schedules that served as ways to avoid her fears. This was Rachel's first real relationship too—a surprise to Emily—though Rachel had had her first kiss years before with a bunkmate at camp. It evened out, Rachel said, because she'd never done anything with a boy, and Emily had. Emily often—especially now—wished she hadn't, but she kept that to herself. *This is Rachel*, she sometimes thought to herself. *With me.* Awed. With disbelief, waiting for the part where she woke up. And then there would be a love note in her mailbox or a message on her answering machine and her heart would skip a beat.

The Saturday before midterms they had a party in Rachel's dorm apartment. Rachel's roommates were all gone for the week-end—*a first*, Rachel had said, *we must celebrate*. They decorated that afternoon with construction paper chains, which reminded Emily of Sukkot and Rachel of Christmas trees. They set out alcohol and crackers and spinach dip and nonalcoholic fruit punch.

As the guests started arriving, Emily's crowd-shyness emerged, and she realized how differently she and Rachel experienced a party. Rachel was effervescent, a whirl, while Emily was drawn to the corner of the couch. Sporadically throughout the evening Rachel made her way to Emily's lap, leaning back with Emily's arms around her. Then up again to greet a new guest, pour some-one a drink, adjust the floral arrangement she'd bought on a whim to cover the scratches on the institutional table. Emily watched

Rachel circle the room and give all the straight girls flirty pecks on the cheeks, and she felt the beginnings of jealousy. But then Rachel returned to Emily, their eyes meeting followed by their lips and tongues, the kiss a long one, and Emily felt centered again.

Emily thought perhaps it would happen that night. But when all the guests had left, she felt timid. Rachel's energy had waned, and she joined Emily on the couch, yawning and sending a wavy arm towards the mess before resting her cheek against Emily's and closing her eyes. They fell asleep stretched out on the couch in each other's arms, Emily oblivious to the pain in her left shoulder and leg which were cramped against the wooden edge.

Waking up in the morning to a sleeping Rachel curled around her, it finally felt real. After all those weeks of excitement, tension, nervousness, butterflies. Later that day, after Emily had helped Rachel clean up and spent a few hours in the darkroom printing the last batch of prints for her assignment, she called her brother Zack, to tell him about her girlfriend.

"Are you going to tell Mom and Dad?" Zack asked.

"Eventually I will," Emily said. "It's too important not to tell them. But it's about me loving Rachel, it's not about labels or politics or anything, and nothing's that simple for Mom."

"I bet Dad flips out," Zack said. "Not about that she's a woman. But Daddy's little girl dating *anybody*. He won't show it though."

Emily hadn't thought through that far, but she knew Zack was right. "What do I do about that?" Emily asked.

"Nothing," Zack said. "He'll get over it, he has to let you grow up sometime. Just don't expect him to be a cornucopia of dating advice."

For her midterm Emily had to hand in a portfolio. Even though it was only going to the professor, Emily tried to select photos which said the least about *her*: zooms in on Rachel's face, the outdoor fashion-style shots, a couple of Rachel reading, one where Rachel was eating Shredded Wheat and making a face, one from the haircutting adventure. No kissing pictures. But Emily knew more of the story could be read from the gaps, and from the last photo: Rachel looking up from doing the dishes, in what was unmistakably Emily's dorm room. When Emily came to pick up her portfolio, her teacher pulled it out to look one last time and said, "That photo's a treasure." And then, "I hope for your sake it lasts."

Emily started to say something about the composition but the teacher shook his head. "It's the way she's looking at you. Her eyes." Emily then admitting to herself, yes, this was why she liked that image. It was a photograph of Rachel in love with Emily.

My girlfriend. Emily liked to say the phrase, began using it whenever she could. Identity labels were elusive—lesbian, bi, queer, dyke—but Emily didn't care anymore about the unanswered question of her potential with men, because she was with Rachel and wanted to stay that way, forever.

Rachel herself identified—emphatically—as a lesbian. She had come out to her best friend during high school and now was out to every single person she knew, except her family. *You have to understand my parents,* Rachel had said, but Emily couldn't fathom her girlfriend in any closet.

They made love for the first time. Rachel's hands exploring her body, the way they tangled gently into Emily's pubic hair as the two of them lay together in Emily's bed, made her feel beautiful, truly beautiful, for the first time. Emily moving her own hands, slowly, still unsure if this was her, what she wanted, what her body craved physically, afraid to find out it didn't and shrink back to a world of men who scared her. Emily moving her hands and the unexpected softness, and then her mouth and how was it she seemed to be the one taking initiative, her mouth tracing down Rachel's body. Tasting her nipples and moving on. Tasting lower, teasing Rachel's belly button as Rachel gently played with Emily's hair and scalp, then lower and here Emily paused. Here she felt the panic could she do this did she want to, go slow go slow go slow and she did go slow, taking her time to get there, and somehow figuring out she could go slow and not have to say it, not have to tell Rachel she was still scared. And then her tongue tasting Rachel's groove. She still didn't have language for the body parts, language she could speak, but there was expression she'd learned from one of the drummers she'd photographed, a term for accompanying singer-songwriter-guitarists on the hand drums, *giving groove,* and when she'd heard it the sexual connotation had seemed so obvious, a name for the place and a name for the action. It wasn't a phrase she'd ever said aloud but one she thought to herself, as her tongue and her lips explored, *I'm giving Rachel groove.*

She didn't know how long to go on, when to stop, was Rachel going to orgasm from this? Was she doing something wrong? But then Rachel was moving, saying *kiss me,* and so Emily moved back up and kissed her with this new taste moving between their mouths. Kissed her and remembered, they'd never exactly talked about safe sex, just that Emily had never done anything unsafe and Rachel had only kissed a few people. It had seemed okay but now Emily was second-guessing herself, was sex between safe people enough to constitute safe sex? And Emily remembered, cold sores, you had to watch out for cold sores, but neither of them had cold sores so it was okay. And Emily relaxed and concentrated on kissing.

And then Rachel moved down Emily's body, with her lips. Her hands sliding down Emily's side making Emily shiver even though they weren't cold. And then Emily could feel Rachel giving Emily groove, and she didn't know what to do with her hands, with her anything, was she supposed to do anything or just lean back and enjoy it? And then, and then, and then she felt it so close and there it was, wow, not big like when she used her hand or a doll's head but little and *there* and Rachel had just done that to her, she had just done that, and wow. And she felt Rachel's tongue pause and then Rachel asked *did you just come?* and Emily whispered, *yeah,* and Rachel climbed back up and they lay in each other's arms speaking only with the little motions of their bodies. Emily thought maybe Rachel had fallen asleep but Emily lay there awake, awake, holding Rachel and thinking to herself, *we just made love.*

Emily expected it to happen again, again, to become a thing they did. But it didn't. At first Emily chalked it up to time, schedules, interruptions, Rachel's nervousness about making noises that roommates might hear. Then to the long weekend Rachel spent with her grandparents—they talked on the phone every night, but still it took a while to get used to being in person again with someone, didn't it? Rachel started worrying about what she would do after graduating, and Emily wondered what they would do if Rachel moved away.

Emily herself was planning to stay in Philadelphia, living off her savings and doing photography, though she hadn't told this plan to her parents yet. Rachel was looking for activist jobs, jobs where she could help people, especially queer people. "Ooh, this is perfect," Rachel said one day, surfing the net. "Program Director for the LGBT center at Philadelphia Community College."

Emily looked over her shoulder. The job *did* look good.

Rachel was already opening up her word processing program and beginning a cover letter. "Dear Sir or Madam, I am *the* perfect candidate for this job. Allow me to tell you why." She kept typing and Emily sat back, imagining Rachel in an apartment down the street from her, dinner together every night, a good morning kiss before leaving for work.

A draft was printing out, and Rachel handed it to Emily to look over. Emily started reading, then looked up. "I guess you'll be coming out to your parents if you get this job."

Rachel's face fell. "I hadn't thought of that. Maybe I can just say I haven't found a job yet. Nah, that won't work." Rachel took the letter from Emily's hand, skimmed it, and crumpled it up. "Forget it."

"Rachel," Emily said. "You can *do* it. You can do the job, and you can tell your parents. I know you can." But nothing Emily could say would make Rachel change her mind.

Emily had been thinking more and more about coming out to her own parents, talking to Rachel about where and when. It was time. Emily wanted her parents to know, wanted them to meet Rachel. Then Rachel's parents called unexpectedly one Friday morning and said they were coming to town on Saturday.

"You have to go," Rachel told Emily. "They can't see you. They'll figure it out."

Emily lay in Rachel's bed, pajamas on, watching as Rachel ripped down everything from her door. Down came the rainbow stickers. Down came the Ani Difranco poster, the *Philadelphia Inquirer* article, the photograph with Rachel's beautiful breast, the photograph of the two of them kissing.

"Why are you just lying there?" Rachel asked, frantic, shoving books and the pink triangle posters into a drawer underneath her sweaters, "Get dressed. Help me at least."

"They're not coming until tomorrow," Emily said, but Rachel was already too flipped out to hear, scanning scanning scanning her room for anything she'd missed.

Rachel sent Emily back to her dorm that morning with a heavy box of dyke paraphernalia, *wait till they're gone,* and Emily wondered when—whether—Rachel would piece together her fragmented life. Rachel seemed convinced she'd never have to tell them. Wasn't Emily reason enough? Rachel was reason enough for Emily, Rachel was reason period.

That Saturday was Gay Youth Pride downtown. Rachel had had the flyer taped to her door for a month, and Emily had imagined the two of them hand in hand at the march, role models for the high schoolers. Instead, Rachel was taking her parents to Manayunk for the day, far away from any setting that might provoke questions. Emily decided to go to Pride anyway, alone. It was amazing how many people she recognized from campus, how many she actually knew. She felt the beginnings of community.

In that community, across the crowd, Emily glimpsed a face she recognized from eighth grade and hadn't seen since: Spencer. She couldn't wait to tell Rachel.

"Are you sure it was him?" Rachel asked. They were back in Rachel's dorm, and Rachel was flipping channels. "Why didn't you talk to him?"

Emily shrugged. "And say what? Hey, look, we're both queer? I know he saw me. He was hanging on some guy the whole time, and holding court like he used to do in middle school. I didn't feel like being part of his entourage again."

"Well at least you know why he got weirded out when you asked him to a dance." Rachel flipped from MTV to a home shopping channel.

Emily stared at the cubic zirconium diamond necklace on the screen, confused. Rachel's parents had left that afternoon, and after dinner Emily had arrived with the box of paraphernalia, a pair of pajamas and clean underwear on top. Rachel still seemed distracted, out of sorts. Emily couldn't put her finger on it. She wondered if it was PMS. "Are you expecting your period?" she asked.

"No, I got it two weeks ago when you did, remember?" Rachel glanced at Emily, then back to the screen, now showing someone's home-videoed dog tripping over a Frisbee.

"What happened with your parents?"

"Nothing. We went to that restaurant, we walked around. I told you. They want me to work for my uncle's company after graduation." Rachel turned off the television. "Let's just go to bed."

In bed Rachel became more attentive, and they were kissing and touching and letting their hands wander to now-wet areas. Emily was getting more and more aroused, when suddenly Rachel's hand slowed, then stopped. "I'm too tired," she said. "I'm sorry."

Emily's body moved involuntarily against Rachel's hand for a few moments, and then Rachel shifted to her usual sleeping position and her hand was spooning Emily's stomach, out of reach.

Two nights later, Rachel called it off, over the phone, *friends, okay?*

"I don't get it," Emily said.

"What don't you get?" Rachel's voice was bitchy and weird, unfamiliar.

"Why you want to break up suddenly. Can we talk about this?"

"I don't know what there is to say. I just can't go out with you anymore."

"Is this about your parents? Did they say something?"

"No. I have to write a term paper, Emily. I can't talk right now."

"Do you—" Emily said, but Rachel was already saying goodbye and hanging up.

Emily paced her apartment waiting for Rachel to call back with some explanation, say it had all been a joke, although what kind of joke Emily couldn't imagine. She fiddled with the camera, not shooting anything: putting the fifty millimeter back in its case, reattaching the zoom, zooming in on inanimate objects, the chair, now the desk, now the dust bunnies, click, click, click, knowing they were bad shots.

She sat on a bench in a deserted corner of College Green, click, click, click, with no film in the camera, what else could she do? What was the right thing? How could she get Rachel back?

Then inside again and the answering machine blinking and a message from Rachel. *I'm sorry, I didn't mean to be a bitch, I didn't want to hurt you, it's just too much for me right now.* Emily biked across campus, entered the dorm and knocked on Rachel's door. *Do you still love me?* she asked, when Rachel opened the door, and Rachel answered *I don't know.* And Emily tried to find the answer in Rachel's face but it wasn't Rachel's face anymore.

Emily didn't remember if anything else was said, how she left, just crying and crying and somehow making it to Sean's apartment, fumbling with her Kryptonite bike lock until it fastened to the iron rail, and then Sean's arms around her. She fit inside Sean's hug in a way that felt good, safe, necessary. He let her fall asleep on the sofa, crying, his chest for a pillow, those safe arms for a blanket. In the morning he made her breakfast and said, *it's her loss* and *it sounds like she was just scared,* and Emily said, *well I'm scared too, I was scared too, I didn't run away.*

That's part of what makes you special, said Sean. *Hopefully next time you can find someone who's ready to be with you.* But Emily felt as he said it that there wasn't going to be a next time, and when Sean said that after a while it would stop hurting so much, Emily didn't believe him.

After the breakup, Emily found herself skipping classes, and actually missing an exam that brought her grade in the course down from an A- to a C and not even caring. She was thrown and disoriented. She had the urge to run off somewhere where no one knew her, but after skipping another day of classes and getting lost in the King of Prussia Mall, that urge left her too.

"You're not coming home," Mom had informed Emily whenever the subject of what to do after graduation came up. "This town is no place for an educated twenty-something." Emily hadn't argued—she sensed the need for physical distance from her parents, even if she couldn't articulate why—but she wondered if her mother would be any less insistent if they lived in a real city, a place like New York or Boston where you might realistically choose to live in your twenties. Emily had flirted with the idea of going somewhere exotic, but place wasn't at the top of her list of concerns.

"Have you visited the Career Services office?" Mom would ask next in these conversations. At first the answer was no, and then it was yes, and that still wasn't enough for Mom. "You could work for a newspaper," she offered. "How about as a program director for a Jewish organization?" She had plenty of suggestions, but none of them interested Emily.

"Emily, you need to find a job," her father would chime in. "You forget—you won't have homework, you'll have time to do photography *after* work."

It didn't matter how much Emily had followed her family's rules, had followed the path they set forth, had achieved, had excelled: it never seemed to be enough. She didn't often compare herself to her brother, but when she did, it seemed that he was having more fun. And despite all her parents' worry about Zack—which was far from insignificant—they didn't seem to love him any less.

Zack was back in Seattle, after a month in Oregon and a brief visit home. Every so often now Emily would get a postcard from him. Zack never said much about where he was staying but scrawled notes like *here's a picture of the largest ball of string in the world* or *everyone says that when you look down from a mountain, people look like ants, but they really look more like short caterpillars* or *have you read any Raymond Carver, you'd like him Emily, his stories are like your photographs.*

Emily had come out to her parents while Zack was home, defiantly, almost daring them to say anything: *My heart was broken two weeks ago. Her name was Rachel.* Her father, in the front seat of the car with Zack, let her mother do the talking, but later he hugged Emily just as hard as he always did when something hurt. Her mother said carefully, *I'm sorry that happened to you Emily,* and *thank you for telling us,* and then asked question after question, *how long did you know this girl? were you dating? how long have you known you were gay?,* until Zack rescued her with a story about a ventriloquist he had met in the train station. But Mom, too, hugged Emily like she always did. Emily's sexual orientation was no big deal; it was her lack of an acceptable career plan that threatened her parents.

In April one of Emily's photographs made it into print, second place in the *Your Best Shot* section of a national photo magazine. Publication and a hundred dollars. Emily took it as a sign that was time to follow her own compass.

She graduated on a warm May day in black cap and gown and rainbow tassel, without a job or the intention of getting one. She tried not to stare at Rachel, marching ahead of her with black tassel, turning away whenever Emily attempted to catch her eye. Zack's last postcard nestled in Emily's pocket, a substitute for his physical presence. Emily and her parents and grandparents posed by the Ben-Franklin-on-a-bench statue for the obligatory cheesy photo, then had a late lunch at Emily's favorite restaurant. Mom beamed with pride. Grandma Novak kept grasping Emily's thigh and saying *my bubbeleh,* and Grandpa Novak snapped picture after picture and said how elaborate the food was, and Dad kept tousling her hair like he'd done when she was little and saying *my baby's a college graduate.*

Emily felt like she'd accomplished something real, not in graduating but in all the individual accomplishments her graduation represented. There were papers and projects, and the intellectual history exam she'd studied harder for than she'd ever thought possible, and the science class she'd barely passed, and the sheer endurance of thirty-four courses over four years. There was weight to the degree.

"Aren't you glad you stayed with your education," Grandma asked, "instead of gallivanting like your brother?" *It isn't gallivanting,* Emily wanted to protest, *he's learning something too,* but she knew better to bring that up. She nodded, mouth full of pea mint ravioli.

"And what's next?" asked Grandpa.

"Emily is joining the ranks of the unemployed," Dad announced.

"Really?" said Grandma. "I thought the school helped all the students secure employment by the middle of the spring term."

"That's just the business and engineering students," Emily explained. "The liberal arts students don't usually find jobs until after graduation."

"So do you have interviews lined up?" asked Grandma.

"Maybe you can talk some sense into her," Dad said. "Emily's decided she doesn't need to have a job like the rest of us. I don't know how she's expecting to pay rent or feed herself."

"Uy," said Grandma.

"She's not coming home with you?" Grandpa asked, as Mom shot Dad the *not here, not now* look and Emily felt the tension return to her jaw. She'd thought at least her actual graduation day would be focused on her accomplishments.

"I'm staying in Philly. I have money saved up and I'm going to work on my photography this summer, and I'm not discussing the fall until closer to the time," Emily said. She tried to say it politely, since she wasn't mad at her grandparents, but she didn't want to be having this conversation.

"We're helping Emily move in this afternoon," Mom said. "She found a nice place to sublet for the summer, and it even comes with a bed and a desk so she doesn't need to buy furniture. We told her that she wouldn't be happy coming back to Connecticut and she decided it would make more sense to stay in Philly for now than try to relocate." Emily knew that Mom was trying, for appearance sake. Mom's true feelings were closer to Dad's. "It's such a great city. I've really enjoyed visiting her here." Mom smiled at Emily.

"The campus is gorgeous," agreed Grandma, and they talked about the perks of Philadelphia for a while, safely off the subject of Emily's future. Then the conversation shifted again, to Grandpa's garden, and then lunch was over and they walked Grandma and Grandpa Novak to their car to return to Queens.

"Well, good luck to you, whatever you do," Grandpa said to Emily. "You're smart, you'll figure it out."

"Come visit us during raspberry season," said Grandma, as they drove off.

All Emily really wanted to do was take pictures. She'd found a cheap sublet and figured that the money accumulated in her bank account from babysitting and summer jobs and her bat mitzvah would last through the summer and maybe even a little longer. She would build up her portfolio, one good photograph each day, and at the end of the summer she would walk into the stock photography agency on Walnut Street and ask them to buy her work, and then fall and beyond would take care of itself.

The first days were idyllic. Waking up naturally, no alarm clock, around eight. Orange juice and cereal and then a shower with the sun streaming through the window and yellow shower curtain, casting a glow throughout the bathroom. There was a used bookstore down the street and Emily would wander inside, find a book to read on its little front balcony for a while. She would take pictures of the stacks of books on the landing, on the chairs, on the tilting bookcases. She photographed the berries on the tree outside. *They're mulberries,* someone told her, passing by and picking a few which he popped in his mouth. She tasted one too, the surprisingly bland flavor outshone by the simple fact that here in the middle of West Philadelphia was a mulberry tree and she could eat its berries whenever she wanted. She rode her bike downtown to the big Borders bookstore and then to the photo store where she bought more film and then along the river by the art museum. She got a library card. She photographed the men selling vegetables at the Italian Market, who grinned into her camera as they showed off perfect ears of corn. She photographed the new coffee shop around the corner. She learned from one of her roommates how to make eggplant parmesan, and she photographed the dish coming out of the oven. There was something wonderful about everything, its newness.

On Wednesday of the second week, Emily took five rolls of film and a backpack full of chemicals to the school darkroom. The building was locked, but Emily still had a key. She'd never gotten around to returning it and reclaiming her security deposit. She let herself in, nodded at the guard at the other end, and entered the outer darkroom.

No one else was around. Emily procured the largest film developing tank, which held five rolls of film, and loaded her film on the reels in the complete darkness of the inner darkroom. Once all five rolls were loaded, she returned to the light of the outer darkroom, turned on the radio to the Temple jazz station, and prepared the chemicals. She listened to John Coltrane and to someone she thought might be Dizzy Gillespie as she poured and agitated first the developer, then stop bath, then fixer.

The negatives were already hanging to dry when a guard came in, a different guard than the one she'd recognized earlier. Hungry, Emily was trying to decide whether to come back for the negatives later or dry them with the hairdryer. The hairdryer method didn't take very long, but sometimes negatives would curl from the heat.

"Can I see your Penncard?" the guard asked.

Emily reached for her pocket, then remembered she'd lost her Penncard during graduation. It had probably fallen out on the football field. She had been annoyed only because it meant she couldn't use it for student discounts that summer. "I lost it," she said.

"How did you get in here?"

She tried to figure out whether it was smarter to admit she had a key, or to say the other guard had let her in. Would the other guard still be here? "It was open," she said. "I'm just developing negatives—I'll be done really soon. I'm from Penn—I can show you." Emily reached for her backpack and then realized she'd emptied it of everything else in order to fit in the chemicals.

He looked annoyed. He looked fairly new, not about to be lenient. "I can't let you be here without a Penncard," he said.

"What about my negatives?" Emily asked.

"What do you have to do with them?"

"Just dry them and cut them up to put in negative sleeves," Emily said.

"Fine," he said. "And then you have to go."

Emily waited for him to go back into the hall, but he wasn't moving. He was going to stand there until she finished. He looked impatient. She plugged in the hairdryer and directed it towards the first long strip of negatives.

That night, over Indian food, Sean asked her, "What are you going to do now?"

"Well I guess I can't use the darkroom anymore," Emily said. "I don't know when this guard works, and I don't want to get caught in the middle of something by another guard who won't let me finish."

"Is there another darkroom you can use? The Art Institute?"

"Their security is even tougher," Emily said. "I can develop film at home I guess. In the downstairs bathroom or something. No one ever seems to use that. And I can do my printing in Connecticut—I was going to go visit in August, maybe I'll go up once in July too. It's not ideal, but I'll manage."

"You need your own darkroom," Sean said.

"I know," said Emily. "But I need a house first, to put the darkroom—it goes in the basement—and to get *that* I need a lucrative photo career, and to get that first I need to have a good portfolio."

Sean laughed. "Good luck. What about color? Can't you do color photography in the meantime?"

"I need to learn more. It's expensive to do well."

"Excuses, excuses."

"And it's not my vision."

Now Sean nodded in understanding, and Emily remembered that most of Sean's own work was in black and white. "I only really like doing color when color is the subject. Maybe in the fall, when the leaves change. How's your film going?"

Sean sighed. "Ran out of money again. I can keep editing, but I can't shoot more than about five minutes of footage until next payday."

"I'll treat you to dinner," Emily said, as Sean shook his head. "That'll give you at least an extra couple of minutes this week—you can treat me back once the film is done."

Sean was drinking Sprite, and Emily liked the way his fingers looked holding the glass full of bubbly liquid. She reached for her camera, which sat next to her in the booth. She adjusted the light meter on something else nearby, so he wouldn't see what she wanted to shoot and become self-conscious, then focused on Sean's knuckles and a strip of bubbles and pushed the shutter.

Emily kept shooting all week, letting the undeveloped rolls of film accumulate. Developing film wasn't as rewarding when even contact sheets were a month or two away. She had paid to have contact sheets made at the photo store from the five rolls of film she'd developed at school, thinking that might be a workable solution, but even without ordering prints it was expensive. Four bucks a roll plus tax. Which was nothing compared to their prices for movie film—no wonder Sean was always broke.

Doing laundry one day, Emily noticed a sink in the basement. Maybe she could set up a darkroom down there? She wasn't about to ask Dad to transplant *his* darkroom to Philadelphia for her, not when he was still on her case about getting a job. She dug out a few photo magazines and catalogs from the mess in her room, grabbed a pad and a calculator, and sat on the porch for the next few hours taking notes and making calculations. Decking out a really nice darkroom like the one she'd been imagining in her head was expensive. The mounting press alone was over a thousand dollars. The leftover bat mitzvah money might cover part of it, but the only way she could afford it was if she also used money that her parents had put in her name when she was little, meant for emergency or for something like grad school or a retirement fund. There was a difference between using money she'd been given for her bat mitzvah that was intended to be spent on *something important when you're older,* and using money she had been given by people who loved her but disapproved of what she was doing.

That afternoon a bank statement came in the mail, along with the May utility bills, and Emily got the first inklings that her money was shrinking faster than she'd expected. *How much does it cost to live?* Emily had asked her parents that fall. They couldn't give her solid numbers, *it depends on this, it depends on that, you need to get a job and a place to live first,* so she'd asked the Career Services counselor, who had tried to come up with numbers. Those numbers had convinced Emily that her summer plan was reasonable, but they were much lower than Emily's already-frugal spending.

The next day it was overcast, so the sun didn't stream through the window and Emily showered in dingy yellow rather than the energizing glowing gold. She ate her Cheerios as usual and drank the last of the orange juice—she would have to remember to pick up another carton—and then slung her camera bag as usual over her shoulder and headed outside. She sat down on the front steps for a few minutes, deciding where to go, another action that had become routine. Her route would always bring her past the mulberry tree but beyond that it could take her anywhere.

What Emily wanted to do that day was to take candids, pictures of people. But she would need her subjects to sign model releases if she was going to sell the photos. Emily hadn't created her own model releases yet, although she'd taken a book out of the library on the subject. More importantly, she hadn't figured out how to approach strangers to ask permission. She preferred to zoom in from afar, to watch people who were oblivious and snap the photo at just the right moment, then disappear without them ever knowing. So Emily headed towards the bus stop, and the first bus to arrive brought her to the section of the Schuylkill River by the art museum.

She walked along the edge of the river, uninspired, looking for something interesting to photograph. The subjects that caught her eye at all were too mundane, too man-made and repetitive. Sidewalk and brick and grass riddled with cigarette butts. Emily continued walking, zooming in on tree trunks and rocks and rippled water, occasionally even clicking the shutter, but the composition was all wrong, too boring, too much like photographs she'd already taken.

It was eleven o'clock and it was getting hot and Emily realized she was hungry. She opened the granola bar she kept in her camera bag. Crumbs. She noticed a food truck outside the art museum and headed over. The truck sold sandwiches and hot pretzels and gum and candy. Emily bought a pretzel with mustard, the cheapest option that would stave off her hunger, and sat down on a nearby bench.

She focused her camera on the pretzel, but the pretzel texture fought with the texture of the bench. The image wasn't worth recording. Emily put down the camera and took a bite of the pretzel. Maybe next time she saw Grandpa Novak she would borrow his macro lens again and take close-up pictures of pretzels, so close that all you could see was golden brown and mustard and oversized pieces of salt.

After finishing the pretzel, Emily caught the bus back downtown, buying a slice of pizza for two dollars and fifty cents that she ate on Market Street while watching pigeons. Pigeons were fun to watch but not to photograph. Emily had taken a lot of mediocre pigeon pictures before admitting to herself that she didn't like the aesthetic of how their shape showed up in the frame. The sun was beating down, and Emily was sticky even in the shade. She wiped her forehead with her shirt. She had planned to go home and read about model releases but right now all she wanted was air conditioning.

Emily wandered in and out of a few stores before deciding that it was hot enough to justify a movie ticket. Two hours of cool air and special effects, then sticky sweat again.

Back home it was too hot to concentrate on model releases, even with two fans going and the windows open. Emily gave up and took a shower, wishing the bathtub wasn't so grimy so she could soak there with a book. After showering she was hungry again and it was dinner time, so downstairs to the kitchen, sweating as she moved, opening mostly-bare cabinets and wondering if it made more sense to go out for dinner.

Emily added up the day's expenses in her head. Six dollars for the movie and two for the pretzel and two-fifty for the pizza and three-twenty for the bus because she had run out of tokens. That was a lot. She didn't want to pay for a restaurant dinner, and she wasn't in the mood for yet another chicken cheesesteak.

She threw away the vegetables that had rotted in the crisper and opened the freezer. One frozen turkey frank. Emily microwaved that and ate it standing up, no bun. Crackers in the cabinet, cheddar cheese in the fridge. Emily ate those sitting down, right off the cutting board. In the morning she would go to Thriftway. Not tonight because it would be dark before she finished shopping, which would mean paying for a cab to get home safely.

Still hungry, Emily filled a large mug with ice cream and brought it upstairs, where even the ceiling fan wasn't doing much against the heat. She tried calling Sean. He wasn't home. She took another shower and then lay down naked under the ceiling fan, hoping the phone would ring. It was eight o'clock. After an hour of staring at the fan turning, she gathered the energy to reach up and pull the string to turn the light off and sleep.

The next morning there was only half a bowl's worth of cereal left, and the milk smelled funny even though there were still two days until the expiration date. Emily realized she'd also forgotten about buying orange juice. Leaving her camera behind in favor of an empty backpack, Emily biked with a growling stomach in the opposite direction from the mulberry tree, towards Thriftway.

Sixty-two dollars and thirty-seven cents later, Emily was back at her sublet with sore shoulders, hungry and hot and sweaty and thirsty. She tilted her face underneath the kitchen faucet, drinking as if the sink was a water fountain, and then stuck her whole head under to be soaked.

She made her way through a whole row of Ritz crackers with Nutella and glass after glass of lemonade as she sat in front of the kitchen fan, trying to get the energy to go back out. It would be a perfect day for photographing Reading Terminal

Market—indoor, air-conditioned—but Emily had already done that twice. It was too hot to go to the zoo. She was bored with her neighborhood, and with downtown—always the same tired subject matter. She could feel the sweat dripping from behind her knees. Somewhere, someone was probably photographing knee-sweat.

As the days went on, Emily took fewer and fewer pictures, spending more time inert near fans and listening to the recordings of her friends' voices, *leave a message after the beep.* She spent seven hours straight one day on the internet at the public library, trance-like from the screen, searching first for her cousins' names as she had done periodically—unsuccessfully—since freshman year, and then for names of everyone else in her family. Her cousins would be eighteen and sixteen by now. Old enough to go to college and drive, or get knocked up and slit their wrists, or run away. Emily had absolutely no idea who they would have grown into. She searched her own name, and a page came up with her email address and a few photographs, a placeholder for the website one of Sean's friends had promised to teach her to make before he graduated. She had checked that email address at least once a day since freshman year. She left the library and stepped back into the sweltering outside, dejected. If her cousins were looking, they would have already found her. There was no point anymore in imagining.

Even on days when Emily woke up to the shining sun and photographed something beautiful right outside her door, there was still the rest of the day to fill. There were unplanned expenditures, like an iced mocha or an Indian buffet lunch purchased so she could be inside air conditioning. Emily's stress exacerbated. She didn't want to admit it, even to herself, and she didn't feel like she had a right to complain—no one around her had the luxury of not having a job.

Emily was used to spending a lot of time alone, but this was different—no knocking door-to-door in the dorms for someone to eat with, no regular activities to break up the days. She'd thought that with so many roommates there was bound to be someone to hang out with, but that hadn't turned out to be the case, and really, Emily didn't want to be hanging out. She wanted to be living the photographer's life she had dreamed about forever, and she'd thought all she needed was this unpressured stretch of time. So why was she lying under the ceiling fan at eight o'clock at night, too hot to move, lying naked with soaking towels underneath her that were seeping moisture into the subletted mattress, lying inert with her eyes numbed at the ceiling when it was barely even getting dark outside?

It didn't occur to Emily that this was rejuvenation time, that photography came with a cycle of creativity and processing, that if she had access to a darkroom she could be making progress right now without the pressure to capture. Instead, inspiration seemed to evaporate with the arrival of the heat wave.

It spiraled. It spiraled and spiraled and Emily couldn't tell that it was spiraling, couldn't remember when it hadn't been like this. *You need structure,* her father kept saying. *Get a job, you'll be happier if you have a job, if you have structure, you can do photography on the side.* But that's what Emily had been doing, photography on the side of school, and it hadn't been enough. She had felt chained. She didn't know what it meant that this, now, *making the commitment,* wasn't enough either.

"How's your money holding up?" Mom asked, over the phone.

"Not too well," Emily admitted.

"Are you *surprised?*" Mom's voice was mocking. "Living costs money, that's why you need an income."

Emily moved the phone a couple of inches away from her ear so she could wipe off the sweat. "I'm going to have an income, Mom. As soon as I start selling my photos."

"Well are you even *trying* to sell them? It sounds like you're just building a collection of undeveloped film. Have you sent that butterfly photograph to a magazine yet? What about entering that photo contest we saw advertised in the paper your graduation weekend?"

"I'm concentrating on building my portfolio," Emily said defensively.

"What about selling your work at a crafts fair? We were at a crafts fair last weekend and your photos are at least as good as what we saw there."

Mom didn't have the know-how to give real advice on this—advice that would take Emily from where she was now to where she wanted to be—but she was convinced of her rightness, convinced her way was the only way. Emily didn't know what magazine to send to and didn't want to sign away all her rights like the photo contest required. She was pretty sure but couldn't prove that a crafts fair would cost a lot of money up front without bringing in enough money or even exposure to make it worthwhile. She started reading more books to find out some of these answers, but the library didn't have much and buying the books meant her checking account was shrinking even more, and when Mom asked her point-blank how much money she had left, Emily deflected the question because the honest answer was that she didn't know.

Emily didn't have the language—or was it the perspective?—to call it *depression*. She hadn't made the connection between this and what had happened to Grandpa Irv after he got sick. She didn't understand that this was what had happened to Mom after Grandpa Irv died. She only knew that she'd made this commitment and now instead of being outside, somewhere, taking pictures, exploring and shooting beautiful things, instead of reading the book on macro photography or the one on *how to sell your photos* or trying to find a yard sale darkroom she could make do with for a while, she was spending her dream summer lying on a mattress under a fan, sweating and crying and wondering if any of this would ever change.

Have you sent out your photos yet? her mother kept asking. *Why not?* And there were a million things Emily could say if her mother wasn't using that critical tone, if her mother hadn't acted like she knew everything in the world about selling photos, if her mother had asked in a way that allowed for Emily to be mixed up and stuck and fumbling through.

Do what you need to do with your photography, Zack said when Emily told him about these conversations. *Don't let Mom and Dad talk you out of it.* But Zack didn't know any more than Emily did what it was she needed to make this work.

It was August and Emily sat underneath the kitchen fans with her checkbook and a pad and a pile of bills and receipts. When she subtracted the July electric bill, with two more bills and most of the receipts still not factored in, the number crossed the line. The past few weeks had been a farce, an illusion that Emily was still supporting herself. Her earned savings and her bat mitzvah money were gone. The next thing Emily bought would be paid for by money from her family, and the thing after that, and the thing after that. The money was there, and it was hers to use, but it meant she had failed.

She was alone in the kitchen and she smashed her hand against the wall, then began knocking things over, chairs and grocery bags, throwing cans of beans against the cabinets, crying. It wasn't fair. No one had told her that even a frugal life was *this* expensive, that the money would disappear *this* fast no matter what she did. She was angry at her parents, she was angry at Penn, she was angry at God who probably didn't exist, she was angry at Sean and at Zack for not having a magic answer.

"Damn you, Rachel," she hollered as she threw a box of orzo, which hit the edge of the sink spew-flying. One orzo hit her in the space below her right eye, and she brushed at the spot. "Damn you for leaving me." She threw another can of beans, which dented and scratched paint off the cabinet. "Damn you."

She threw a can opener, tore the calendar someone had left lying on the table completely in half. She pushed the table itself, which screeched until it keeled over on two legs, spraying up more orzo, sending the bills and receipts into a jumbled mess. She kicked the refrigerator door and yelped as the pain registered, stumbling backwards and tripping on a can of tomatoes. She landed splayed on the floor, choking on tears, exhausted. "Damn you all."

It might have been hours later when Emily finally moved from that position, carefully collecting the pieces of paper that were hers and leaving the rest. She didn't tell anyone what had happened. She hid out and eavesdropped instead as a few of her roommates came home and speculated and eventually cleaned up most of the mess, and when her parents invited themselves down the next weekend, she didn't say no.

Mom and Dad arrived and they hugged Emily and they took her out to eat good meals and they let her cry and they hugged her again. They drove her to the ocean one afternoon and her mother wrote down recipes for how to make easy healthy meals. Her father flipped through photo catalogs with her and talked about equipment he could loan her and the extra black stuff he had in the basement for covering up windows if she wanted to make a darkroom. Together they helped Emily with the tangible things like dishes in the sink and food shopping. They drove her around in the air-conditioned car to evaluate safer neighborhoods where she might want to move. Emily didn't understand why the phone conversations made things worse while her parents in person made things so much better, but she wasn't arguing, just soaking it up, grateful. Maybe she couldn't do this alone after all. At least she had tried.

Her parents still were emphatic that she not move back home, which might have angered Emily if she had let herself feel it, and they didn't think anything would be better if she went to another city—*unless you have a job there*, her father said, *but even then*—but they suggested that once she had found a new place, she come back home to Connecticut for a week to rest. After signing a lease on an apartment a block away from Sean's, and registering with a temp agency, Emily did just that.

It was stressful to take care of yourself, Emily had discovered, and simply having someone else who would cook for you or do the dishes or come with you to buy tape and photo chemicals was an incredible thing. Her father came with her to a few yard sales that Saturday in Connecticut, and they found an enlarger, a good one, which was expensive but an excellent deal, and Emily decided this was a tool she was meant to use. And her father said, *well, it could be an early Chanukah present.* Emily had thought that she needed to buy it herself, that psychologically she needed to do this whole thing herself, but somehow it felt okay now to accept the gift. She'd tried *by herself* and now she was going to see what would happen if she had a little help.

Later that weekend she borrowed Mom's car and drove around the woodsy areas near Litchfield and she parked the car in different places and walked around and photographed. Everything was beautiful. She sat at the edge of Bantam River and watched a pair of ducks, not photographing, just watching and watching and occasionally quacking at them and listening to them quack back. She sat there for an hour maybe, long after the ducks swam away, still watching. It was like staring at the fan and yet completely unlike that, *rejuvenating,* because she was in nature and little things *did* change out here, like dragonflies landing on a reed, instead of everything being stagnant in a room.

Her father helped her develop that roll of film that night, and Emily made a contact sheet and some prints the next morning, after a slow beautiful walk around the neighborhood. They drove down to Queens in the afternoon, just the two of them. They picked raspberries and zucchini in Grandma and Grandpa Novak's backyard and went folk dancing with her grandparents, and then spent the next day in Manhattan. Emily hadn't brought her camera. She and Dad wandered around New York, visiting Chinatown, watching a Neil Simon play. There was something liberating about not having a camera. Not having to be careful it didn't get stolen or remembering to pick it up from the coat-check in a museum or from under her feet in a restaurant. Not having to look so hard for something to capture, to keep. New York wasn't beautiful in a *keep* kind of way.

In Connecticut Emily had found a mostly-empty childhood journal she'd ceased writing in when she was twelve or thirteen, and on the drive back, she wrote, *I think it's getting better now. I hope it is.*

When the sublet ran out at the end of the month, Emily moved to her new apartment downtown, a one-bedroom with a tiny living room that could be turned into a darkroom if she didn't mind rinsing the photos in the oversized bathroom sink. She read every book on personal finance she could get her hands on. She got a temp job at the library, and signed up for another class at the Art Institute, and the depression began to lift. *You need chains,* is how she explained it to Sean one day, *but what's different now is that you choose them yourself. How can I pay rent and still have time for photography? That's a question I have to keep at the forefront.* She learned, slowly, to create elaborate structures for herself, complete with elaborate loopholes, to trick her mind into being creative without falling back into the downward spiral.

Meanwhile, Mom and Dad had finally been allowed to visit Zack and reported that the six-person co-op where he lived was a little grungy and run-down, but the people seemed nice, and Zack seemed happy there. They sounded almost disappointed. Emily spoke to her brother every couple of months now, him sending postcards and her sending emails in between. He was working part-time as a waiter and part-time at a camping store, and Emily wondered how much of the family money *he* had spent in the nearly three years since he'd left home.

Sean had completed a short film that fall, scrapping his first two ideas in favor of an artsy, gritty, black-and-white observation of children on a playground, and on a lark he submitted it to a couple of film festivals as well as to NYU film school. Emily was as excited as he was when he got the NYU acceptance, even though it meant that he would be moving.

It was springtime. Emily's third temp job at the library was about to become permanent, a word Emily had translated in her head as *I-can-quit-when-I-need-to.* She liked her co-workers and being around so many books and not having to touch her family money to buy film or pay the rent. Emily showed up at Sean's apartment on Wednesday to meet him for Indian food, and he was literally jumping on the couch. Kissing his Super 8, he looked all of fourteen years old, as cute and joyful as Emily had ever seen him.

"I'm in, I'm in," Sean sang. "San Francisco! Independent! Film Fes-ti-val! Heeeeere we come!" He high-fived Emily with his free hand. His film had been selected, and even NYU paled next to this unexpected news.

"Woohoo, San Francisco," Emily shouted, letting her own exhilaration loose. Proud of her friend's success. Letting herself acknowledge that expense be damned, she *did* want to be there for it.

The next morning, Emily was having second thoughts about the cost, but it turned out that by automatically putting ten percent of each paycheck into a savings account, Emily had saved just enough to cover a plane ticket to San Francisco and three nights' stay in a youth hostel. She decided that this would be the perfect end to her life as a temp. Particularly when Zack agreed to take the bus down from Seattle to join her.

Crocuses and then tulips were appearing on the landscape. Color was on Emily's mind—did she want to shoot color?

The man at the stock agency had been friendly when she showed up unannounced. He had looked at her portfolio. He had complimented her eye. "Color," he had said though. "It's a business. The clients want color, even if they end up converting an image to black-and-white. Color sells. And slide film, Ms. Novak, *always* shoot slide film. Digital, maybe, in a few years. Not yet." The agency wouldn't touch negatives, he'd said. "Come back and ask for me when you've got a thousand slides I can sell," he'd said. "Five thousand, even better. But you've got spunk, girl. I'd take a gamble on a thousand for spunk."

So Emily brought seven rolls of color slide film with her to San Francisco as an experiment.

Her friends from the Art Institute had scoffed at stock agencies—*your art might be used to sell dog biscuits*—but Emily's art on dog biscuit packages could mean film, a new lens, airfare to photograph at the New Orleans Jazz Festival. Also nicer dog biscuit packaging. Money wasn't evil, and photographing sale-able beauty was preferable, for Emily, to a fifty-plus-hour-a-week career or a sideline as a coffee barista to afford the necessary expenses of her chosen art form. Emily hadn't figured it all out yet, but she had never *not* photographed something she wanted to photograph, and as long as that stayed true, she figured she was doing okay.

So seven rolls of thirty-six shots each, color slide, an experiment. New landscape meant fresher photos, maybe cliché maybe not but definitely fresher, and Emily had set her goal, one hundred sellable slides. Daunting but not impossible in a four-day weekend, and as Emily waited for her plane, she began: close-up red bits in the candy bin, the bustle of greeting at the arrivals gate, electric guitar sans amp being played by a teenage boy oblivious to the crowd around him.

She met up with Zack at the San Francisco youth hostel where they locked up their bags and began exploring the city, seeing more than Emily would have thought possible in a single day. It was nice that it was just the two of them, and they talked and talked like no time had passed at all since the days of playing on the tire swing in the backyard.

Zack was the one who first noticed the murals, pointing out one then a second. Then waiting patiently each time as Emily, reverent, photographed. Murals all over San Francisco, one brighter and wider and longer than the next. Color texture color color, and Emily would sway her body prayer-like to focus. Here, surely, art and market came together, these tic-tac bursts of color, these close-up fragments of beauty, like a bit of souvenir holy water to take home.

Emily photographed her brother, new dreadlocks and grins, and she photographed little kids climbing on a Buddha statue, and in the Castro she photographed men. Men alone, men with men, men in drag. She photographed hands and rainbows. Then, in the corner of the lens, purple-streaked hair, and Emily's heart thumped forgetting all that had come afterward but no. It was someone else. Of course it was. And Rachel was long-gone anyway and a heart-breaker and a fraidy-cat and even now even so Emily wished for her sometimes. But this purple-streaked hair wasn't Rachel's, and last week Emily had heard a rumor, Rachel moving in with someone else, a boy. Zack was up ahead waiting and Emily let down the lens and there were two women passing by, a couple hand-in-hand. One of them smiled at Emily, that knowing *hey fellow gay chick* sparkle in her eyes, and for just a moment Emily felt frisky, San Francisco frisky. Then men again and Zack up ahead waiting but the Rachelness feeling was gone and it was better that way.

And it was *vacation*. Emily and Zack's legs dangled onto the pier, watching boats. Zack and Emily walking uphill on the windiest street ever. Standing outside a church just to hear its beautiful choir. Buying cotton candy, that childhood-forbidden sugary-air snack. Lying on the grass in Golden Gate Park and honest-to-goodness *napping* under the sun's warmth, until bee buzzing opened her eyes to sky so beautiful and Emily taking pictures again. Talking long into the night.

Zack Day.

Day two was Sean Day, but it began with Emily waking up before Zack and savoring the calm of a bowl of cereal and the pattering of other early-risen travelers on a west coast morning. This was when Emily found the courage to look up information about the next Philadelphia Open Studios and compose an email asking if it was too late to participate. By the time Sean found her inserting her second dollar-for-five-minutes-of-internet in the youth hostel lounge, she'd already pressed *send* and was copying down a phone number to follow up when she returned, and she was plotting what could hang where.

Sean plopped in a chair. "I'm nervous."

"You are?"

This was their friendship—no preludes, no *how was your flight, when did you get in,* just dive right in to the important stuff.

"For the Q&A afterwards," Sean said. He raised his hand, waving it like an impatient audience member. "What's the existential meaning of the tiger in the penultimate scene?" He deepened his voice. "Wouldn't you agree that voice-over narration is a cardinal sin of filmmaking, and was your use of the device *intended* to be *ironic*?"

"It won't be that bad," Emily said, but she hadn't been to enough of these to be sure. Anything else she could think to say suddenly sounded like her mother's voice, so she was quiet for a moment.

"What if they think I'm a fraud?"

"Well, for starters," Emily said, "You're not."

Sean didn't seem convinced.

"Do *you* think you're a fraud, Sean?"

Sean started to nod, then shook his head. "I think I'm a student."

"Bingo," said Emily. "Start there. Do *you* like your film?"

Now Sean smiled. "Yeah."

At that Zack appeared in the doorway. "I'm so hungry I could eat a student film," he declared.

Sean scrambled to his feet in a boxer stance. "Not mine you won't." Then he laughed and put out his hand and Emily formally introduced them. He had film-related commitments for the next few hours, so the three made plans to meet up after the screening, and then Sean departed with a bow, noticeably more cheerful than he had been ten minutes earlier.

Emily and Zack found good seats in what Emily was glad to see was a packed theater. She had already seen the film, of course, but it was one thing seeing it with Sean and his film crew and quite another seeing it in a crowded theater on a big screen.

"That was *cool*," Zack whispered loudly to her as the credits rolled. "Hey, there's your name." *Emily Novak*, right under Sean's parents in the list of thank you's. That part Emily hadn't seen before. She grinned, feeling the smile stretch across her face.

They stayed for the other short films and then the Q&A session with the filmmakers—Sean intelligent and professional in front of the audience, not even flinching when someone *did* ask about the significance of the stuffed tiger—and then sat outside for a while, Zack watching the throngs of people, Emily photographing them.

When Sean joined them, the line was out the door for the restaurant they wanted, so they wound up stretched out on a patch of grass eating burritos. "Wish I was staying long enough to go camping," Sean said. "I didn't even get to see a redwood tree."

"When does your flight leave?" Zack asked.

"Eleven tomorrow morning."

"Let's do it." Zack looked at Emily. "You in? Mount Tam?"

Mount Tamalpais was a good forty-five minutes outside the city, according to the flyer Emily had read earlier in the youth hostel. Emily looked at Zack strangely. "How? We don't have a way to get there, we don't even have a tent."

"You got a stash of camping gear somewhere?" Sean asked.

"You in if I do?"

"Sure."

"Can I borrow a couple of quarters?" Zack asked Emily.

She dug three out of her pocket and handed them to him, and he headed to a pay phone across the street. When he came back, his arms were raised, victorious.

"Score," Zack said. "A tent, two sleeping bags and a blanket, *and* a car to borrow."

"How?"

"Oliver's cousin," Zack said. "We just have to fill the gas tank and get it back by noon."

Once they were piled into Oliver's cousin's car with the gear—Emily still in disbelief that this was actually happening—Sean insisted on making a stop at a place called The Stinking Rose. He emerged grasping a paper bag, plunked a quarter into the meter where the car was idling, and ushered the siblings to a nearby bench.

"There are melting concerns," Sean explained cryptically, "otherwise I'd wait for the woods."

"What is it?" Emily asked.

Sean pulled a pint-sized container from the bag with a flourish. "*This*," he said, "is nothing other than *garlic ice cream*."

"Garlic?" Zack sounded intrigued.

"No, thank you," said Emily.

Sean pointed a plastic spoon at Emily. "Do not mock. It is the initiation rite."

The San Francisco trip marked the beginning of a definite and steady upswing in Emily's happiness. Two years out of college, Emily had adjusted to the idea of a day job, appreciating health benefits, paid vacation days, and the tuition remission plan that subsidized occasional advanced photography workshops at the Art Institute. She kept a list taped to the wall by her bed of things she needed to learn and do to *get somewhere* as a photographer. *Make portfolio*, the first item on her list, had been crossed off and later supplanted by *build library of 1000 slides to sell to stock agency*. Her library was already at nine hundred something slides, even after having recently tossed some images that didn't meet her standards anymore. Other items on Emily's list included *learn how to legally establish small business, find name for business, get quality b/w negatives every time, learn zone system, learn flash photography or how to work without it!!,* and *try magazine photojournalism(?)*. Awareness of Sean's parallel quest in film school energized her when the list felt daunting.

Emily cringed at the quality of most of her older photos now—shooting slides and spending too much time in the darkroom with shoddy negatives had made her acutely aware of the technical skills she had been lacking. Yet more and more people were saying she had a gift, that she could go places with this, and even her parents had come back around, thanks to the day job. Emily had sold a sizable number of her *Textures of Philadelphia* photographs at the most recent Philadelphia Art Council Open Studios.

She'd bartered with a former classmate for some marketing help, and out of that her music shots had started getting some notice, and the subway musician series she'd done at the Art Institute had been displayed in a gallery downtown, leading to Emily's being featured in the newspaper's "One to Watch" section.

It was Friday evening in mid-July and Emily was in her apartment darkroom, printing. She heard the phone ring and turned down the stereo so she could listen to the message. *Hi Emily, it's Mom, Shabbat Shalom, I hope you're doing something fun. I'm calling about your brother, nothing's wrong don't worry, but please call back tonight or tomorrow if you can. What?* A pause. *Oh, your father says Shabbat Shalom.* Beep. The darkroom clock read nine o'clock. She would call Mom back later. Emily had been working all day, in a groove, and knew she needed air soon and people contact. It wasn't time yet to stop, though. When you were in a groove, it was best to honor that.

Another four hours passed. Emily had one more print she wanted to finish when she heard the sound of her neighbor in the hall. He was an amateur photographer. He had invited her over to see his portfolio when he first moved in, and she didn't like his work much, and he wasn't someone she would choose as a friend, but sometimes they would talk. Mostly Emily would extend an invitation when she was going stir-crazy from being alone, and sometimes he would come up and knock and say he was getting take-out, did she want to take a break? It was past one in the morning. Too late to call anyone. Emily knew that if she opened the door, she'd lose a few minutes and expose the test strip that was still in the developer, but if she didn't she would have gone the entire day without human contact. She opened it and called out a hello.

His Kramer-like hair was wilder than usual, emphasizing his premature bald spot, and he seemed breathless, excited to see her. "I just got back from this seminar," he said. "It was amazing. There's one more day."

"What kind of seminar?"

"You have to go too," he said. He wore an Ansel Adams t-shirt and black jeans.

"What kind of seminar?" Emily asked again. "Is it about photography?" How would he be attending a photography seminar she had never heard of?

"Yes," he said intently. "Photography and *life*. *Life*. It's about *everything*."

Emily was confused, and her neighbor was talking and talking. He was using words but not quite making sense. She was too tired to focus or to figure out how to cut him off.

Emily wasn't sure what to make of these interactions. Once he started he could talk for a while. He usually talked to her about his frustrations with life, his dreams of doing photography full-time, not this mumbo-jumbo. She liked the superior feeling of telling him how to enter contests or how to dodge or burn a print. A couple of times she had wondered if she might like him, but it was a mixed-up feeling. She wasn't attracted to him physically—*repelled* would be closer to the truth. Her feelings towards him were more like the kind of feelings a therapist might have towards a patient.

"We talked about fear," he said now. "Things we've been afraid to say. Like, all this time, I've never hugged you. We talk all the time and sometimes when I leave, I just want to hug you, and I'm always scared to say it."

Emily looked at him, this man in front of her saying these things. She had thought it too. There were some people you hugged and some you didn't and she wasn't sure what made people fall into one category or another. "Well then," she said. She stepped forward for a hug. But he held on, he wasn't letting go when she loosened her arms. He held her tighter. She tightened her arms again, okay, sometimes people didn't quite get hug length. Eventually it ended. She stepped back. He stepped back. Emily wanted to say goodnight now and finish her print and go to bed. He kept talking.

He was telling her about the seminar. A mass of people packed in a room with no bathroom breaks. Rules. Language they had created for concepts Emily knew by other words. It smelled of cult.

She asked questions, trying to figure it out. He answered. She was almost sure it was a cult. Her mind was fogging up, exhausted. He was inviting her to come back with him the next day. He was telling her he loved her. *What?*

"I keep telling myself," he said, "she likes women, forget about it, but it doesn't go away. You're—I'm in love with you. I can't help it. I'm in love with you."

Emily didn't know what to say. The silence was too uncomfortable, too loaded. "I need to finish printing and get to sleep," she told him.

"I want you to have a wonderful sleep," he said. He stretched out his arms. "A goodnight hug?" Emily didn't know how to say no but as he hugged her the skeevy feeling crept through her body and he whispered, "The seminar starts at eight A.M. tomorrow, I hope you'll be able to make it."

She turned the deadbolt behind him, slid down with her back against the door, and shuddered.

Why her?

Emily was brought back again to college, freshman spring. A day Emily now tried to forget. It was just one day, it had happened years and years ago now, why couldn't she erase one day?

He had been a junior, an acquaintance who was in a fraternity and lived on another floor. He had been knocking on doors looking for people to split a pizza with for dinner, and it had wound up being just him and her, in Emily's dorm room.

In her dorm room telling him about her family. Then him kissing her and it was unexpected and it was new and it felt good and he asked *is this okay* and she nodded and whispered yes. They were sitting on the bed because it was either that or the floor. The pizza box was on the floor, open, one slice left, Emily kept her eyes open and she could see the cheese half-slid off. He guided them both into a lying down position, kept kissing her. She kissed back, the good strangeness of tongues and teeth. His bulge on her crotch feeling good between their jeans. But then his mouth was on her breasts without asking—like *yes* had been a carte blanche ticket—and her breasts felt like udders.

Udders.

Emily hadn't liked it, didn't want him there, but wasn't she supposed to? But it felt unbalanced that he could be doing those things to her without something comparable for her to do. His shirt coming off didn't count for anything—he didn't have breasts, he could do that in public. Then his two fingers were on her jeans between her legs rubbing. Something she *could* match and he tried to guide her hand down but she didn't want to feel his penis. Did that alone mean she was one hundred percent lesbian? She didn't want him touching her there either, she hadn't wanted any more than the kissing, not with him. Not on something that couldn't even be called a date, something that had only taken place because he'd gone knocking down the hall and no one else had answered.

It had been different with a girl, with Rachel. Because she was a woman? Because they were in love? It had been even, and gentler.

Could it have been that way with Sean, if she'd met him freshman fall? Emily could almost imagine having sex with Sean now, almost imagine it being comfortable. But the desire wasn't there, the attraction seemed to belong in a different place inside her. Because it was friendship? Because he was a man?

And now this neighbor. Emily's mind replayed the hug, and she shuddered again.

But Emily had liked the junior's crotch up against hers. She liked the bulge. She imagined sometimes she'd like it poked out of boxers, shirt on, clothes on. She imagined not him and not Sean and not the neighbor but some hot mystery guy. Not even kissing. Not the scratchy face. Not intimacy, not conversation. Just the hard penis greased up and moving inside her until she came.

The next morning Emily checked the clock before going downstairs to fetch her newspaper, making sure it was late enough that the neighbor would have already left for his seminar, and tensing up anyway as she opened the door. For the next few months, Emily would continue to avoid the neighbor, tensing whenever she entered and left the building, until he finally moved away.

As she drank her orange juice that morning, she studied the yellow pages, reading entries under *therapist* and *psychologist* and recognizing among them the name of one Rachel had—unsolicited—recommended to her way back when. She reached for the telephone, but called home instead, spooning Cheerios into her mouth as she dialed.

"Your brother's coming home next weekend," Mom told her. "I don't expect you to rearrange your plans since he gave us all *so* little notice, but I thought you'd want to know."

"How long is he staying for?" Emily asked.

"I hope he still has his key," Mom said. "We have tickets for a play at Hartford Stage and I am *not* rescheduling, we bought those tickets months ago."

"How long is he staying?"

"Two nights. He's been home once in the last two years and he can't give us more than two nights."

"You were just in Seattle visiting him," Emily pointed out. "Well, which nights? My schedule's relatively open next weekend, I might be able to come up."

The nights were Friday and Saturday nights. Emily rearranged her Friday schedule with a co-worker, and finally got the courage to call the therapist's office right before she left. She arrived in Oaktown late Friday afternoon, just in time to bring her bag upstairs and use the bathroom before sitting down to Shabbat dinner. They hadn't had a Shabbat dinner together, all four of them, since the night before Zack's high school graduation.

It was a beautiful mid-summer evening, and Mom had set out dinner on the front porch, saving the candle-lighting for closer to sunset. Dad invited Emily to do the kiddush, and she did, the long version, trying to make it sound nice rather than rushing through the prayer. Zack cut the challah and said *motzi*.

"Mmm," said Zack, heartily. "I almost forgot how good your challah tastes, Dad."

"Let's say the *Shechechiyanu*," Dad suggested. "In honor of this special day of our whole family being together." Emily looked around, at her whole family, at the table set before them, at each of them individually. "*Baruch ata adonai*," Dad began, and they all joined in, smiling, almost—but not quite—peaceful.

Mom served the chicken, one leg each for Emily and Zack. "There's more," she said, "but I know you both like drumsticks."

"Mmm," Zack said again, with a mouthful of chicken. Home-cooked food agreed with him. Or maybe it was just being home again. Emily couldn't take her eyes off her brother. She hadn't seen him in over a year. He had grown muscles, his body filled out his clothes more. His hair was longer, the dreadlocks gone. He glowed.

As they ate, Zack told them more about the trip he would be leaving for on Sunday. He would be hiking the Appalachian Trail, a so-called "reverse hike," starting in Maine and continuing as far south as he and his trail mates could make it before the snow started. "When I come back," Zack said, "I may sign up for some classes."

Emily watched Dad's face light up. Mom stopped mid-chew, then swallowed, and Emily could tell she was trying to stifle emotion. "You mean *college* classes?" Mom asked carefully, as though by her saying the word he might change his mind.

At Dad's urging, Mom had rescheduled the play to Saturday and purchased two more tickets. All four of them were making an effort that weekend, and it seemed to be making a differ-ence. Driving to Hartford next to her brother in the back seat, Emily remembered other drives, drives from before Mom's parents had died, when Mom would pack car food and tell them as they traveled all about what they were going to see—plays, museums, once an opera of Hansel and Gretel. Once a magic show. She remembered figuring out how the magician did a particular trick with his newspaper, teaching Zack how in the car on the way home, fooling Mom. She remembered Dad singing as he drove.

"Dad?" she asked, hesitant. "Do you remember the song about the foxes in the boxes?"

"All the foxes on the hillside," Dad sang promptly, "all the foxes in their boxes." He stopped. He had never been good at remembering the words to songs. "What came next, Emily?"

"I remember," Zack said, singing, "All the foxes in the boxes and the boxes with the lockses."

Now Dad sang again. "And the loxes on the bagels and the bagels on the fox nose."

Emily and Zack were both laughing. She remembered when Dad had made up this original nonsense song, driving Emily and Zack and Adena to Hebrew School. She and Zack had been competing to see who could read Fox in Socks the fastest, and Dad had broken out into these ridiculous lyrics, which had gotten more ridiculous each time they drove somewhere.

Dad was still singing. "And the sockses on the foxes in the boxes with their loxes smelled of cream cheese to the foxes without bagels on their fox nose."

Mom was laughing too. "You still remember that from when they were little, Elliot?" she asked.

"Yes," Dad said.

"No," Zack said, "Some of those are *new* lyrics."

"I must say," Mom said, still laughing. "I may never eat a bagel the same way again."

"Aha," said Dad. "But will you share it with a fox?"

Emily couldn't remember when she had laughed so hard.

Emily dutifully attended therapy once a week upon her return to Philly, but she couldn't elucidate why she was there. The therapist had stiffly-permed hair, a foundation-covered face, a bare office with one framed Monet poster and a dusty wicker-covered box of tissues. Emily knew nothing about her.

"Why didn't you just tell your neighbor you needed to go?" the therapist asked. "It was one o'clock in the morning. You didn't need to stay and listen to him. You certainly didn't need to hug him a second time."

Emily stared blankly, her mind not processing. "I wanted *him* to go," she said finally.

"It sounds like you have some definite issues around boundaries. Emily, did someone ever not listen to you when you said *no*?"

I'm not allowed to say No. Emily bit her tongue so the words wouldn't escape her mouth. Where did that come from? It was true, though. It was true. An image flashed through Emily's mind, her teenage self hunched on the toilet, underpants around her calves, otherwise naked. Bathroom door open wide, shivering from the cold, and her shouts of *close the door, close the damn door at least,* having no impact on her father's footsteps, stomping away in fury. Emily shivered now involuntarily. And then another image, an older memory of Dad tickling her, under her arms, and Emily squealing, *No Dad, Stop It, Don't Tickle Me,* and Dad tickling tickling tickling.

Emily thought to herself, *But That's Not Abuse.* But her arms were tight, squeezing.

The therapist was waiting. Emily could feel her eyes on Emily's body, on the changing body language. Emily couldn't read what was under the foundation, behind the professional mask, but she sensed it was somehow dangerous. Not quite as competent as represented on a business card. Not quite kind enough.

"No," said Emily, her arms still tight.

Emily wouldn't return to that therapist. She decided that maybe she would choose a different one, maybe the one a co-worker mentioned, or the one who looked friendly whenever she opened the door to the shared waiting room. Someone who wouldn't push Emily into uncomfortable places.

When Zack returned in November from the Appalachian Trail, having made it *almost* as far as he'd hoped before the first snowstorm hit, he moved back in with Mom and Dad, using their faculty tuition benefit to take classes at the local colleges where they each taught, working and saving up enough to put himself through a semester at the state college the following fall. Mom and Dad's initial doubts had manifested in not providing Zack financial support beyond not charging rent while he took classes. Soon, though, both of Emily's parents were giving her glowing reports of her brother's studies and had agreed to pay the two years' in-state tuition that her brother had asked for. Zack had always been smart; now he was also focused.

In another year Zack had officially matriculated at the state college with junior standing. Emily couldn't help thinking that taking time off had been one of the smartest decisions he had ever made.

"He's learned more than me," Emily told her therapist. This therapist came with a messy homey-feeling office filled with books and art that reminded Emily of her favorite teachers' offices, and in some way that Emily couldn't explain even after a few months of weekly meetings, she simply felt genuine.

"Is it a competition?" asked the therapist.

"No, that's not what I mean. I mean, *my* way was supposed to have been the right way. Going straight from prep school to the Ivy League. And instead I have a degree that's not worth anything and it took me two years after graduation to really start learning the things I needed to know."

"So you're really upset about *your* education."

"I'm upset about being lied to. If someone had told me earlier what *I'd* need... and not pretended the degree was a silver platter..."

"Life doesn't work that way, Emily," the therapist said.

"I wish it did."

"You're on your own path now, Emily," the therapist said. "*You've* been telling *me* that you're doing what you want to do."

But I'm lonely, thought Emily.

She was spending most of her nights now on her music photography, shooting open mics and local shows mostly on spec, selling prints and publicity rights and occasionally being commissioned for a CD cover. When she wasn't shooting, she was usually printing or handling the business side of things or trying to catch up on sleep and laundry and dishes. The money was starting to look decent, if you looked at the sum rather than how much it worked out to per hour, but she wasn't earning nearly enough to quit her job, or even go down to part-time, and it was exhausting. Every couple of months, Sean would come to Philly, or she would give herself a weekend off and take the train to spend time with him in New York.

One weekend in February, when Sean had bailed on a hard-to-schedule visit because his girlfriend was sick with the flu, and Emily had agreed to shoot a jazz trio she'd never heard of before, just to keep herself from dwelling on the frustration, Zack called up and announced that he was passing through Philly that very evening to see that very same jazz trio and did she want to go out for a late dessert afterwards? Of course she did. She invited her brother to crash on her couch, but he was traveling with the new woman he was dating and they had already reserved a motel. Oh, and by the way, she would be joining them for dessert, of course.

That evening, it started to snow, a wet nasty snowstorm, and Emily had the urge to crawl into bed at six-thirty and stay there. She *did* crawl into bed, and lay there for fifteen or twenty minutes with her eyes closed, letting the conflicting voices in her head go back and forth, until the one that had been getting stronger ever since the first fall after college graduation took control and got Emily out of bed and dressed in snow gear and out to the bus stop. She had learned that small treats like a bus ride or a nice restaurant meal provided a particularly helpful bit of fuel, in larger proportion than one might expect. So she ate pad thai and read the historical novel she had taken out of the library that afternoon and then headed across the street to photograph the show.

Zack hadn't arrived by the time the show started, and Emily was quickly drawn into the music and the challenge of capturing these unfamiliar musicians. When she did finally spot her brother across the room, it was during a trumpet solo. Too dark to see more than a silhouette of Lalaina next to him, and not the right moment to go over and be social. Instead, Emily concentrated on the soloist. There was power in the way she held the camera, moved confidently, waited for the right moment. A power that had been with her for years, brought alive by the weight of camera meeting hand, then meeting eye. She would frame a composition and focus for a while, then finally shake her head. Race to a spot a few feet away, focus something else and click. Turn again, zoom, focus, wait. Wait. Then a click, and a nod of satisfaction. She didn't notice Zack's new girlfriend looking in her direction, nor the way she touched his hand and gestured.

When the set was over, Emily made her way to where Zack and Lalaina were sitting. She could hear them talking before they saw her approach. "—watching her move, at that show at Penn, I felt envy for the first time. Not that I hadn't often envied the way she was treated, but never what she did or who she was. I'd always felt that if I wanted the things Emily had I could have them, I had just chosen differently. But this way Emily could see, this confidence, was something I knew I didn't have and wished I did."

Emily stepped back and stood in the darkness for a moment, letting a few people pass before she approached further. Then Zack noticed her, and called out, and she stepped forward and was introduced.

They wound up in Chinatown, where Emily ate dessert and Zack and Lalaina ate what amounted to a late dinner, having been delayed by the snowstorm and arriving in Philly just in time for the show. Emily watched the two of them together. They had met in the fall and only recently started dating, but Emily witnessed a sophisticated sort of chemistry, a compatibility unexpected if you considered the two of them separately. Strangely, it wasn't race that would lead to that confusion, even though Lalaina was light-skinned Black and Zack was recognizably Jewish. It was the combination of clothes and hairstyle, perhaps. You wouldn't expect the two of them to even interact.

Zack was, well, Zack. Flannels, jeans, outdoor layers like the cover model of an outdoor catalog would look after wearing the same gear for years. Lalaina was stylish, feminine, hot. The polar opposite of Emily. No, not exactly. They were three points of a triangle, Emily the un-cool not-quite-butch not-quite-androgynous definitely-not-femme dyke, Zack the masculine comfortable-with-gender-bending no-effort-into-clothing naturally-cool guy, Lalaina the cultivator of style, who didn't need to show cleavage to draw attention, whose clothing and movement was its own artistic expression, who said more with earrings and a scarf and a smile than most people said with their entire body but whose whole body spoke. In a still photograph, you might expect Lalaina to walk out of the photograph to someone completely different. In an audio recording, you would sense a three-way intellect and want to join the conversation. But if you watched the motion, you would sense a three-way friendliness, an attraction towards Lalaina that

Emily was trying to hide, and a sense of potential between Lalaina and Zack. If you kept watching, you would see Emily witnessing the potential, rooting for it even in her envy. You would see Lalaina genuinely interested in Emily, leaning forward, eyes engaged in the conversation, even as her fingers massaging a knot in Zack's neck revealed her physical desires. In therapy the next day, Emily wouldn't mention the tangled feelings within her, hoping that in not giving them words they would go away, and this would prove to be a wise strategy, as the unexpected crush would then easily morph into a genuine familial relationship with this woman who would become her future sister-in-law.

Meanwhile, when Lalaina stepped out to use the restroom, Zack leaned in to Emily and whispered, "I hope I don't mess this one up."

Sean came up to visit in March, last-minute, agitated by something he didn't want to talk about. Emily thought maybe he was
thinking about breaking up with his girlfriend. He tossed a scarf
around Emily's neck, adjusted it for style, and dragged her out
to a nearby bar, where soon they were both flirting with the cute
flaming bartender. There was something freeing in the dynamic for
Emily, something enjoyable and even arousing about flirting with a
cute boy stranger who wouldn't be interested in more. After their
first round of drinks, the bartender brought them each a pome-
granate martini on the house, and told Sean, "If I wasn't working,
I'd ask you for your number."

"Sadly, I'm rather taken," Sean said. "Or I'd kiss you right here."

The bartender made a slow and sexy motion with his tongue,
and grinned. "If that changes, you know where to find me. Just
ask for Mikey."

Emily noticed that Sean carefully hadn't mentioned the gender of
the person he was taken by, and when Mikey moved to the other
end of the bar, Sean whispered, "I *so* needed that queer energy."

Emily definitely understood.

They both watched Mikey's swish from behind as he poured
someone else a drink. "Lickable," said Sean.

Mikey bumped hips with the other bartender, a woman, and
leaned in and said something to her, then she turned around
and looked at Emily and nodded. A moment later they both came
over to Emily and Sean. The woman bartender was just as hot as

151

Mikey, but wore an engagement ring. "Her sister," Mikey said to Emily. "Adorable, twenty-three, single. Also an artist. We're setting you two up." The woman bartender scribbled a name and phone number inside a pack of matches, and Mikey handed it to Emily, gently clasping her fingers. He winked. "Call her."

Emily and Sean left a large tip and headed out into the night, tipsy and exhilarated. Sean grabbed the matchbook and pulled out his cell phone, and before Emily could stop him, he had set up a date for Emily for the following Saturday evening.

The week was a bungee jump between elation and terror for Emily, landing somewhere near hope but closer to dread on Friday afternoon when Emily returned from work to feed her cat and get ready for her date. What did one do to *prepare* for a blind date? Emily changed into her nicest pair of jeans—a pair already worn once since doing laundry—and kept on the shirt she'd had on at work, since the shirt she'd originally wanted to wear was covered with Andy's cat-hair. She didn't notice until she was unlocking her bike from the rack that her shoes didn't look good with the jeans—*dorky* would be a more appropriate word. Oh well. This girl would need to like her as-is anyway—Emily wasn't about to change for anyone.

Her date was sitting at a table sketching in a notebook when Emily entered the café, which boosted Emily's hope quotient, especially when she had a brief flashback to Rob from the train. The girl's name was Mary, or maybe it was Marie. Somehow Sean had wound up with the matchbook where it was written down. Mary-Marie stood up to greet Emily. She had dyed-black long hair and wore a baby-doll dress, but most noticeable of all were the plaid knee socks. Campbell plaid, a green-blue-yellow-white pattern Emily recognized from neighbors who had gone to Catholic school. Emily wasn't quite sure whether this girl was weird or cool. She guessed cool, but it felt like a pop quiz that even her brother and Sean might not be able to pass with confidence.

The date progressed, in the awkward interesting fashion of blind

dates where the verdict isn't clear from the outset. It was flattering, in a way, that Mikey the bartender saw something in Emily
that might be a match. Something unique and quirky, a little bit
wild. Marie showed Emily one of her drawings, Rainbow Brite talking to the Hindu god Ganesh. Clearly she was talented, regardless
of the subject matter, and again Emily felt out-cooled, like she
was missing something. She wasn't quite sure what to say about
the image. But as the conversation went on, Emily began to sense
the age gap, and suspected that Marie's drawing—and outfit—were
more indicative of a search than of the arrival they purported to
be. Marie was talking in one sentence about barely making rent
with a part-time retail job, and in the next about maybe traveling
around the world that summer, and in the next about wanting to
work on a farm. Emily was intrigued by this girl with the plaid knee
socks, and wondered if she might wind up becoming a friend, but
it was growing clearer that this wasn't a romantic match.

And then Plaid Knee Sock Girl mentioned, almost out of
nowhere, "I had this Used Band-aids of the Stars collection when
I was a kid."

Definitely *weird*. Probably also *gross*. By no means *cool*. But was
Emily being too judgmental? Was it possible that a Used Band-
aids of the Stars collection *was* cool, and Emily still wasn't cool
enough to realize it?

"How did you get a Used Band-aids of the Stars collection?"
Emily asked. "I mean, how did it start?"

"Well, I guess it started with Keshia Knight Pulliam's Rainbow-
Brite band-aid," Emily's date said. "We were four. We were friends,
this was right before she got famous. Our moms were friends, and
we were beeeeeest friends. So one time before she moved to New
York for the show, we were playing at my house, and she had a
Rainbow-Brite band-aid on her finger. I was jealous, because my
mom only bought the regular band-aids."

This, Emily could relate to. Getting hurt at Adena's house
had always been slightly tempered by the *Supergirl* and *Sesame
Street* band-aids.

"So Keshia gave me her band-aid."

"And you kept it?"

Plaid Knee Sock Girl shrugged. "She was my best friend. I was four. I put it in my jewelry box, and later I could never bring myself to throw it out."

Okay. Emily could understand that. And this girl had been friends with Keshia Knight Pulliam. From *The Cosby Show*. That was pretty cool. Even if they had only been preschoolers at the time. "What about the rest of the collection? How big is it?"

"Um—I'm not sure."

Where would you store a used band-aid collection? Would it all fit in a jewelry box? Would you label each one? Did Emily really want to know these answers? Maybe it would be a good idea to change the subject.

"Wait, no, I do know this," Plaid Knee Sock Girl said. "It was three."

"Three band-aids?"

"Yes. One from Joey from *New Kids on the Block*, I got that at the mall when I was nine. My friends and I were waiting for *hours* for autographs and then they left right before we got to the front of the line, but we'd watched Joey pick this band-aid off his ankle and toss it on the floor before he left and my friend dared me to pick it up."

Three band-aids. Three was barely enough to call something a *collection*. But *New Kids on the Block?* Even at age nine Emily had had better musical taste.

"The third one I got when I was fourteen, my wild phase, I was plastered at this bar. I had a fake ID and it was right after a Yankee game and I was flirting with this guy with a tiny band-aid on his forehead, I ripped it off and kissed him, that's how I got his attention, and I must have stuck it in my pocket because it was there the next day. He fingered me in the bathroom before I threw up and passed out. I found out from my friend Sherry later that he was the Yankees' new designated hitter."

"Um." Emily wasn't sure what to say to that one. Was it time to end this date?

"Oh, but wait, I'm wrong about the number. There are actually four. Four band-aids. I actually added a fourth one last week."

A used band-aid collection was definitely *not* something one added to as an adult. If anything, it was an embarrassing childhood story you—or more likely, your relatives—pulled out sometimes for laughs, like the story of Adena stripping in synagogue when she was three. And probably not something to be shared on a first date, no matter how comfortable you might feel.

Emily listened politely as Plaid Knee Sock Girl described Used Band-Aid Acquisition #4, former property of lesbian musician Melissa Ferrick.

"I had *such* a crush on her when I came out," Plaid Knee Sock Girl said. "I mean, her music helped me come out, you know? And so there I was, in the restroom before her concert, and there she is, looking in the mirror. And I'm completely tongue-tied." Emily kept listening, knowing that as soon as she left the café, she would be calling Sean to tell him the story, and that Sean would quickly spread it further. After all, it wasn't every day that someone, encountering a semi-famous musician in the restroom, and witnessing that musician toss a band-aid into the trash, would hide out in a bathroom stall for half their concert, waiting for the entire restroom to be empty of people, then steal the trashcan and search through it to reclaim said band-aid.

I may not know why I'm single, Emily thought to herself as Plaid Knee Sock Girl described the thrill of the score, *but I know why you are.*

When her photos began getting stale and there was nothing and no one new that Emily wanted to shoot, the loneliness came. It came in waves. *Lonely* wasn't a constant for Emily the way *busy* was. She had found a rhythm. The mechanics of printing, cataloging slides and negatives, and sending out images kept her moving and kept her on an even keel. These were rituals she performed in homage to the joyful moments of the first sight of a new image. None of the *wows* from others could match that feeling of seeing her best images for the first time, and Emily supposed that was what kept her hooked and kept her honest. She would have traded much of this life for love—even the *wows*—but not the moment of capture, and not that moment of first sight.

Photography was changing for her, though. There was no denying it. Now she thought about marketability. *Will someone hang this on a wall? Would it illustrate an ad or a textbook?* She thought about streamlining workflows and digital conversion and whether shooting the band whose music she hated would pay for a new spiffier camera. She *liked* the challenges—creative in their own way—but photography was much different for her at age twenty-six than it had been in the beginning.

Her day job paid rent and the day-to-day everything and a little bit for retirement. Her photo sales—from the stock agency and music gigs and a website and occasional group shows—paid for All Things Photo, including some vacations and the photographs

Emily would take Just Because, photographs that wouldn't sell or that she would never place a price on.

Every so often, Emily would take out her very first Pentax and she would photograph herself. Naked, black-and-white film, developed at home in her darkroom and stored away under lock and key but still. Emily would make those photographs and study them. Emily face-to-face with her distance and her fears and the moments of vulnerable honesty.

What she saw: Emily still protecting herself. Not open to love. Not open.

How was she succeeding with photography? How was she still getting attention as an *artist*, for photographs of other people?

She was photographing people who were open without one-on-one intimacy. Watching closely, zooming in to frame what her subjects didn't—or couldn't—hide.

At the library, Emily had made friends with some of the grad students. Mostly the smokers, because they would often be standing outside on her breaks. She would stand upwind of them and talk. One of them, Wendy, regularly stopped at the same food truck as Emily, and they got in a habit of having lunch together on Thursdays.

Conversations were meaningful, thoughtful. Emily liked the way Wendy scrunched her nose when an idea was percolating, drummed her fingers on the nearest surface whenever she got excited. Wendy waited without interruptions for Emily's sometimes-slow replies. She added new features to Emily's weekly straw-wrapper sculptures.

"I don't want to get in a relationship again until I finish grad school," Wendy had told them all outside the library one day. Plus Wendy was straight, and smoked. So Emily tried to ignore what she sometimes took for chemistry.

Zack called one night to tell Emily he was engaged. He was twenty-four by then, and in his last year of college. Emily tried to wrap her head around the word. *Engaged.* It was so far from her reality. Sometimes it felt like everything with Rachel had been imagined, that Emily was still someone who no one would ever want. She expected to be alone forever.

Zack—engaged.

"Don't tell Mom and Dad," said Zack, "but Lalaina's pregnant."

"Is that why you're getting married?" Emily asked.

"No," Zack said firmly, and Emily didn't doubt that he was telling the truth. "But it *is* why the wedding's so soon."

Soon there was going to be a new human being. Emily made photographs and now Zack was making a person.

At lunch the next Thursday, Emily tried not to show surprise when Wendy said that she had started dating one of the other grad students. "I wasn't looking for anything," Wendy said. "You *know* I wasn't looking for anything." But Emily could see in Wendy's face that she was already becoming smitten. Had Emily been *too* cautious? *Too* respectful? Had she missed an opportunity?

Might there still *be* an opportunity?

Emily felt her fingers reaching for the camera by her side. She didn't pick it up, but she noticed it happening. Emily's version of retreat. Instead of asking what she wanted to ask, she tried to sound happy for Wendy, asked encouraging questions. Tried to pretend that friendship was all she'd ever wanted.

Zack called a few more times that season, each time more angry and frustrated at their parents, who were less than thrilled that Lalaina wasn't Jewish, and weren't holding back their feelings very well.

"Lalaina and I should have eloped, *then* told Mom and Dad," Zack said to Emily.

"Like that would have gone over better?" Emily said.

"If Lalaina didn't care about family being there for the ceremony, it would have been worth it."

Mom called too. "Your brother is making things difficult, as
always," she said. "We're offering to pay for things, I don't know
why they can't wait to get married until after graduation. And I
don't see why he won't at least *talk* to her about converting. She
could even take the conversion class and *then* decide."

Her dad, on the other extension, made a disapproving sound.
"It won't make a difference, you know that," he said. "She's not
right for him. If only they figure that out before going through with
this stupid thing."

Emily held her tongue and let them rant, not knowing what—if
anything—she could say that wouldn't somehow make the situation worse.

"My brother and dad aren't speaking," Emily reported to Wendy
at lunch one Thursday a few weeks later. "And my mom wants to
know if I'm bringing a date to the wedding."

A half-shaped straw-wrapper sculpture rested on the table
between them.

Emily thought she saw Wendy's eyes flicker for a moment at
the word *date*, before Wendy's hands moved to the sculpture, but
neither one asked or offered.

Years later, when Wendy was married to someone else and had
two kids, they would run into each other in the Seattle airport and
Wendy would bring it up. "There *was* chemistry at the beginning,"
Wendy would acknowledge. "But I could tell you weren't ready to
go there either. And that conversation about your brother's wedding was when I knew it would never get explored."

In the moment, though, Emily merely felt the weight of what
such a question might open up, in so many realms, and futility
again triumphed over courage.

"My brother and dad are speaking again," Emily reported the

following week. She didn't mention the nightmares she'd had in between, the ones where Zack, or Dad, or Mom, started driving away into ominous landscapes, ones where she called and called and no sound came out. She didn't mention the worst one, the one where Dad turned into Aunt Ninian in the hospital room, the flailing arms, the screaming of someone, who was all of them, in the bed, Dad-Aunt Ninian yanking out the breathing tube.

"I got that job," Wendy reported. "I'm moving to Austin right after graduation."

Zack and Lalaina were married that springtime on a scenic hill in Dalton Park by a rented Reconstructionist rabbi and Lalaina's Unitarian minister cousin. Emily was glad that Lalaina's brother was a wedding photographer, that she could relax for the occasion. *Relax* maybe not the right word, as she stood solo with her hands in her pockets. In her mind Emily photographed Lalaina's mother's tight lips as she registered her daughter's barely-showing stomach. Dad's clenched teeth as the minister slipped in a *Jesus*. Mom's full-body disapproval overshadowing the planted smile. There would be more tension to come.

But for now: Zack and Lalaina's glowing love eyes, as the drizzling began and they all rushed across the street indoors to the reception.

And a few months later: Benji. Little toes and big brown eyes and a beating beating heart and oh why were they moving all the way to Seattle? Emily held her hours-old baby nephew and looked around her at Lalaina and Zack and Mom and Dad and wondered how it was that God and her family could create someone so perfect.

"Oh, *hell* no," Zack was saying to Dad in the hospital corridor, a few hours after Emily and her parents had met Benji for the first time.

Emily looked from one to the other, wondering why Mom was taking so long in the cafeteria. Dad had just discovered that Zack and Lalaina were planning a bris for Benji but not a religious conversion, and the conversation wasn't going well. "I subscribe to patrilineal descent, Dad," Zack said, "like both the Reform and Reconstructionist moments. I'm Jewish, therefore Benji is Jewish enough to have a bris. No conversion needed."

"We did not raise this family either Reform or Reconstructionist." Dad's voice was rising. The veins in his neck showed.

"Since when do you subscribe to every ruling of the Conservative Movement?" Zack replied forcefully. "Do you keep a kosher home? Are you shomer Shabbat? So why the hell is matrilineal descent suddenly your be-all end-all?"

"What happens if Benji wants to move to Israel one day? Did you think about that? He's not Jewish according to their laws. What if he wants to have an aliyah in his grandparents' synagogue?"

Their tones frightened Emily, but she couldn't stay quiet any longer. "Dad, you're entitled to your opinion, but this isn't your decision."

"Tell your brother he's making a stupid mistake."

Emily took the train up from Philadelphia again the day before the bris, spending the night at Adena's to escape the family conflict. Adena and her parents would be missing the bris itself to go to a cousin's wedding, and Adena was in law school now, so visits and even phone calls were few and far between. The two stayed up late, catching up.

The next morning, on the eighth day of Benji's life, when Mom rang the bell to pick up Emily, Emily was surprised and relieved to see Dad sitting in the car.

"I thought you weren't going," Emily said, putting on her seat belt.

"Of course I'm going to the bris," Dad said. "This is my family, I wouldn't miss my grandson's bris."

Emily didn't ask any more questions, and she did her best to tune out her parents' latest rants, and soon they were pulling into her brother's crowded driveway.

Zack and Lalaina were living for the summer in a house off-campus, house-sitting for one of Lalaina's professors who was on sabbatical, as Lalaina finished her Masters thesis and Zack worked with an outdoor summer program for troubled youth. Come September, Benji and Zack and Lalaina would be heading to Seattle. Zack had a teaching job lined up this time, and Lalaina would be employed part-time as a social worker, but they were moving because Zack loved Seattle so much he'd begun his job search there, and because most of Lalaina's extended family lived throughout the Pacific Northwest. Meanwhile, both families descended on the borrowed house to celebrate Benji. The only ones missing were Grandma and Grandpa Novak, who hadn't been able to exchange their tickets and instead had called earlier that morning from a cruise ship docked somewhere in Greece.

Emily wandered through the strange house, overwhelmed by the crowd and waiting for a turn with the baby and disoriented, and still full of amazement that this beautiful tan-red howling creature was *her* nephew. Wanting to soak this up, knowing that she would be on a train back to Philly the next day. Praying that in the meantime no one would bring up the tensions and feuds that continued to erupt within her family like a crusty old volcano.

Mom was hurt that Zack was choosing to go far away again, and this time taking her newborn grandson, and Dad was still angry—or perhaps anger was simply a masquerade of hurt—at Zack's first decisions about Benji's religious upbringing.

But all was forgotten in the moment of blessing. Mom and Dad all pride in the cutting of foreskin, Lalaina biting-lip pale like any mother watching this for her son. Zack's voice solid as he read the Hebrew prayer and then English words of his own.

Benji's lungs, loud.

People began to disperse, gathering around the buffet table, taking plates to chairs and corners, as Benji kept wailing. Not quieting even to nurse.

"Give him Manischewitz on your finger," someone said, but Lalaina and then Zack both shook their heads.

Then Mom took Benji from Lalaina and magically he stopped crying, Emily watching it happen.

Mom whispered to Benji, kissing his bare forehead, softly bouncing him up and down. Emily felt on edge. She crept away, wandering, brushing her way through the crowd, one direction then another. Disoriented and mad but unable to admit mad hurt. Wanting to be the one so loved in Mom's arms.

Emily made her way through the kitchen and turned the corner to see Dad tickling one of Lalaina's nephews.

Curly-hair seven or eight. The kid was laughing, wriggling, trying to tickle back. Emily's arms squeezed and tightened involuntarily against her torso. Dad was laughing too, having fun. His eyes flickered onto Emily for a moment and he smiled in invitation, still tickling. *Say something,* Emily thought to herself. *Say something.* But her words had frozen along with her body.

A while later, Emily was sitting by her self on the backyard swing set, a plate of egg salad in one hand. The back door opened and Dad came towards her. "Why don't you come in and join everybody?" Dad said.

Emily shrugged. "I'm fine here."

"Emily, come join us. Did you meet Lalaina's cousin Tyrone? He works for a newspaper not far from you, he says they're always looking for photographers. You should talk to him."

"Dad, I'm not really interested in working for a newspaper."

"You never know what it might lead to. It doesn't hurt to have a conversation."

"I just want to sit here, okay? Just leave me alone please."

"What's the matter? This is supposed to be a *celebration*."

"Dad, just leave me *alone*." Emily screamed this, near tears and not knowing why.

Dad moved closer to give Emily a hug, and Emily felt her arms fly out and hit him away. They kept swinging—"Emily—." Both anger and shock in Dad's voice. Now her feet were swinging too.

She sensed rather than saw a clear passage—jumped—rolled onto her ankle—ouch. Scrambled back up and ran, kept running until the end of the block. Out of breath, she slowed. Crossed the street, feet moving slow motion the next block, then turning the corner.

Now, where no one could see, she leaned against the stop sign, eyes closed. *What now?* Then, *Benji*. She would have to go back.

She circled the extended block, crying, not crying, not under-standing. Once back near the house, she could see her father in an upstairs window, showing someone something on the computer. Emily slipped back inside through the side entrance and sat down quietly in the living room, near the now-sleeping Benji in his bassinet.

Conversation at the other end of the room, women conversa-tion. Emily half-listened to Aunt Sarah and women she didn't know, watching her nephew sleeping. He stirred. She moved closer, spoke to him softly.

"Want to hold him?" Lalaina was at her elbow.

Emily smiled.

"Sit down," Lalaina gestured to the rocking chair. Emily sat, and Lalaina handed her Benji, now slowly waking and his eyes so brown and big for a body so small. And Emily held him close and rocked and rocked.

Once the crowd had thinned, Zack started up the barbecue grill and a couple of the cousins took charge of grilling burgers. Benji was back asleep, this time upstairs where it was quieter. Emily stretched out in the grass with her portobello burger, watching the few kids that were left race each other around the yard. Lalaina's nephew ran up to Dad, who stood talking to Emily's uncle.

"Tickle me Mr. Elliot, please tickle me," the kid begged.

Dad complied, his hands on the boy's shoulder as he kept talking to Uncle Max. The kid squealed, laughing, and almost immediately shrieked, "Stop," and tried to get away.

Dad stopped.

"Why did you stop?" the kid asked.

Dad resumed tickling, but only half-paying attention, the other half on what Uncle Max was saying. He stopped again after only a few more seconds.

The kid frowned, his face showing disappointment, and then came over to Emily, who had been watching. "Tickle me please?" he asked.

Emily was not sure what to make of any of this. Not sure how to digest the fact that Dad stopped when this kid said "stop" but not when Emily did. "I don't tickle people," she said. "Want to go on the swing set?"

"Nah," he said, scampering off before Emily could ask his name, then tugging on her father's sleeve until he looked down. "*Please* tickle me again?"

Dad started tickling, a full-fledged tickle monster now, tossing the kid over his shoulder, putting him down, going for the rib cage and the back of the knees as the kid squealed and laughed and finally ran away in the direction of the swing set.

Zack was watching now too, glancing up and back as he fiddled with the fire.

The kid began climbing up the fort connected to the swing set. When he reached the top, he let out a whoop and began waving his arms. "Bet you can't get me now, Mr. Elliot," he shouted.

Zack looked over at Dad, who was making faces at the kid, but not moving towards the swing set. "All the fun I missed," Zack said, "by not being ticklish."

"Is it okay," Emily asked her therapist on the next visit, "*not* to deal with something? Just not to go there?"

"Sure," said her therapist. "But there's a cost. Either way, there's a cost."

Emily thought about that comment, often, over the next few years. She tried personal ads. She tried speed dating. She was known among her colleagues as the queen of the first and second date, and she even made a few friends that way, but she freaked out when it came to getting physical, and she rarely made it to date three. And yet, the costs of dealing still seemed too high. She let the physical distance from her family protect the façade of closeness which was, at least, familiar, and was something she still needed, even if it kept her from something else she wanted.

It had been a long time since Emily had let her heart out, and the physical without the heart sounded nice until it came to acting on it. If she tried hard, she could still remember Rachel. She could feel the length of Rachel along her body, Rachel's toes tracing the arch of Emily's foot. She could feel the wetness, Rachel's fingers, her lips. Rachel more confident than Emily at first, both of them new, and that changing, subtly, quietly, unrecognized, until Emily wasn't afraid and Rachel was. Maybe it was a fear of reconciling her life, maybe a fear that Emily wasn't enough, maybe Rachel just wasn't ready. Emily didn't know. Wouldn't ever know. Didn't think Rachel knew either. She imagined Rachel being lured by an insistent inner voice that had pulled her away, wrapped her up in a safety blanket, left Emily with the fear.

Emily visited Seattle for Benji's first birthday and again for his third. She came home to Connecticut—or met up with family in New York—three or four times a year, her parents coming to Philly less often, Zack and Lalaina and Benji coming east for Thanksgiving and usually Passover as well. Sometimes the visits left her with an ache of emptiness where a partner might belong. She still felt like a teenager whenever she walked through her parents' front door—something her therapist told her wasn't uncommon. Yet as Dad and Mom and Zack's new family settled into *their* rhythm, family time had become less volatile and largely something to look forward to again.

All this time, Emily had been applying unsuccessfully for various artist grants. Prompted by a request from one of her colleagues, she had also returned to photographing people, the kind who weren't separated by a stage. She had started with colleagues' children, then Benji's birthday party, then a pre-school class where a friend taught. When the news came that Lalaina was expecting once more, Emily was inspired to pitch a different sort of photography project on her next grant application, one she had been contemplating ever since Benji was born: a series on modern American families.

Emily wanted to watch other families tick, see what mattered to them, discover how their histories played out in the day-to-day. She wanted new ways to understand her own. If she was honest with herself, she might have admitted that she wanted answers without vulnerability, although she would soon rediscover that the quest would bring her closer to the places she feared to go.

When the grant came through, Emily arranged a two-month sabbatical from the library to do the actual shooting. In Philadelphia she photographed a lesbian couple—friends of friends of friends— who had adopted a special-needs child. What did it mean to be special? What were needs? What if someone had given that much attentiveness, care, to the parts of *her* that felt unfinished, quirky, lost? What if she could feel that unconditional love and patience no matter what she did? Emily had thought that this photo session would take her in another direction, towards sacrifice and limited options, but her unspoken questions, seen through the images, centered upon the choices that one could make about how to care, how to give. Her lens spoke of the many things that could go awry in the creation of a human being, but also of gratefulness and kindness and the depths of love.

Next, Emily photographed her old Connecticut neighbors the Hendersons. They had lived with three generations under the same roof until Keith and his siblings moved out, and they still filled their evenings with full-volume aggressive bickering and just as full-volume affection, sometimes combined in the same sentences. Emily filled her lens with both, wondering if she had it in her to be as vocal about either.

Emily's third shoot took place on the outskirts of Seattle, at her brother's newly-built house. On the cross-country flight she felt nervous in a way she hadn't experienced since the Rachel photographs. She understood now that photographing your own family wasn't something to be taken lightly.

Zack had offered to pick her up at the airport, but Emily wanted her body to know how to take her back home. So bus then cab, then her own two feet to the front door. Lots of hugs all around, welcoming. An introduction to the room where she'd be staying, an invitation to settle in and rest up before dinner. Zack telling Benji on the other side of the mostly-closed door that Emily would come back out in a little while. Emily kicked her shoes off to rest briefly on the bed, then was up again, loading film and somewhat shyly padding back to the living room.

It was late Friday afternoon. Lalaina sat on the couch next to four-year-old Benji, reading him a book about Harriet Tubman. Zack played with baby Sam. Emily took a few pictures before settling in on the couch, her older nephew quickly climbing into her lap. She kept the camera ready beside her as they gathered around the dinner table and lit candles. Zack rested his hands on each boy's head to bless them, one after another. Emily's hands automatically reached for her Pentax as Zack spoke to Benji in a voice too low for her to hear.

Emily composed the image carefully, knowing that more than one click of the shutter could ruin the moment. She could see her brother's devotion to his son, Benji's adoration of his father. Then Benji took Emily's hand and squeezed. "Squeeze Mommy's hand," he coached her. "That's how you pass the love around the circle." She passed the love along while Lalaina hummed a tune from her own childhood.

Dinner was a colorful vegetarian couscous dish, a far cry from the cans of tuna Emily often shared with her cat. Emily felt something cracking open inside her. Benji pointed out the ingredients to his brother, teaching him the colors red, green, and yellow. Lalaina and Emily laughed at his pronunciation of "turmeric." When he finished, Zack talked in language appropriate for a four-year-old about the many generations of Jews who had observed some form of Shabbat.

Zack was at complete ease, sleeves pushed up on his cable-knit sweater, talking to them as the teacher he'd become. His storytelling was much more engaging than Hebrew School had ever been. Benji listened attentively, interrupting periodically with questions, and even Sam seemed to be paying attention.

Emily thought about the lives she and Zack had chosen for themselves, the costs of those choices. She remembered her eight-year-old brother at the dinner table, *what did God do on the eighth day?* The inquisitiveness and the rebellion and the question that mattered perhaps more than any of them had realized at the time.

"I like the rituals," Zack said later that night as Emily helped him with the dishes. "Even when I change them. It's still a way to connect to a part of me, and to share that part with my sons and Lalaina."

"What are you going to tell the boys," she asked, "when they ask about the eighth day?"

"Mom and Dad never did get comfortable talking about God," Zack reflected.

Emily shook her head. "Not really."

"Hard to teach something you're unsure of yourself. I guess I'll just tell them I don't have the answer." He turned the water on to rinse a plate, then turned it off. "And that part of growing up is trying to figure it out."

Emily sat with that for a while. Wanted to end the conversation on this note, a good note. But couldn't. "Why can't you just apologize?" she asked. "Mom called me again this afternoon. Why can't you just say you're sorry for not telling her about Benji's chicken pox and be done with it. You know she overreacts about that stuff."

"Why do you still let them control you?" Zack asked, an edge to his voice.

Why did you leave me? But she couldn't say that, couldn't risk him leaving again. And now he had hit a nerve that only he could help her figure out, because he was the only person who had grown up in the same house. "What am I supposed to do?" she asked.

The question came out raw, too raw, and she wanted to take it back. Flee to safety.

A wail came from upstairs, and then the sounds of Lalaina calming baby Sam. Zack tilted his head for a moment, listening. "She's got it," Zack said. "But if he hears us, he'll want to come back downstairs." He toweled off the last dish and unlocked the back door. "Shall we take a walk?"

Emily nodded, afraid to meet her brother's eyes. Afraid to speak. Her brother squeezed her shoulder. She felt their ages shift, snap into place, and for once there was a relief to it, a relief to letting go of being the older one. She felt how deeply, how long, she'd needed that.

Once they were heading down the block, Zack resumed the conversation. "We've never functioned quite right as a family since

Gram died. Mom being depressed all those years. Dad not knowing how to respond, because Mom's family contradicts what he
believes about the inherent goodness of family. All four of us living
in that house and not talking about it and not dealing with it."

It was all true and Emily had never once heard it spoken aloud.

"I'm not the only one who ran away," Zack continued. "You did
it by hiding in the darkroom. Dad still does it—ever notice the
way he suddenly needs to use the bathroom whenever something
comes up he doesn't want to talk about?"

"And Mom gets her migraines," Emily added.

"Careful," Zack said. "Most of those are real."

"Most. Why are you defending her?"

"I'm not defending her," Zack said. "I'm just—forget it." He
paused. "You're turning thirty, Emily, and you're still scared to
make waves because you never learned how to deal with the
debris. You saw Mom's family fall to pieces and so you think that's
what happens whenever there's conflict."

Was Emily ready to be having this conversation?

"It's not," said Zack. "People fight, they do what they need to
do, they get mad at each other—and they get it on the table and
then they work it out. But if you let them bully you into being
a pawn—"

Emily watched one foot step in front of the other.

"Dad's always been paranoid that something's going to happen
to us," Zack said, "and *he's* overreacting, but *you* buy into it, and
that's how he gets you to do what he wants." Emily sensed Zack
looking at her. "I don't mean he does it *consciously*. But you did
call them as soon as you got off the plane, didn't you?"

"That doesn't mean anything."

"And you emailed them your whole itinerary. I doubt you even
go visit Sean overnight in New York without telling them where
you'll be."

"That's *safety*," Emily said.

"Safety? If Sean knows you're coming, and you don't show up, don't you think he'd notice? Maybe even get in touch with Mom and Dad if something's seriously wrong?"

"Fine, point taken." Emily felt the edge in her voice. Zack didn't respond. "So what's the magic trick? *You* didn't ever buy into Dad's paranoia."

"Doesn't mean I wasn't affected," said Zack. Emily looked at him now. "There's no magic here, Emily. I reacted in the opposite way. I did a lot of stupid stuff—and no, I'm not talking about pot. I mean stupid rock climbing shit." He paused. "Luck is the only reason I'm still here."

"Are you saying that's all *Dad's* fault?"

What does Zack mean, luck is the only reason he's still here?

"It's no one's fault, Emily. Crappy things happened to Mom and it filtered to the rest of us."

Crappy things happened to Mom and it filtered to the rest of us. Emily thought about that. If crappy things hadn't happened to Mom, perhaps Mom might have balanced out Dad's overprotective-ness. Emily might not feel so deep down broken. And Zack might have—well, if you went down that path, Benji and Sam might not be here.

They were quiet for a few minutes, walking. Emily heard a cat meowing, and crickets, and other familiar night sounds.

"It wasn't easy dealing with the invisible," Zack said suddenly.

"Mom's depression, you mean?"

"There was—do you remember a photo you took in high school? Of Dad? The night the Median got raided and a cop brought me home? It was hanging in Main Hall, part of a class exhibition I guess, and I saw your name so I stopped. And there was this pic-ture of Dad. I just stared at it. I swear, I must've been ten minutes late to class, just staring at this photo. I didn't even think about how it was yours, or a photo, it was just Dad in this horrible way that no one ever talked about. There was something—I want to say *validating*—something honest about having this picture exist. That there was some proof out there that Dad had this side of him which no one outside our family ever saw. They all thought he was just this mellow guy all the time."

"I never told him I hung that picture," Emily said. "I never showed it to him or Mom."

"No," said Zack. "But you took it. You made it visible. Which was more than I could do."

They let that settle, quiet again, as they turned the corner and the house came back into view. They passed one neighbor's yard, then another. They were almost home. They were the same age now.

Ask.

"What happened when you were rock climbing?" Emily asked.

Zack studied her. Emily sensed he was trying to decide if this was an interrogation, or just a question. It felt like both of them were younger again, like simply talking about this topic had brought them back to adolescence. They were back in the front yard, and Zack climbed the porch steps and sat down on the swing. Emily sat down next to him.

His knees were bent, and when he stretched them out, the swing pulled back. Zack let it rock like that as he talked, stretching and bending his knees.

"I was hanging onto this rock that was coming loose," Zack said, "and I hadn't clipped in right. I'd been distracted or something. We were climbing a mountain that was beyond my skill and I was being cocky. Shit, you don't want to hear all the details. You really don't. I mean, basically, I fell. I lost my footing. I could have fallen many many feet and cracked my skull open. But I only slipped a few inches. There was a rock in the right place."

Quiet. Emily listening, wondering if that was the end of the story.

"What I remember," Zack said. "Is rolling a fat joint when we got to the bottom. I was so freaked out and could barely wrap my head around the fact that I could have just lost my life. I'm here telling the story to my buddies, adventure-style, you know. And this climber, we'd met him the day before, his name was Bill. I'm telling the story and he says, if you knew what you were doing you wouldn't climb yourself into trouble in the first place."

Emily watched her brother, who was looking at something that wasn't there, back at the mountain. She saw fear in his face, defiance, the opposite of the mature confidence she was used to seeing now.

"I was pretty pissed at him at first," said Zack, his voice slow. "Who the hell does he think he is, saying this to me. He wasn't taking my attitude though, he just spoke all calm and soft-spoken. He said he could tell from my eyes, from the impatience in my limbs, that I was not composed *here*," Zack put his palm to his chest, "or *here*," Zack's hand moved to the crown of his head. "Doesn't matter what the conditions are outside, Bill said to me, you gotta be there inside, you gotta be able to be making decisions every second, you gotta be *on*. When you're thinking about the top, you're not *on*.

"And I'm listening to this guy, but I'm kinda taking it with a grain of salt, and I knew he could tell. Then he asked me how my foot felt. Tired, I said. My whole body is tired. No, he said, how does your *foot* feel. Your right foot. Focus on it. And so I tried to focus on my foot and after a few moments I said, my toe itches. Which toe, he asked me.

"I pointed to the toe. I was barefoot, my legs stretched out. What else, he asked. There's a muscle along the top that feels cramped up, I said. My big toenail is still irritated from being compressed all day. The bottom side feels relieved to not be touching the ground.

"I was a little nervous at this point, who *is* this guy, where's he going with this, particularly when he pulls out a Swiss army knife. I mean, my friends are giving each other *let's ditch the guy* looks, one of them had already gotten up to take a leak, but something tells me to stay.

"So Bill opens the scissors on his Swiss army knife, wipes them off on his shirt, and leans over to my foot. No athlete's foot lurking around? he asks me. No sir, I say. And then he clipped my toenail, real carefully, cornering and smoothing off the ends but not cutting so close it would dig into my skin. And the other toes? he asked, when he was done with the big toe. I wriggled them, reached down with my right hand and felt each toe. Fine now. But they're long enough that they'll probably start bothering me in a day or two. He clipped those toes too, just as carefully, then returned to the big toe and cleaned out the grooves with his fingers. Clean fingers, I noticed. Unusual for a climber. Then he massaged my entire foot with his palms and fingers. Stand up, he directed when he was done. I stood. How does it feel? I directed my attention to my right foot. Much better. Could you hike on it in the morning? Yeah, I said. Would you want to? Yeah. And the left one? No. I mean I could hike on it but it feels like it'll hurt. Not just sore. More like I'd be hurting something. It's cramped up."

Emily could feel her own feet cramped now, both of them. She wriggled her toes, flexed, made circles with her ankles.

"See if you can give that foot the attention it needs, Bill said to me. And then do the same for the rest of your body. You stretch out in the morning and you know what your body can take. If you're not in shape for endurance, you'll be mis-stepping towards the top of a tall climb. That's not to say you'll fall—you might, you might not. But you've put yourself in a situation where *not* falling is a matter of luck. At that point, if you're smart, you'll start back down. But either way you'll feel crappy at the bottom. Recognize the feeling before you start, you'll just pick a smaller mountain. Reach the top and you won't be thinking, that was a small mountain, you'll just be thinking, that feels good."

Emily's feet still felt cramped, but not quite as much. Now she stretched her hands, the fingers as far back as they would go, then recurled more loosely.

"It was funny," Zack said, "how this guy spoke what sounded like wisdom and he still focused on getting to the top. I asked him about it and he said, dude, if you want to stop and smell the flowers, plant a garden. Climbing's all *about* the top. Getting there all sweaty and drinking water from your pack that tastes like heaven. Looking down at where you've been and knowing there are always other places you can go."

Zack was looking off into the horizon, his story finished. Emily was looking at Zack. She was glad someone had been there at this point in Zack's life when she and her parents had failed to be.

"I'm still angry at you," Emily said. "I have been, for a long time."

"I know," said Zack.

Emily photographed seven families total, the remaining four beginning as strangers, each shoot both harder and easier than she'd anticipated. Each teaching her something unexpected, pushing her through another form of discomfort. Once the sabbatical was over, Emily spent a few frantic weeks of late nights and weekends printing her best images. She was proud of these photos, and of her own growth.

Through some combination of serendipity and tenacity, and perhaps also talent, Emily had been offered a two week show at a tiny gallery in New York. This would be followed soon thereafter by the grant-sponsored gallery exhibit in Philadelphia. Mom and Dad decided to attend the New York opening, since it was closer. Grandma and Grandpa Novak came too, as did Sean and his new boyfriend and some other relatives. A handful of strangers also came and went throughout the evening. Emily stood in the middle of the gallery, sipping occasionally from a plastic cup. It felt good to watch, letting her photographs speak for themselves. It felt good to hear her relatives say nice things, to murmur "thank you" and smile, to listen to Sean and Uncle Max debate which images they liked best. And it definitely felt good to watch one of the strangers pull out a checkbook while the gallery owner stuck a couple of colored dots on the wall, knowing that this ritual represented the most money Emily had ever received for a couple of photographs.

The next Monday began with Emily back on the same crammed bus to work she'd been riding for years. Afternoon meant dealing with yet another rude patron about overdue books. When Emily pulled out another can of tuna for dinner that night, she discovered a reoccurrence of ants in the the cabinet. The highs from photography, as good as they might feel in the moment, were always fleeting. Even though Emily had no other plans, she wasn't sure that that this life in Philly was what she was meant for forever. A piece or two was still missing. A line from the Passover Haggadah ran through her head, as it had every so often, *they had not intended to settle in Egypt, but only to sojourn.*

Later that fall, Emily found herself in the middle of another appreciative crowd. It seemed that everyone else she knew—as well as many she didn't—had come to the Philadelphia opening. The gallery was packed. There were dots next to more than one photograph. That morning, an article about the show, complete with an interview and reproductions of three of her photographs, had made the cover of the Arts section of the *Philadelphia Inquirer*.

It felt like success.

It felt like an arrival in a way, the culmination of something that she'd been striving for from the day she'd tentatively broached the topic with her parents of studying photography in college. It also felt familiar. Except for the wine and cheese, it was just like showing work in college or high school. Not so far off from show-and-tell in kindergarten. *Look what I did! Look what I saw! Isn't this neat?*

It was comforting to realize this, and, just as back then, it was thrilling to have so much attention on something *she* had created.

When Emily got home, it was late. She was still on a glorious high from the night. She walked through the apartment, opening the windows to feel the air, pausing at each and every framed photograph.

"This one was my first experience with liquid light," she told

Andy, who meowed and continued washing himself. "That one was on the cover of the *Penn Gazette*." She stopped for a long time at the most recently framed image, Zack blessing Benji. "I think *this* one is my new favorite."

As she brushed her teeth, Emily was surprised to hear the phone ringing. She spat and rinsed before answering.

"It's Lalaina. Have you heard from Zack at all today?"

"No," said Emily. "Did something happen?"

"I'm not sure," said Lalaina. Emily sat down on the couch next to Andy, petting him as Lalaina continued talking. "He hasn't come home. He had a doctor's appointment this morning, they'd done some blood tests on him and he was going for a follow-up to find out the results. I'm worried—I think they might have found something. It's not like him not to call."

"I wouldn't worry," Emily said automatically, but even as she spoke the words she knew she had no context for them. Her hand had stopped moving.

"I'm sorry for calling so late," Lalaina said. "It must be, what, nearly one a.m. by you. The thing is, I had this crazy idea he might have hopped on a plane and gone to your parents', but I didn't want to freak them out and I thought you might have heard something."

"I haven't," said Emily. "Not since last night when they called to wish me a good opening. I can call you if I hear anything, though."

"Please," said Lalaina. "And how was the opening? I really wish we'd been able to be there."

"It was wonderful," Emily said. "I still can't believe how many people want to see my photographs."

In the morning, both her parents were on the line. "Emily, we have some bad news," Dad said. Dad's voice sounded close to normal, so Emily knew her brother wasn't dead. She sat down anyway, awkwardly, the corner of the hard kitchen chair digging into her thigh.

"Is Zack with you?" Emily asked. "Lalaina called last night looking."

"I just brought him to the airport," Dad said.

"To Seattle?" Emily asked, postponing whatever it was, wanting these mundane facts. She fit four fingers in between the coils of the phone cord. "Does Lalaina know?"

"They spoke," Mom said. Her voice was breaking up. She was trying not to cry but not succeeding. "She knows. Elliot, can you?"

"Emily," Dad said. "Zack has cancer. He has leukemia."

Cancer. After all these years of her family expecting drug overdoses, car accidents, stupid preventable tragedies. Emily knew her mother was seeing this as a foreshadowing of the phone call she had dreaded since Zack's adolescence, *your son is dead*. But Emily knew Zack was a survivor, Zack was invincible. Zack would be someone in his eighties who had had leukemia when he was twenty-nine.

Emily's fingers were tangled in the phone cord now, cutting off circulation. She was curled up in the chair, her other arm hugging herself underneath her thighs. Her mind and body were disconnected, body knowing the possibilities her mind couldn't or wouldn't process.

Her parents were on the phone reassuring her, *the cure rate is better than it used to be, Zack has a good shot.* But Emily wasn't worried about Zack. She was worried about her parents, who thought Zack might die. She was worried about herself, still their child, not quite as independent as she let everyone believe.

Later, Emily would worry also about Benji and Sam, just for being young and in the middle of something.

Right now, curled up in her Philadelphia kitchen miles away from all of them, Emily's thought was not *my brother has cancer* but *will Dad fall apart too this time?*

When she got off the phone, Emily decided to clean up her kitchen, doing dishes and wiping the stove, piling up the paper mess and moving it to her bedroom. She was trying to clear her head, because even though Zack was not going to die, it was still a thing. It was still something that would shake her family once more. And so Emily wanted her head a little clearer. She would call Zack that evening after he landed. She would call and make sure he knew he wasn't allowed to die.

She tried to move slowly and deliberately, but her mind was still racing, barely even room for Zack because there were still images left to print, thank-you notes to write, cat food running low, a compliment she wanted to remember, someone's business card she was supposed to do something with she'd already forgotten—and her hands were shakier than usual for some reason and a juice glass slipped out of her hand into the not-quite-empty sink.

And then Zack called. Emily knew she was supposed to be the one to call but there he was on the phone from some airport waiting for a delayed connection and she had broken glass to deal with and she wanted to say, "Can I call you right back?" thinking twenty minutes was all it would take to clean it up, forty until the whole apartment was clean, but you couldn't do that. Even if he had been calling from home you couldn't do that. So she stayed on the phone.

"I just want you to know that Life Savers are my airplane sucking candy of choice," Zack said. "So there's nothing to worry about."

"Life Savers?"

"Yes. Feel free to send me packages of toothpaste to deal with the side effects. But that's not why I called. See, my son Benjamin is playing a Pilgrim in his preschool Thanksgiving play, and he asked if you would be there. I explained that it was impractical given the distance between Philly and Seattle, but I also promised to extend the invitation. So there you have it, and that's my plane that just started boarding."

And then Zack had hung up to catch his plane, and Emily knew that he knew not to die, and she knew that she was invited to Benji's Thanksgiving play. But instead of thinking about Life Savers or her nephew in a Pilgrim costume or even the broken glass in the sink, Emily was thinking about Not-Mom. She was remembering walking up the staircase of her childhood home, hearing the horrible sound of Not-Mom crying, louder and louder.

"It's still cancer," she said to Sean that night. "I don't know what I'm expected to do. I don't know how much it's going to mess up my family. I don't know how to be an adult in this. I want to go home to Oaktown and crawl into my bed and have both my parents tuck me in and tell me it'll be okay."

Sean didn't say anything, letting Emily keep talking.

"When Gram and Grandpa died," Emily said, "my mom fell apart. What if that happens to my dad?" Emily was near tears, though they wouldn't come, or maybe she wouldn't let them. "I hate this."

"What's your schedule like this coming week?" Sean asked.

"Flexible I guess. I was taking most of the week off because of the exhibit, and to do some printing of the images I sold in New York."

"Go home," Sean said. "Take your negatives if you want, but go home. It sounds like you need to be with your family in person for a while. You can call me if you need to."

"What if it's bad?"

"How bad do you think it will be?"

"I don't know."

"Would you rather not know? Emily, it's gonna be hard, the whole thing's gonna be hard, but I don't think it's gonna be as bad as it was when you were thirteen. *Nothing's* as bad as it is when you're thirteen."

"Maybe."

"If I thought it would be that bad, Emily, I'd go up with you. But I think you need time with your family. Maybe I'm wrong, but I think you'll be glad."

Mom and Dad were already packing for Seattle when Emily called that evening. "You don't need to come," Mom said. "It's just a chemo session. Lalaina said they could handle it."

"She should come if she wants," Dad said to Mom. "Emily, if you want to come, just book a flight into SeaTac for tomorrow afternoon or evening, so we can pick you up, and let me know so I can reserve another hotel room. We'll pay, don't worry about the expense."

"Do you think something bad is going to happen?" Emily asked, on the verge of tears again. It almost sounded like Dad was planning for a funeral.

"No," Dad said. "I just think it's important for family to be together. I don't want you to be all alone in Philadelphia worried about Zack. I think we'll all feel a lot better once we've seen him."

It was uncanny how Dad and Sean sounded so much alike sometimes. Emily flew out the next day and Dad met her at the airport. He hugged her, and she held on, and he didn't let go until her tears were ready to stop for a while. She could tell he'd been crying too, but he was still Dad, still taking charge as they checked her into the hotel and then headed to the restaurant where Mom was waiting with Zack and Lalaina.

Mom, too, acted strong, joking with Zack as they ate, although Emily saw the handkerchief poking out of her clenched fist, and noticed as the evening progressed that Mom would excuse herself periodically, her face a little redder upon each return. And Mom *looked* fragile, a too-skinny dancer's body but bent, like you could reach out and break a bone with your bare hands, just snap it, brittle, in two. But no one talked about the cancer that night, and it was almost as if this was a regular vacation, wandering around in shops until it was time to go home and relieve the babysitter.

The next morning, early, but still late by Emily's east-coast body clock, Emily and her parents ate a quick continental breakfast in the hotel—none of them actually eating much—then drove to Zack and Lalaina's house.

Emily wouldn't actually be going to the hospital. At first she thought she would be watching Benji and Sam, but as Emily and her parents were pulling into the driveway, Lalaina was pulling out, both boys in the back seat. "I'll be back as soon as I drop the boys off," she called out. "Door's open."

Then it was Mom and Dad and Zack and Emily alone in Zack's house, waiting, and Emily was suddenly thirteen years old again, in the back seat of the car, praying this time, *Zack, please drive us out of all this.*

Dad was pacing.

Mom was cleaning the dishes left from breakfast, scouring the stove, taking a toothpick to the groove where the sink met the counter.

Zack was his teenage self, unreadable.

Is he scared?

His lips were moving.

His fingers were tapping. No, not tapping. Drumming. Playing something. Now Emily could see the invisible headphones.

A car slowed. Emily sensed her father's pause first, then heard the sound. Then her father's pacing again. Emily fiddled with an imaginary camera at her waist.

Another car. Dad's pacing stopped. "Lalaina's back," he announced. The running water stopped. Mom appeared in the living room. A car door slammed. Zack was still drumming his fingers, nodding to something none of them could hear. Key turning in the lock.

"Are we ready?" Lalaina asked, opening the door. Suddenly it was normal again, talk and bustle. Lalaina pointed Emily to the remotes and the bookshelves and the food in the fridge, Zack hollered out for Lalaina to leave Emily the extra key, Mom asked Zack where to find his jacket. And then they were gone, out the door and piling into Dad's rental car while Emily watched from the window. And they drove away and Emily slid down on the couch and—

—trying not to think.

Not to think.

She had been racing for months now—the show, the prints, the galleries, interviews and day job and little things like answering phone calls and putting labels on postcards and doing layout and and—

—and what to pack for the airport and how to get someone to take over her shift and canceling the blind date scheduled for tonight and adding an out-of-office message to her email

—and last-minute laundry because she'd run out of underwear—

—and now—

Nothing.

Nothing.

Emily closed her eyes.

Disappeared somewhere.

Behind her eyes: speckled light-black. Inner-thumb color. Glowing shapes, star-pricks, dragonfly wings. Inner-skin glowing speckle-prick.

Then a clank-thump.

Heater? Something falling? Mail. Slot-clank, floor-thump.

Hum of the fridge—

Emily zoned into the hum of the fridge. Then a bird. Then voices down the street.

Her right knee was cramping.

Twinge on the left side of her lower back.

Sock damp under toe.

After a while, she opened her eyes. Stared, not seeing, head not moving.

Felt hunger coming on, breakfast digesting. Sat with that.

Eventually, Emily shifted her knee, then flexed her back. Then, slowly, feet on floor, stood, walked in her breath to the kitchen. Opened the fridge.

When the family returned home, Emily was reading *A Natural History of the Senses*, a plate with crumbs of an almond butter and jelly sandwich and the core of a pear next to her. Zack headed straight to the upstairs bathroom.

"He's a little nauseous," Lalaina told Emily. "But it went okay."

Mom headed upstairs, saying she wanted to check on Zack.

Emily went over to Lalaina to give her a hug. Lalaina held on tight. Soon she was sobbing. Emily held her, rubbed her back. "I didn't want to break down in front of him," Lalaina said. Her voice was solid-shaky. "But oh my God, watching those tubes, the red flowing through, I don't know how we're going to get through this."

"You will," said Dad. He put his hand on Lalaina's shoulder, squeezed. "You're strong, both of you. I was proud of you both in there."

Lalaina's grip on Emily loosened. Emily led her over to the couch, helped her sit. Lalaina sank into the pillows, drained, yet strong.

Dad eyed Emily's plate. "That looks like a good idea," he said. "Lalaina, shall I make you one too? No, sit back down, rest up a bit. Emily, check and see if your mom wants a sandwich, then keep Lalaina company and I'll bring out lunch when it's ready."

Zack was sitting on the bathroom floor, knees up, back against the wall, sipping from a paper cup. Then shivered, stuck his shaky cup-arm in Mom's direction, leaned over the toilet, dry-heaved.

Emily stood in the doorway. Mom held the cup in one hand, rested the other on Zack's forehead. "I think that's it," Mom said.

Zack shook his head.

Mom glanced up at Emily, then back to Zack, handing him the cup again, running her hand up and down his back in a gesture that reminded Emily of their early childhood as he stared at the cup but didn't sip.

"I had no idea," he said.

"If only I could trade places with you," Mom said.

"Don't wish that Mom," said Zack, his voice hoarse from vomiting. "Don't wish that." He leaned back over the toilet bowl.

Mom looked up at Emily then. Emily both wished she hadn't seen the incredible helpless anguish in her mother's face, and felt thankful for it.

"Lunch?" Emily mouthed.

Mom nodded, then angled towards Zack and shook her head.

Emily nodded. "Zack, I'm downstairs if you need me," she said.

The hand clutching the rim of the toilet gave a weak thumbs-up.

Back downstairs, Emily gave her father the lunch orders.

"How are they?" Dad asked.

Emily shrugged. Dad scraped the last bits of jelly from a jar.

"It's like when we were little," Emily said, "and one of us had the flu. I almost think it's worse for Mom." She watched her father spread almond butter on another slice of bread. "You seem okay."

"It's no picnic for me either," Dad said. "Actually, I left the room during the actual procedure. Sat in a chair in the hall. Told Zack stories for three hours—he could hear me from where I was, and I think it calmed your mother and Lalaina too, but I just couldn't watch."

This was new. "What if Mom and Lalaina weren't there?" Emily asked. *What if it was me, and I needed you?*

"Then I guess I'd be in there," Dad said. His voice was firm, almost cracking a joke, but Emily noticed his face momentarily pale. "We do what we have to do, Emily. And we do what we can."

He handed Emily two plates and gestured towards the living room. "Start eating. I'll bring this one up to Mom and then come back out with the drinks."

Zack and Mom soon joined them downstairs, Zack resting in much the same position that Emily had been in just a few hours before, but almost immediately Zack jumped up and rushed upstairs again. Dad and Mom exchanged a look, and Lalaina started getting up.

"I'll go," Emily said. She was the only one who had already finished her sandwich.

Zack was dry-heaving again. Emily filled a new paper cup with water and sat down on the edge of the tub, waiting for him to pause.

"I gave up pot when I became a father," Zack said, after taking a sip of water. "Might be time to start again."

Involuntarily, Emily let out a laugh, then tried to stifle it.

"It's ok," Zack said, laughing through shivers. "Gotta laugh where we can. There was a kid today. Doing chemo in a frog suit. He made the nurses promise not to serve up his legs in a French restaurant if he died." Zack looked at Emily. "It was awful, Emily. Kid wasn't old enough to ride a two-wheeler without training wheels. And here he is with a bald head getting his blood shot up with red poison. I just sat there for three hours thanking God it was me in that chair and not Benji."

"I wish it wasn't either of you," Emily said.

Zack put his palm up in a such-is-life gesture, then dry-heaved again. When the heaving stopped, he leaned up from the toilet rim. "So how does it feel to have *Modern American Families* finally out in the world?" he asked.

They stayed for two more days, flying back after Zack's second chemo. Lalaina was rock-steady, and Zack was Zack, except for the nauseous period after both chemotherapies, where he would puke and groan like he had a hangover.

Lalaina had arranged for Benji and Sam to stay with her parents for those first two days, so on the afternoon of the in-between day, Emily and Mom and Dad headed over for a visit. The boys were happy, excited to show Emily the new sandbox in their grandparents' backyard, thrilled to have three new people to play trains with. The adults, too, got along.

Driving back to the hotel with her parents, Emily listened as Mom told her how Zack had flown straight from his doctor's appointment across the country and taken the Connecticut limo to Oaktown, to their door.

"Your father was at a faculty meeting," Mom told Emily. "I didn't expect him for a couple of hours. I was in the den. I was on the computer, the only time I can get on the computer is when your father isn't home. The window was open, it was warm so the window was open, and so I heard someone pulling in the drive-way and someone get out and the car leave, and that was odd. I thought first it was the neighbor."

Emily wished her mother would hurry up, get to the point of the story. She didn't need all these details. But Emily also knew that these were the last details of Mom thinking her son was healthy.

"Then I thought maybe somehow Dad's car had broken down," Mom continued, "and someone had given him a lift home. I didn't know. I got up and I looked out the window and I saw Zack, coming towards the house. No bag. Paper grasped in his fist. I knew then something was *really* wrong."

Dad, at the wheel of the rental car, passed Mom a packet of tissues and checked in on Emily through the rear-view mirror. Emily sat frozen, listening, wanting yet not wanting to hear. Mom looked straight ahead.

"I met him at the door," Mom said, " and he just fell into my arms. Sobbing, clinging to me like he was a baby. Emily, I was so scared. I thought maybe something had happened to Lalaina, or Benji, or Sam, but then why would he be *here*, why wouldn't he be with them? And so then I thought something happened to all of them, maybe a fatal car accident. So when I finally realized I could see the crumpled paper he was holding, I could make out some of the words without letting go, when I saw the word *leukemia*, I was almost *relieved*." Mom gasped. "Relieved. Oh God. It's awful. It's so awful."

Mom was sobbing now too hard to speak. Dad reached for her hand, leaving his left one on the wheel, and picked up the story.

"When I came home two hours later," Dad said, "Zack was lying face down on our bed, asleep or close to it. His feet hanging over, your mother scraping dandruff from his ear in one hand and holding a tissue to her face with the other. She hushed me quiet and I sat on the edge of the bed and read that piece of paper. That's how I found out."

Dad took his hand back, using both on the wheel to make a U-turn. "He'll be fine," Dad said. "I told him he'll be fine." Emily could see his eyes in the mirror, betraying the confidence of his words.

"Maybe," Mom said. "He asked me," Mom said to both of them, choking up. "He asked me, 'What's best for my kids?'"

Mom, telling the story now, said to Emily, "I want to ask you if I told him right, but I can't give you that burden too."

The story opened the floodgates. Emily asked questions she had been wondering forever and others that she'd asked in the past and wanted to hear the answers to again. About ballet, about Mom's family growing up. Mom didn't answer everything, but she shared more than she ever had before. Later, alone with Dad, she asked Dad about Mom. And the next day, Emily went with the other four to the hospital and witnessed her family *not* fall apart. And the thirteen-year-old inside her began to feel a little less scared.

The chemo continued, and life did too. Emily spoke to someone in her family at least every other day, and when there wasn't any news—*the usual chemo, a little less puking this time, a longer wait because the nurses were short-staffed today*—she would talk with Zack or Lalaina or Mom or Dad about something else. She learned that her father had picked up chess again, and that Lalaina liked the glass artist Chihuly, and that on Mom's commute to work every morning she tried to name three things she was grateful for.

Sometimes, though, the conversations with Mom and Dad would deteriorate into fights. Emily was angry and she was scared. Why wasn't all the cancer gone yet? Why were they recommending *another* six weeks of chemo? She lashed out at Dad: "Why didn't you marry someone who doesn't have cancerous genes?" She shouted at Mom: "How come you're not paying for Zack to go to one of those famous cancer centers?" She yelled into the phone at both of them: "How come you won't come down and visit *me* for a weekend? Do I have to get cancer for you to make the trip more than once a year?"

The fury lost context, and so when the big breakthrough confrontations finally took place, Emily didn't even know how the conversations started. She just knew she was saying—finally actually saying—to Dad, "When someone says *stop* you ALWAYS need to stop."

"It's just tickling," said Dad. "You liked it."

"NO," said Emily. "No. You *always* need to stop."

He was laughing at first, not getting it. Not taking her seriously. *He might not ever fully get it*, Emily realized.

"*Always*," Emily said again. She was silent, staring at a stain on the wall.

"I'm sorry," he was saying now, and Emily could tell he was finally letting himself hear the impact, the upset and rage that Emily was still carrying. "I'm sorry," he said. "For whatever I did that wound up hurting you."

It was something.

In later years, Emily would attend various groups where other participants told stories that sounded both deeply familiar and not quite the same as hers. She would wonder which of the fancy terms or acronyms that drew these humans together might apply to her parents, which patterns were relevant to her own family's dynamics. The experience would be both validating and frustrating, especially when she tried to engage in discussion with each of her parents and repeatedly found herself—another new word—*gaslit*. But it would still be useful to hear other people's stories. It would give her energy to keep trying, as well as permission to let go.

The other conversation was messier, harder. Emily felt the daggers going back and forth across the phone wire, both parents on the other end. Emily: That Wasn't Right, What You Did To Me About My Cousins.

"Emily," Mom replied. "That was *years* ago."

"And it's *still* messing me up."

"Emily," said Dad. "You're an adult."

"There's not a statute of limitations here, Dad."

"Do you *want* to find them?" Dad asked.

"I want Mom to talk to Aunt Ninian again," Emily said. "I shouldn't have to do all the work."

"Your mother wasn't the one who stopped speaking," said Dad, as Mom interjected, vehemently, "I am *not* doing that."

Emily was silent.

"I have no need," Mom declared. "Ninian said everything she had to say in front of our mother's deathbed, and I am not subjecting myself to that again. It's the past, Emily."

"It's *my* present," said Emily. "What did she do besides that one thing that was so bad?"

"Can we change the subject of conversation please," said Mom.

"No."

"I'm hanging up then."

"No you're not," said Emily. "That's what you did with everyone else in your family, and *I still need a mother.*"

Mom was silent now. Then, "Fine. You want me to drag this out. Don't you think *I* needed a mother too?" And then Mom was centering the conversation on herself yet again, claiming the spotlight and the victim role both. Emily zoned out for a moment, returning to the conversation as Mom was saying, "My mother was convinced that everything *I* did was wrong and everything Ninian did was right, even when Ninian married that drunken lout who beat her up and threatened your father with a knife—"

"My ex-uncle did *that?*" Emily interrupted, shocked.

"No, her first husband," Mom said. "The one she swore everyone to secrecy about when she got remarried. The one Ninian pawned Great Aunt Gertie's pearls for."

"I'd forgotten about that," said Dad.

"What?" asked Emily.

"Gram," Dad said, "took the money your mother had set aside for our honeymoon and gave it to Ninian to bail that bastard out of jail. That's why we went to Niagara Falls for our honeymoon instead of Hawaii. And when we got back, Ninian had pawned half of our wedding gifts to go with him to Vegas—"

"And my mother called *me* selfish for being upset. Do you believe me now," Mom asked, "when I tell you my family was mentally ill?"

Maybe.

"What about Grandpa Irv?" Emily said.

Dad used a low voice meant to imitate Grandpa Irv. "Daisy, listen to your mother."

"How come I never saw any of this?" Emily asked. "They always seemed normal to me."

"Emily, you're talking about a woman who was capable of actively hiding breast cancer for half a decade, and the child who lived with her for the greater part of thirty-seven years."

"What about my cousins?"

"What about them?"

"Are they ill too?"

"I have no idea. Can we change the subject now?"

"Yeah." Emily wasn't sure she wanted to keep talking about this either. Not *all* of this was new information, but it was certainly a lot more concrete than anything she had heard before, and a lot nastier.

She hoped her cousins had somehow escaped, had grown into people she wouldn't mind knowing. They would be twenty-six and twenty-four now—old enough to be done with college, if they had gone. Old enough to have children. They could be in jail, dead, married, strung out on heroin, working in a nail salon or an auto parts store, auditioning for bit parts in Hollywood, locked in a psych ward—anything was possible.

To mark the occasion of Zack's remission, Emily sent her brother a three-foot-tall tube of Life Savers and a card that played the first two lines of *Siman Tov u Mazel Tov* when you opened it. Grandma and Grandpa Novak turned the second Passover seder into a party, filling their home with *YAY ZACK!* balloons and a fancy matzah meal sheet cake. The whole extended family came to celebrate, and Emily let her nephews—now four-and-a-half and two—take picture after blurry picture of the festivities with her new Pentax digital SLR camera until Benji's best shots began to illustrate the magic of this new medium. Dad and Mom were beaming, Lalaina looked worn out and grateful, Zack's face had a new seriousness and his whole body held a smile.

Time with family went by too quickly now. They were so spread out—Philly, New York, Connecticut, Seattle—and for the first time, Emily wished they were *all* closer, maybe an hour's train ride away.

Unfortunately, the remission didn't last long. By fall, Zack's leukemia had come back, and the chemo wasn't working this time. Emily flew to Seattle to be with her brother when she could. Her life otherwise was focused on her photo career, her cat, and Wednesday night Indian food with Sean, who had recently moved to nearby New Jersey. She had pared the day job down to twenty-four hours a week, maintaining her benefits. Maybe one day she would be able to let it go completely, but even long-time professionals were feeling the increasing pinch of digital's impact on their stock photography income.

Emily thought about Gram, over and over, the images coming back. The tubes coming out of Gram's nose. The usually-stiff curls limp and mussed against the off-white pillow. Emily didn't know if that was the lump she had seen through the sheet, or just breast. Wanting to see for herself and yet shuddering at the possibility, holding tightly to her father's hand. How thin and frail her grandmother looked in only a hospital gown, the skin on her arms wrinkled and sagging, the blue veins showing, the shape of the bone jutting against her wrist. It was as though all you had to do was lie in a hospital bed and suddenly you would look older, sick. Had Gram really only been sixty-three? If she'd lived, she would be in her eighties now.

After all these years, Emily still had to stretch to find good memories to cover the others. The hand crushing a new crisp ten-dollar-bill into hers. The head turned for a kiss. The birthday checks. The stiff grey-white streaked hair, which Emily hadn't understood as a child until her mother explained hairspray. The plastic ice-cream-shaped cup and the bent straws Emily had asked for and gotten at the supermarket one summer, when Emily and Zack had spent a week with each set of grandparents while their parents traveled. The pleasant memories were distant.

Who was her grandmother? Aside from these memories, Emily had only her mother's few stories to go on, the ones Emily sensed were too colored to give her the answers she needed. *Why did Gram die? Why Zack? Am I next?*

Emily found herself treating her own life with more urgency. All at once, she wanted to get buff. She had disdained gyms, hated most forms of exercise besides riding her bike to the photo store, but suddenly she wanted her body in its peak form. Whatever that might mean. She wanted muscles. She wanted to *feel* her body, be aware of herself as a physical being.

She started at Sean's favorite Philadelphia gym, where he promised there was a personal trainer who was nothing like the gym teachers she'd once had. There were strengthening exercises, and exercises to get her heart moving faster. There was the feeling of a shower after a sweaty workout. There was learning to not care about being naked in the locker room, beginning to look admiringly at others naked. There was a rock-climbing wall, there were kayaks, there was biking along the river, there was rowing to try out.

Don't overdo it, the trainer said, but Emily found herself filling her empty hours with body motion. She wore athletic wear when exercising, men's pants and a photographer's vest when she wasn't. Then a new haircut, designed to keep the hair out of her eyes as she moved. And sometimes, not always but sometimes, heads were turning.

Emily's head often turned in response, but something held her back from action. She was still more comfortable watching others open up.

Music photography was fast becoming the most lucrative part of Emily's photo business, and it came with an added bonus of live concerts filling some of her spiritual needs. There was something wonderful about being surrounded by people and stimulation, yet being able to lose yourself in the music as it transported your mind. Emily would often bring her camera to concerts featuring multiple performers, knowing that a few free well-chosen shots could easily gain her a new client or two. She'd approach the performers after the show with portfolio under her arm, business cards in hand. *I shoot musicians. Call me.* At one of these shows, she met Jess.

Jess was energy on stage. Intensity. Power. Cross Ani Difranco with John Coltrane and add in something Emily had never witnessed before. Jess had performed two songs and won over the crowd, Emily letting down her camera after the first few notes, closing her eyes, and just listening, listening through to the end of the song. Then remembering and lifting her camera again and discovering just as much beauty in the motion. Click, click. She wanted not so much to capture as to keep trying.

Jess already had a photographer but asked to see Emily's portfolio, admired her work. They crossed paths at a handful of other shows, a few minutes of conversation each time. Once Emily asked, *want to go for lunch?* and Jess said *sure when I get back from this tour*, but it didn't happen. The musician-fan awkwardness hadn't completely gone away for Emily, and Jess was nice and seemed sincere but not in a way that went beyond the moment.

Time went by. Adena got engaged and Zack went into the hospital and came back out with a worse prognosis. Emily was feeling down and alone. This feeling had scared her into vigilance ever since the summer after college. The best trick of all was a concert, but there was no one Emily wanted to hear in Philly that weekend. She set her search radius a little wider and soon discovered that Jess was playing in New York at the Fez.

Emily's bus got to the city mid-afternoon and she wandered the streets, people-watching. As she was browsing the new issue of *ArtBeat* at a magazine stand, she heard her name. Figuring it was meant for another Emily, she looked up instinctively anyway. A familiar face. *Meet the amazing photographer Emily Novak*, Jess was saying to the stranger next to her. And then, *Emily, meet my cousin.*

Handshakes, small talk.

"Do you have your portfolio with you?" Jess soon asked. "I'd love for my cousin to see it." Emily didn't. All she had in her backpack was her sweatshirt and water bottle and a travel pillow for the bus ride home.

"You're taking the bus back *tonight?*" Jess asked. "It gets sketchy."

Emily shrugged. It had seemed not any less sketchy than traveling alone to a youth hostel after the show, and cheaper.

"I just came for the concert. I lived for four years in West Philly without even getting mugged, I'll be fine."

Jess looked at her cousin, who nodded. "I'm not going back to Philly until Tuesday," Jess said, "but if you want to crash with us at my aunt's apartment, I can drop you at the bus station tomorrow morning."

"You sure?" Emily asked, looking from one to the other. Street smarts were bound to fail you eventually.

"There's plenty of room," Jess' cousin said. "You'll have to sleep on the couch, but we have extra pillows and towels and all that."

It sounded good to Emily. A bare hardwood floor would sound good to Emily right now, if it meant sleeping in the same apartment as Jess. "Thanks."

"Thank *you* for trekking all the way up here," said Jess. "See you after the show."

Ethiopian food for dinner. Emily's mood was up again. She'd played with a four-year-old on the bus, discovered a new photographer she liked in *ArtBeat* magazine, eaten a tasty healthy meal. Her brother was out of the hospital and might be well enough to come to Connecticut for Rosh Hashanah. The weather was clear and bright, with friendly faces in the few existent clouds.

Then the show. That fix Emily wanted. Jess and her guitar filling the universe, too cool for words. Some people attained coolness so effortlessly, like they'd been born with it. That was Jess. Emily could tell she wasn't *trying*, she just *was*. Emily envied it. Envied this thing that could never be her. Emily photographed certain musicians to capture this coolness, to feel it vicariously, to possess it in some small way.

Jess told stories to the crowd. She played one guitar after another like she'd received it in the womb. She broke a string midsong and continued on five strings without missing a beat, flirted with someone in the front row, winked at Emily. She was powerful up there, only a few physical feet away but untouchable. But then for one song, Jess sang *a cappella*, and that's when Emily noticed Jess' hands. They hung down by her sides, small, trembling a little. Like Emily's hands.

Back at the apartment, Jess and her cousin and Emily ate ice cream and played Trivial Pursuit and watched *Saturday Night Live*. The next morning, driving Emily to the bus, Jess was the one to suggest they hang out again.

Their friendship built up first, with desire underlying. A caring, honest, friendship. It felt like talking to Sean sometimes. It made Emily wonder what might have unfolded with Wendy, if she hadn't moved away. Emily talked to Jess about her mom, about her lost cousins, about her brother. And there was space now for other conversations, conversations she hadn't dared broach in the days of the therapist. New conversations that could be slowly parceled out, bits with Jess, bits with Sean, rather than opening up so vulnerably to one person who might fail her.

The bond between Jess and Emily grew, slowly but steadily. More time together. Conversations deeper. And then one evening they were out by the river. Emily was conscious of that. They were out by the river, not alone in a room. Emily said, "I don't want to hurt you." Said, "I want to kiss you." Said, "I don't want a one night stand."

And Jess said, "This is stronger than that." But she looked deep into Emily's face, asking, *yes?* Searching.

Searching, Emily knew, to see if Emily believed it too, or if it was only desire speaking. And then they were kissing on the riverside, and talking, and kissing again.

Emily called Sean, bursting with the calm joy of it. Then she called Zack's number, Lalaina answering. *It's bad here today,* Lalaina said to Emily. *Tell me something good. I need to hear something good.* Emily told Lalaina her something good. She would call again later and tell Zack too, sometime in the afternoon when he might be awake.

She called home next, but the words got stuck in her throat when she heard their voices. Her news could wait. Dad busy on the computer researching for anything, anything, that might beat the leukemia. Mom packing to fly out west again. Zack wouldn't *give in*, would he?

In the shower at the gym, Emily followed the instruction card hanging from the shower head. One breast, then the other. Then she shampooed her hair and washed her body. She wondered, if she felt a lump, what she would do.

Emily thought about Gram. She now had both Jess and Sean to talk to if her head got messy, so it finally felt safe to go there. She kept it inside though. Private in a different way. Something no one else could help her answer. She imagined her grandmother on a particular day, that day her mother had commented about her grandmother's cough, tried to get her to go to a doctor. Suicide, the word Emily's mother eventually used. Emily couldn't comprehend her grandmother's actions, didn't trust her mother's interpretation as the final word. She needed reasons.

Emily imagined that day, the day of the last phone call from her grandmother to her mother before the breast cancer had been diagnosed:

The Lump was larger. Gram looked at it that evening, felt it, like she did every evening when she changed into her nightgown and robe. Like she wanted to do all the time now, but didn't except in the bathroom because someone would see. She was almost used to the coloring. She could feel pain in her lungs—had it spread? Exhaustion from breathing—she'd had to fight it sometimes when her brother Lou showed up. She sometimes let herself imagine what it would be like, how long it would take. She imagined it happening at night. One night she would go to sleep and it would all be over. She didn't imagine beyond that.

Until death do us part was the vow. It was hard to remember the good days, the dashing man who'd swept her off her feet, slipping four-line rhyming poems into her pockets, asking her father for her hand and then getting down on one knee. She had learned how to dress and move her body in such a way that men noticed, that they looked past her face. She had felt *wanted*, dating men in secret, going farther than her Orthodox father would have approved of, always carefully stopping above the waist. She had enjoyed it—but her heart had stayed at a distance, until *he* had appeared. The unexpected one.

It had been so hard to *stop*, at first—in fact, their first time happened after the engagement, before the wedding. Her pregnant soon after. Was it the factory job that had set off his mood, or the miscarriage? She'd never liked the act, the way he became possessed. The first time had hurt, and her friend Helen, already married, told her it was like that in the beginning. Then they had waited until the wedding and she found she felt different about him when he was less of a mystery, when she saw him everyday and cleaned his underwear and heard him snore.

Then the miscarriage, a time she wanted not to revisit. It would have been a boy. After a while, they had tried again. There was the first girl—Emily's mother—and a second. And mostly dry spells, coexistence. His mood came and went.

It was not happy. The closest thing to what might be called joy was the rush from a cigarette. Some days were better than others. After they got a television there were the soaps, those were good. There was the feeling just after dusting, everything briefly clean and complete.

Since he got sick, days were measured more by what *didn't* happen.

She had been coughing all day. Just a cold, she figured, but the cough sounded nasty. If it went on too long she could feel it deep down. She wasn't going to think about the blood she'd coughed up. A one-time occurrence. Although this cough kept hurting in the same place. "You should see a doctor, Ma," her elder daughter had said over the telephone. But Gram imagined the prolonging. This lump was *hers*, her way out. And if she let a doctor get involved, even if all the prodding of private places and the cutting out of body parts didn't lead to dying, she would be deposited on the other end into a different life, one that wasn't hers.

When her younger daughter persuaded her later that week, *let's check out that cough*, it was the thought of morphine that allowed her to cave in.

Emily sensed this as truth, somehow. Maybe not the literal truth—though it could be—but a truth of who her grandmother was. Not someone spiteful, vindictive. Someone scared, so deeply scared and alone, someone without enough good to keep her going. Emily wanted to trade in her blood, not be related to someone so destined for death, for capitulation. Emily wanted to live. She wanted her father's bloodline to be pulsing through her body and Zack's, not diluted by the bloodline of her mother's side that seemed out for destruction. She'd blocked off her mother's nuclear family for years now, years, years, often pretending there was no relation, no connection, but she couldn't disown the blood.

Jess was not perfect. Emily learned that quickly, the night her cat had to be taken to the emergency room and Jess was on tour, not even returning Emily's urgent voicemail message until two o'clock in the morning. Jess snored. She was grouchy without coffee in the morning. She wouldn't eat green peppers or hummus. But she also listened better than anyone Emily had ever known. She truly lived her values. She wasn't shy about expressing what she needed. She baked a mean apple crisp. She could make Emily laugh so hard she fell to the floor, and—both in bed and out—she could make Emily's body feel like every cell was created for that very moment.

"Your brother's family won't be making it in," Mom told Emily in late October. "So it may be a small Thanksgiving, unless you're bringing a guest."

"Actually, I invited Jess," Emily said.

"The musician friend you've mentioned? That's great," Mom said. "She's welcome to join us."

"We're kind of seeing each other," said Emily.

"Kind of? What does 'kind of' mean?"

"Kind of." Emily was glad this conversation was happening over the phone.

"Emily, you're an Ivy League graduate, you can use words better than that."

"Fine. We're sleeping together, we love each other, she's not my girlfriend, we can see other people, she's one of my best friends." *There, that should shut Mom up*, Emily thought.

But Mom recovered quickly. "Are you seeing anyone else?"

"No."

"Is she?"

Damn. She got the jugular, she always did. Emily intentionally wasn't asking Jess that question. They took physical precautions anyway—Jess insisted on it, which Emily appreciated. Emily's dread was the thought of Jess falling in love with someone else.

"I don't know, Mom." Technically true. Evasive. There was a someone Jess was probably still sleeping with occasionally. "Can we change the subject?"

"Emily, I'm glad you're seeing someone. I just want to under-stand a little better. I don't want you to get hurt."

It won't happen. It's inevitable. Both felt true to Emily. Not a conversation to get into with Mom.

"Is Dad home?" Emily asked.

"Yes. Shall I put him on?"

"Yeah."

"Okay. Just let me know when you know what time you and Jess will be arriving and how long you'll be staying."

"I will. It's a month away, we still haven't figured it out."

"Well let me know. Okay, here's your father, love you."

"Love you too," Emily said to Mom, over Dad's *hello, my favorite daughter.* "Hi, Dad."

"So you're bringing someone home for Thanksgiving?" Dad asked.

"Yeah, Jess is coming with me. We've kind of been seeing each other."

"Mazel tov," Dad said. "I hope she likes anchovy pizza."

"Actually," said Emily, wondering if this fact or Jess being nomi-nally Jewish would make more of a difference for Dad, "she does."

"You've *never* brought someone home before?" Jess said. They were on the way up to Connecticut, Emily driving Jess' truck.

"No."

Jess let out a deep breath. "Way to put pressure on a woman."

"I'm sorry," Emily said. "Do you want to back out of it?"

"I didn't say that. But you might have warned me earlier."

"I was hoping if I didn't dwell on it, it wouldn't be a big deal. For any of us, I mean."

"Your hands are trembling," Jess observed. She put her left hand on top of Emily's right hand on the steering wheel. "Is there anything in particular to *be* worried about, or just that you haven't done this before?"

"Just that I haven't done this before. I think. I mean, with everything they've been through with Zack, and me being perpetually single, I think they'd be happy with anyone I brought home who treated me well."

"I'm trying," Jess said.

"I didn't mean it that way." Emily looked away from the road long enough to make eye contact.

"I know," Jess said, squeezing Emily's hand, then letting go so Emily could navigate the next turn. "I ended it," she said quietly.

When they got to Connecticut, Emily was relieved and pleased to see the photo she'd sent of her and Jess magneted to the fridge, right next to the most recent portrait of Zack and Lalaina and Benji and Sam. Mom and Dad greeted Jess warmly, and for the most part Wednesday night dinner felt like any other dinner with her parents and a first-time guest. Gracious manners. Cloth napkins. Interesting conversation—in this case, Dad asking about the logistics of being an independent touring musician, Jess and Mom discussing Julia Child and the best ways to cook a turkey. But there was a moment right before dessert when Emily felt Jess' gentle fingers resting lightly between her shoulder blades. The simple touch brought these two worlds of Emily's together, and it felt both surreal and completely normal to be sitting there next to Jess, watching Mom scoop out ice cream as Dad rinsed off dishes and put away leftover slices of homemade pizza.

That night on the fold-out couch, limbs intertwined with a snoring Jess, her parents long asleep, Emily suddenly burst out laughing.

Jess stirred. "What?"

Emily kissed the top of her head. "Nothing. The opposite of anticipation. Go back to sleep."

By the time Emily got out of the shower the next morning, Jess was already helping in the kitchen. Emily sliced apples and set the table. Keith Henderson stopped by, sneaking a few crudités before dragging Emily up the street to say hi to the rest of the Hendersons. Then Emily and Jess took a drive-tour around town. Emily pointed out childhood landmarks and new construction to Jess before pulling up at an address she could still recite by heart, where Adena greeted them with huge hugs and they were both introduced to Adena's fiancée.

When Emily and Jess returned from their drive, there was another car parked outside. Grandma and Grandpa Novak had arrived with Aunt Sarah and Uncle Max and one of the cousins. More introductions. More laughter and conversation and food preparation. Mulled cider and musical instruments and crudités by the fireplace.

The Seattle branch of the family called as they were all about to sit down to eat. There was a flurry of activity as people ran around the house to pick up an extension and say Happy Thanksgiving and hear Benji and Sam's rendition of *The Pumpkin Ran Away*.

Finally there were nine people sitting around the dining room table. Dad lifted his glass and said, "Let's take a moment to go around and give thanks."

Dad: "To the God I don't always believe in, for keeping my son alive and giving him a fighting spirit, and for giving us all the strength we need."

Mom: "I'm thankful that my children have found love and happiness, that they understand it's not how long a life is but what it contains." She was choking up.

Emily blinked back tears, and Jess gently caressed the back of her neck.

Grandma Novak, next: "God, you can do better than this. This is my grandson." Dad looked at Grandma Novak and Grandpa Novak nudged her. She frowned at them and continued. "I'm thankful my religion allows me to talk back to God and express my anger. And I'm thankful to be here myself, to witness these hard times from above ground with my wits about me."

Grandpa Novak: "I'm thankful for my wife; my daughter-in-law, who cooked this delicious meal; my son, who married her; my daughter and son-in-law, who did the driving; my grandson Zack and his family, who give us a reason to visit the beautiful west coast; my eldest grandson, who told us jokes for two hours straight in the car; my granddaughter, who comes to visit so I don't have to navigate Philadelphia driving; her friend, who played a wonderful duet with me earlier." He looked around the table, stopping on his eldest grandson, who was eyeing the turkey. "I'll save the rest of the thanks for dessert."

That night, Emily lay in Jess' arms. "Would you ever consider moving to Seattle?"

"Probably not," Jess said. "For the same kinds of reasons you're thinking about it."

Emily knew Jess was thinking about her newborn niece, who lived in Melrose Park, back in Pennsylvania.

"Sean's leaving again in a few months, going to wherever his boyfriend gets a job, which looks like Colorado or Florida. My family's all spread out. I'm an octopus. With tired arms." Emily stretched out her arms and let them flop. Jess took one hand in hers, intertwining fingers, pulling it towards them.

"I tour in the Pacific Northwest. It might not be all that different from now."

"Yeah it would."

They talked with their fingers along with their words.

"I could get there more often than I do. Maybe I could do the recording there for my next CD. If it makes sense for you, Emily, I shouldn't be what's stopping you."

"You think it makes sense?"

"I don't know. It makes sense you're thinking about it. And it's *not* impossible—photography's portable, you get new subject matter, the musicians you shoot play Seattle as much as Philly for the most part. You can get a library job out there if you need it—"

"Maybe I could rent basement darkroom space from my brother," Emily said, thinking aloud, holding their hands still. "So much is digital now anyway, I probably don't need a setup in my apartment." Then she shook her head. "If I were in Seattle I'd just be that much further away from everyone else. Including my grandparents. No, Zack's just gonna have to beat this thing and move them all back east until Benji and Sam grow up."

Emily felt the tears welling up. She let go of Jess' hand. "I hate this, Jess. I hate being so far from *everyone*. I hate that no one settled in the same place, I hate that it feels like re-entry on a spaceship to go from Emily-mode to family-mode. I hate that Sean's moving away again and you're never in town longer than two weeks straight and I'm still living in the same ugly apartment that I moved to after college because that's still the only way to make the money work for this equation."

Jess turned, cupped Emily's face with her hands, smoothed her hair back. "What do you want, Emily?" she asked. "What do you really want?"

Emily looked over at a photo on the wall, the four of them, Mom and Dad with Emily five years old and Zack three, making a dreidel. "The impossible," said Emily.

Zack had gotten sicker. Emily knew this, and she was scared to see him, and yet she was afraid her fear would keep her away long enough for him to die. Emily called often—weekly, sometimes twice a week—and she spoke to Lalaina as often as she spoke to Zack. He had traveled back east for Passover with his kids and Lalaina, and they had all known it would be Zack's last trip home.

In the midst of her fear, Emily received an unexpected piece of mail. It came from the cousin Emily had last seen as a six-year-old, waving at her across Grandpa Irv's grave. The cousin had come across a photo of Emily's in a magazine, and found her address, and would be in Philly overnight for a travel industry conference. She asked if Emily wanted to meet for dinner.

Yes.

Emily arrived early, standing outside the restaurant until some-one caught her eye and headed towards her. It was surreal, seeing an adult face on the cousin Emily hadn't seen for over twenty years. For a moment, Emily thought Ninian had come instead, had played a trick on her. But then the cousin smiled, and the six-year-old peeked through.

"I go by *Abigail* now," she said, when Emily greeted her with the nickname she was used to.

Emily laughed awkwardly. Her cousin used to hate that given name. "Well, I'm still Emily."

They were led to a table, and ordered food, and by the time the appetizers arrived they seemed to have run out of anything to say. Emily had decided beforehand not to discuss Ninian or the deaths or their aftermath—she had learned too much in the intervening years for these to be safe topics. In all likelihood, she knew facts about Ninian that her cousins didn't, and it seemed neither kind nor intelligent to share. They were too old to talk to each other through Cabbage Patch Kids and teddy bears.

"Do you remember the charm bracelet you gave me?" Abigail asked.

Emily didn't. She only vaguely remembered owning one herself, a mid-eighties fad that had swallowed up allowance.

Emily stumbled through conversation, wondering if someone more skilled might have been able to make it flow. She thought how sad it was that someone who had figured so large in her childhood would end up being someone she couldn't find interesting for the length of one single restaurant meal.

She hesitated to mention Zack's cancer. She didn't ask, *why did you wait so long? Why didn't you look for me?*

They departed at the end of the evening without a plan to meet again, barely even a promise to keep in touch. It had been worth meeting, Emily would decide later, but to hush the voices, not for connection. It had reminded her of the people she *was* connected to.

The next day, the work of Emily's day was to buy a ticket, and another after that. Two tickets was a promise. A commitment to keep making these trips, frequently. *For as long as God gives*, was how Emily thought of it, Emily who didn't know if there was a God but had begun praying anyway. This trip she would go for a week.

"Bring your camera," Zack told her when she called that night.

Emily didn't know how she felt about that. She was still grappling with where her art fit into the family. "I want to spend time *with* you," she said. "Not *observing* you."

"At least bring it," Zack said. "At least take a couple of shots.

You might never want to look at them. And I don't want you to show them to Mom and Dad, it's already too hard for them. But take some anyway."

Emily thought about what the pictures she might take would look like in a family album. She snapped pictures of Zack in her head, not trusting herself to get it right, to be humble enough. She wanted to let other people take snapshots, let other people record this occasion in family history. Her brother was dying and it wasn't a truth she was ready to face.

As Emily watched Zack through the lens the first night, she wondered if maybe Zack had asked her to bring the camera for *her*, somehow sensing that the act of shooting, of looking, might help her adjust. Was he truly this unselfish? He couldn't want photos of himself like this, so emaciated, so weak. And she was sure that if he didn't want their parents seeing the pictures, he wouldn't want them on display in a gallery. Rather than ask, she made the choice right then to keep these images private

Zack spent most of his time on the couch downstairs, walking down the block and back in the mornings then seemingly recuperating all day. He read. He wrote in a journal. "Make sure Lalaina burns this when I'm gone," he said one afternoon. "It's not for reading, it's just helping me think a little."

"What have you been thinking about?" Emily asked.

"How I've tried to live," Zack said. "What's been important to me, and the places I messed up."

Emily was quiet for a few moments, reflecting. Should she ask? "Where did you mess up?" She also wanted to hear about his values, but there was more to learn from this other part. She wasn't sure she knew what Zack would say.

"With Kathryn," Zack said. "That's probably my biggest regret, not that I think I could have done it differently back then. But it doesn't matter when you've hurt someone."

Emily wondered whether Zack would have brought up Kathryn if Lalaina hadn't been out with Sam at Benji's soccer game. "I remember you dating her in high school, and then at some point you weren't. But I never knew much about it."

"Hard to know where to start," Zack said. "And it may take a while to tell."

Emily nodded at him to continue, shifting in her chair so her calves were resting on its arm.

"It started even before Kathryn," he said, then paused. "You know how I always needed to figure things out from experience. It was so different from Mom and Dad, who take their lessons from being told things. They didn't know how to handle it. There just wasn't space for that way of being, in a fundamental way. They were too afraid we'd try something and hurt ourselves."

This, Emily knew well. Had internalized.

"So I just shut up," Zack said. "Giving one-word answers when it came to anything important, that sort of thing, because I couldn't stand how they were just *blocked* that way. They couldn't hear me, and I'd figured out it was useless to try."

Emily had learned the shutting up trick from Zack, eventually, but by the time she'd figured it out, she had more invested. More of her opinions came from her parents. Too much of her identity was rooted in their ways of seeing the world. And in a certain way she had become dependent on them. She couldn't rebel in the way Zack had.

"When some of my friends started drinking," Zack continued, "it was yet another thing that was about experience, *what is this experience*, and I tried it to find out. Getting high, too. They were good experiences and so I kept returning to them. My friends and I would have these great conversations, about how the world worked, about religion, that sort of thing, but they only happened when we were drinking or passing a joint. Not that we needed to *be* drunk or high, I realized later, but it was the glue. It made this safe space for us. No one was going to laugh at you or check out as you were talking about something that mattered."

Zack took a deep breath. "But I still didn't really know how the world worked, how the girl thing worked. And in the midst of all that I was in love with Kathryn and we were having sex. I was just starting to make some sense of things when there was a pregnancy scare."

Emily took her own deep breath, imagining her sixteen-year-old brother faced with that, alone. Had *no one* in her family known about it, all these years?

"That basically doomed our relationship," said Zack. "And the thing was—well, the night I got arrested, Kathryn and I were breaking up. It was clear we were over, but there was more it seemed like we needed to say. We were trying. We were still in that intimate place. But we didn't get a chance, because then the cops showed up at Oliver's house, and she just *ran*. And that was it. Very sudden, very—I tried to be macho but inside I was just hurting because I loved her. We both loved each other. We just didn't know how to talk to each other, how to deal with the fact that she'd almost been pregnant and we had different beliefs around that. And there was this very clear sense of *this wouldn't last anyway*."

Emily thought of Rachel, then.

"We tried staying together for a little while after that," Zack said, "trying to get back to the space where we could communicate, but it just made it worse. Mom and Dad were already so angry with me that I deliberately didn't tell them that we broke up. I'm not sure *how* they found out—did *you* tell them?"

"I don't even remember," Emily said. "Probably. I remember hearing about it at school, and being hurt that you didn't tell me."

"You never said anything to me about that."

"I didn't think you wanted to talk about it."

"You're right. Back then I probably would have gotten mad if you'd said anything about it to me. But even so, I still wanted it to be acknowledged. It was this big thing in my life. The first girl I loved."

"I'm sorry."

Emily looked at him, and Zack's eyes met hers.

"I was glad," Zack said, "when you told me about Rachel. I mean, I was glad for you but also for me, for *us*, because it meant you hadn't been keeping something like that from me. You just hadn't experienced it before then."

"I wanted you to know," Emily said. "I'd *always* imagined telling you when I'd fallen in love. I imagined it would be when I was fifteen though. You thirteen, us home alone watching television and he'd come by and knock at the window. That sort of thing. I wanted to be the one to teach *you* about love. Instead I've learned from you. I mean watching you and Lalaina. I can see something of what I'm looking for. Why I don't settle."

"I never knew that."

"Yeah."

"And Jess?" Zack asked.

"It's good," Emily said. She saw Jess' face in her mind, biting-lower-lip love, and felt the shy grin creep its way onto her own face. "I don't have words for what it is, it's not like a traditional relationship or anything. But it's good."

Zack smiled.

"She's here later this week," Emily said. "For a gig. Maybe I could ask her to come by? It's okay to say no."

"I want to meet her," said Zack. "Anyone who can make my sister shine like you're shining now, I want to meet."

Benji came home then, racing into the living room and jumping on his father. Emily saw Zack wince and try to hide it. "Oops," Benji said, jumping off. He explained to Emily earnestly, "I'm not supposed to do that anymore."

Emily watched Zack hug Benji, and she listened as Zack asked Benji about his day and the soccer game. She admired the ease with which he seemed to parent, his tone and instincts making up for the fact that he wasn't moving from the couch, hadn't been able to come to the game. She could hear Lalaina coming up the sidewalk, so she got up and headed towards the door to meet her.

Lalaina was carrying Sam, who was mostly asleep on her shoulder, along with a handbag and another bag. "Can I help?" Emily asked.

"Would you mind taking Sam?" Lalaina asked. "So I can go to the bathroom. There wasn't one at the game."

"Sure," Emily said, reaching for her younger nephew.

"Just take his shoes off and lay him on top of his bed for a while," Lalaina said. "He was running around for most of the game, then he fell asleep in the car. I bet he'll wake up pretty soon."

Emily carried Sam upstairs and laid him on the bed. As she unlaced his left sneaker, he opened his eyes. "Aunt Emily?" he said.

"Hi Sammy," she said.

"Where's my mom and dad?"

"They're right downstairs."

"Is Daddy still on the couch?"

"Yes, he's resting there."

"Is resting like dying? What does dying mean?"

Emily tried to slow her breathing so Sammy wouldn't notice her heart had quickened. She hadn't talked to her brother or his wife about what they would be telling the boys, or when, but she knew they wouldn't lie, and they would try to keep it simple. When had she learned about death? What could Sammy understand at such a young age? What wouldn't frighten him? *Not like sleep*, she remembered reading somewhere. *Don't tell kids death is like sleep, or then they'll be afraid to sleep.*

"It's—what do you think it is, Sammy? Where did you hear the word?"

"Mommy said Daddy is dying. And one day Daddy will be dead, and one day all of us will be dead, but Daddy is dying now so we have to love him and not jump on him anymore. I know what dead means. It means that Daddy won't be here and we have to remember him extra hard. But he's here so dead isn't the same as dying. Does dying mean lying on a couch and not being jumped on?"

"That's part of it," Emily said, gently. "Daddy's body isn't working very well anymore. You know how when you get a cold, you just feel like staying in bed and sleeping a lot? It's a little like that, except with a cold you get better, and Daddy's body isn't going to get better. It's going to keep slowing down."

Emily didn't notice her tears until Sammy asked, "Is it sad? Why is everybody sad? Mommy says it happens to everybody, but she cries a lot too."

"It's sad because we don't want your daddy to die."

"I don't want my daddy to die," Sammy said. He was crying now too.

Emily leaned down and hugged him. She didn't say anything. There wasn't anything to say. There were books, maybe later she could talk to Lalaina and then go to the library and get some books. Make it a little easier for Sam to understand. Benji too. But understanding wouldn't change it. Zack was still downstairs, getting worse. He might have as much as six months, the doctors said, but it was only a matter of time. They'd ceased the chemo, because it only seemed to make him feel lousier.

"I'm not tired anymore," Sammy announced. "Can we play Legos?"

They played Legos for the next hour, Benji joining them, and as they played Emily could hear the murmur of Lalaina and Zack talking to each other. When the voices ceased, Emily leaned over the railing to peek downstairs. She found them both asleep, holding hands, Lalaina stretched out on the carpet next to the couch.

"I'm going to go set up dinner," she told Benji and Sam. "Do you two want to keep playing Legos, or help me?"

"Sesame Street's almost on," Benji said, looking at the Grover clock. "We usually watch Sesame Street before dinner."

Emily stayed for the opening theme song, singing along, then left her nephews in front of the television and crept downstairs to the kitchen. She set the table first, since that was easiest. She wasn't sure what Lalaina had planned for dinner. Lalaina wasn't quite as meticulous as Emily's mother at planning meals, but she usually had something in mind. Lalaina's relatives had also been keeping the freezer stocked with home-cooked dishes. Emily poked around the refrigerator until she found a container of mostly-defrosted squash soup, and then noticed a cookbook on the counter open to a macaroni and cheese recipe.

She put the soup in a pot on the stove to finish defrosting. After that she found the grater and started grating cheese. She had grated almost the entire hunk of cheese when Lalaina came into the kitchen.

"Emily, you are such a treasure. Thank you."

Emily was embarrassed. "I didn't want to wake you up," she said. "I wasn't sure what Corningware to use, though, did I get the right one?"

"That one's fine," Lalaina said. "Sometimes I use the round one, but there's really no difference." She moved around the kitchen, putting another pot of water on the stove to start boiling for pasta, setting a flame under the soup and giving it a stir.

They were quiet for a few moments, Lalaina reading the recipe and Emily measuring the grated cheese.

"How are things with your musician?" Lalaina asked.

"It's hard," Emily admitted. "She's on the road so much, and we sort of figured out from the start a capital R relationship wasn't going to work out. But when we're together, it's so—I haven't felt this way with anyone before." Not even with Rachel, Emily realized. "So comfortable, and *there*, and alive."

"Go with that," Lalaina said. "Not that I'm one to give advice on this stuff. But I think if you've got something good with someone, it's a shame to throw it away just because it doesn't fit some definition."

"Even if it hurts sometimes?" Emily asked.

"Even then." Lalaina dropped a handful of pasta into the now-boiling water. "That's your heart, baby. It's getting exercise again."

When Jess called that evening, Emily made plans for her to come by the following afternoon, before her concert. The boys would be at school and Lalaina would be at work—Lalaina had arranged to go in three days each week, relatives and friends taking turns staying with Zack. In the morning Zack was too sick to take his walk, but he was feeling talkative and he and Emily spent the morning talking, mostly about Emily's photography.

Emily had brought some slides, and after making a few calls, Zack was able to scrounge up a projector to borrow. Once the projector was set up, controller next to Zack, the two of them dove into the leftover macaroni and cheese and some homemade bread that had been dropped off by Lalaina's aunt.

"You've really grown," Zack said to Emily, advancing through a few slides. "The way you're interacting with people in these. They're further away compositionally, but they feel closer."

"I switched lenses," Emily said. "I use a fifty millimeter now almost exclusively, instead of a zoom."

As Zack nodded, Emily felt the simple closeness of his noticing, of someone recognizing this thing, this fact of her over time. It was something she would lose, would lose with Zack, would lose again when her parents died. She hoped she might gain it as well, with Jess, but she couldn't imagine that far into the future to tell. And even so, once you lost the people who knew your childhood, you lost those particular insights, forever.

Jess arrived as they were finishing clearing up from lunch, Zack wiping the table and joking about that being his day's exercise. They sat in the living room, Zack back on the couch, Jess on a chair. Emily stretched out on the floor, legs out, leaning on her arms. Switching positions every so often as her joints got tired.

Mostly, Jess and Zack talked.

Zack asked Jess about her music, questions Emily already knew the answers to, like when Jess had gotten serious about music, what instruments she played. Emily thought he was going to ask Jess how she wrote—most people did, Jess had said—but instead he then asked if she had stories or themes she tried to write about, or if she relied on inspiration.

And Jess said yes, there were themes she tried to write about, that she'd written a lot of political songs but now she was trying to approach those themes on a more personal level, which was harder to get down. She said she'd had a friend who died from AIDS. That when she'd tried to write about that, about her friend, it felt like the songs that came out were really about something else entirely.

Zack nodded, like he understood.

"Does that happen with your photography?" Jess asked Emily, who had been quiet this whole time.

"Well," Emily said, thinking about it, "I guess mostly it's either I get the shot or I don't. I have this image of what I'm trying to get, if I'm shooting a person, and when I see the prints it's either there or it isn't. But there have been times when I've taken a shot and it's a *good* shot, by other people's standards, and it gets used on a concert poster or something like that, and everyone loves it. And yet every time I see it I cringe, because I know it's not right. It's not showing the person's inside, it's not what I was trying to capture."

"I think my favorite shots of Emily's," Zack said, "are the ones where she does capture someone's inside, even if they're not the most flattering images. Especially when it's family."

Jess nodded, and she turned to Emily. "Does it make you feel bad?" she asked. "Showing people's dark sides? Do you worry you won't be able to show their good sides as convincingly?"

Emily nodded. "I wish I were a fiction writer sometimes, then at least I could say *nope that's not my family* but still deal with the hard stuff. Or even a painter, so I wouldn't have to capture the moment *as* it happened. Whenever I shoot family, in particular, I know there's good stuff and I wish I could show it—I have, some-what—but the bad is more powerful."

"I worry about that," Jess said. "I have this one song, I still haven't figured out what to do with it. No one's heard it yet."

"Will you play it for me?" Zack asked.

Emily shot Zack a look, and he smiled at her innocently. "It's my last request."

"That's so morbid," said Jess. "You're trying to manipulate the vulnerable artist into baring her soul."

"No, I'm trying to offer the artist a safe place to grow."

Jess looked at Emily, who was staring at the wall, shaking a little as reality settled in just a little bit more. "I do appreciate that," she said to Zack, softly, "but I think your sister might prefer something a little tamer for the moment. Hand me that guitar?"

Zack reached behind his head for the child-sized guitar that was Benji's and passed it to Jess. Her fingers had to squeeze to fit on the tiny frets.

As she tuned, Jess asked, "Are you scared of death?"

It was something Emily wanted to know, but had been afraid to ask. How was Jess able to ask these sorts of questions so easily? She had a magical way of getting people to trust her. Zack had it too, sometimes, and maybe this was what Emily was seeing, two people who were able to communicate on this very trusting level, very quickly. There was a certain joking that had happened as well, but even that seemed to be rooted in trust. And yet, there was something else too. In Jess' shoes, Emily would have found herself playing the song Zack requested, but Jess wasn't. Emily might have felt less of herself for playing, afterward, empowered and grown and yet stripped of power at the same time. It could have been an awkward moment.

But nothing was awkward now. If anything, Jess' *no* had added to the intimacy. Had allowed her to ask.

Zack didn't answer the question immediately, and Emily wondered if he had heard. Jess strummed, improvising something, and then Zack said, "I'm not scared. A lot of other things though. I'm trying to make peace. I looked up my high school girlfriend yesterday, found a Florida phone number for her. She has a different last name now. I'm not sure if it's fair though to call her. Or too cowardly to write a letter."

"I don't know," said Jess. "There may not be a right or wrong answer for something like that."

"I guess what I'm not clear on," Zack said, "is how much is for my own peace, how much is for everyone around me. And how much is ego, to think your leaving is going to have so much of an impact. But if it didn't, I mean it's so hard for me to think that Benji and Sam are going to grow up fine, and I won't be around for it. It makes me realize, they would still be fine if I hadn't been there from the beginning. And yet I know that my being here *matters*. It just doesn't all compute. The way we aren't necessary to each other, yet we are."

Jess' eyes were glistening, and so were Zack's, and Emily could feel the watery film covering her own as well.

Jess had been strumming this whole time, and now she started playing louder, something that Emily started recognizing as a song. Then Emily was singing along quietly, and then Jess was singing, and Zack had his eyes closed but Emily knew he was listening.

They played and sang and listened like that for a while.

When Benji came home, Jess played a couple of songs he knew. She taught him a couple of chords, and then listened to Benji perform one song *he'd* made up, and then it was time for her to go.

"I don't suppose you're going to make it to the show," she said to Emily.

"Doubtful," said Emily.

"If it's not too crazy, I'll try to swing by here again after."

Benji was watching, so Jess just gave Emily a hug and a quick kiss on the lips. She tousled Benji's hair. She grasped Zack's hands in hers and looked into his eyes for a long moment, then she said goodbye and headed out.

They grilled hot dogs and corn for dinner, Benji and Sam racing around the backyard while the adults ate more leisurely, then talking Emily into roasting marshmallows with them. Dusk came and went. Her nephews kissed Emily good-night with chocolaty-sticky faces, then followed their mother inside for a bath and a promised board game, while Emily and Zack had more good alone time together. Later, dishes long done, upstairs quiet, stars in the sky, Zack headed up to sleep.

Emily sat on the back porch stoop, next to the grill they'd used for dinner and s'mores, watching the dimming fire in the darkness. She was thinking about her old childhood fear, the biggest one, the fear of her parents dying. How that fear had traveled with her into adulthood as she found life as a single person remaining a constant, her norm. When she thought about who she would lean on in crisis, it was always still her parents, and then when she thought about what if they died, she had always thought of Zack. No matter how far away he was, even when he wasn't speaking to their parents, she knew her brother would be there, grieving with her, if something happened to them. And now, he was deserting her. Leaving her to be an only child.

The tears came, fast and furious. Emily hoped the windows were closed so no one inside would hear. Eventually the tears slowed, ceased, and she felt the saltwater on her face, stared into the embers of the burning ash.

Across the lawn, Emily could see the outline of a raspberry bush, even darker than the sky, and on impulse she got up and searched mostly by feel until a lone ripe raspberry fell into her hand. Emily tasted it and a memory she had forgotten all these years began coming back. The family at Grandma and Grandpa Novak's, in the back yard. Zack still in a baby carriage, just beginning solid foods. Grandpa helping Emily pick raspberries. She picks a large one. *Mom, can Zack eat raspberries?* Mom looks at Dad, who shrugs. *I don't see why not.* Emily puts the raspberry between her baby brother's lips. He looks at her in surprise, then moves his mouth—tasting, swallowing—and his face lights up in baby joy at his very first raspberry. Emily, too, is delighted. She hadn't known that *this* was part of the job of being a big sister.

Emily heard Jess' truck engine approaching, closed her eyes briefly, and then moved towards the sound.

They met in a hug, tight, desire and fear and sadness and yes love, and they were kissing too, hot and long, passionate. They didn't need words. They could feel the scars of the past, those spoken and unspoken, and the pain yet to come, and they helped each other to heal in this embrace.

Later, too soon, Emily walked Jess out to the truck, their clasped hands communicating tenderness and love, not promising commitment or longevity but acknowledging something more important: this is real, this matters, this is part of who I am becoming.

Then Emily turned and went back inside.

Acknowledgments

These characters first arrived in my life through a short story, *On the Eighth Day*, which I wrote when I was a senior in college.

That story took second place in the David Dornstein Memorial Short Story Contest for Young Adult Writers and was published in *Jewish Education News* in 2001. It even made a brief cameo in my memoir, *Map. It* Along the way, it received feedback from writers and others, many of whose names and faces I have forgotten by now.

I was haunted by what happened to Zack in that story. I wanted to change the ending. But sometimes characters take on a life of their own, and all I could do was spend more time with Zack and his family.

I wrote a second short story, *I, Emily*, which I published in audio form on my CD *Hear Me Out*. I then tried to write stories from each parent's point of view. That was harder, and slowly my attempts morphed into a novel, which became my MFA thesis, which over a decade became something close to what you are holding. A few agents and publishers considered the manuscript, though none said yes, and eventually I moved on—or so I thought. Along the way, many, many people read drafts and excerpts and provided feedback and encouragement.

When I started writing about Emily and Zack, I was much younger than they are at the book's conclusion. Now I'm the older one, by more than a decade. Curious, I re-read the manuscript in late summer 2022 and brought that new perspective to one last revision, cheered on by friends and family and fellow writers.

THANK YOU to everyone who has been a part of this journey.

And THANK YOU, readers,
for taking these characters into your hearts.